THE KING'S DEBT

A novel by
Samaa Ayman

'He wanted to die, in order to return to the sky,

As if he were a homeless celestial child,

Who had strayed from his father in the maze of evening...

"As if he who kills me fulfils my will."'

Salah Abdelsabur, The Tragedy of El Hallag.

Samaa Ayman

THE KING'S DEBT

Dear Patrik,

You will be missed!

I hope you enjoy reading :-

Samaa Ay

For Giacomo, who held my heart as I wrote.

'La Chambre Séparée' rings through the dark waters and rises, borne by wind beaten mouths singing along, lips and eyes iridescent against 18 swinging lanterns. Faces nestled into 18 boats charging in disparate speed, heading for the siren, slowly revealing itself, calling them, the damning melodies of a 'lusty hideaway', the little common secrets and the not so slight, all here in La Chambre Séparée's celestial perturbation of sea.

Trekking through the waters, elegantly dressed men and women – some concoctions too elaborate than others, yet all unseemly out of place – were more concerned with flattering their destination than paying the sea its due veneration. The men adjusted their ties, their freshly shaved necks itching under the restricting shirt collars, whilst their lovers, wives or mistresses exchanged glances of mutual understanding that the sea is not behaving itself. They concealed their faces frantically to salvage their contoured make-up efforts hours earlier in the making, from the water, as the boats were thrust violently in a continuous encore into the sea, spraying those on board with sighs of satisfaction.

No children nor innocence on board. Nothing to grow but a nascent curiosity, an insatiable hunger carried farther from the shore in 18 boats, their assortment like a pathetic armada of sorts. Overexposed, sun-baked men rowing their oars silently or blasting the noise of their motors further ahead, the display of prominence, of precious breeding, of wealth and the dark comedy in the fact that these three merits remain equal across an array of boats on the same sea, beating against the same waves, seeking the same destination with no point of their journey dividing them save for the shores from which they had embarked and the sands on which their feet treaded.

Day Passed

Samra lost her blood as it flowed, heavy and rushed, and soiled the earth. She ridiculed its steady stream, for it was never something she had considered capable of flowing. To flow, substances needed to be lighter, more penetrable and less loyal.

She was being dragged slowly, her torso clumsily rubbing against the sand. They were talking, their voices beat against her aching skull. Her shirt, trapped against the weight of her limp body pushing against the sand, slid up, pressing past her back and baring her stomach to the sun. Her blood and the sun entwined and copulated. In a surreal way, they always had. She shuddered at the notion of such a union and of how blasphemous it was, its tender rush following the violence their meeting had perpetuated. The vast emptiness of the desert, forever untouched by rain, eternally tinted in red, would remain timelessly resolute.

The movement stopped. The hands grasping her feet released their clutch then dropped her altogether, as the sun touched more of her skin long before a growing siren interrupted the air around. Throughout the torment, she had not uttered a single moan, neither of passion nor pain. Her last scream had rung out what seemed like hours ago, as a hopeless siren signalling no one left alive to save, before her face beat against the ground in a final moment of violence and learnt to pray that God would have her buried right then and there, where she could give herself to the Earth and Sun and be taken as a virgin corpse for the first and last time. But Samra was not laid to rest.

Samra was cursed to relentless bids of unrest.

**

Naktal roared. Its bass hit every corner like a surging flood before scraping right and left to crash centre stage, while Rawan, recluse and wide eyed, peered at herself in the mirror. Her eyes swelled with heat and threatening tears. Somewhat dreading, she sweated at the realisation of what waited outside the dressing room and whom it would target.

Considering the odd appearance of the gaze darting back at her, she thought they seemed almost non-existent, although they loathingly reflected back at her in fierce condemnation. Rather peculiarly, one of her eyes seemed to be looking straight ahead, whereas the other tilted to the side of her face, intensely confused and shaken, deformed in solidarity with her soul. Moments later, they switched appearances so that every time she somehow made attempts to restore her face to its normal state, it contorted once more into an aggrieved rage. Samra glared back in from the reflection, with the same shape Rawan's eyes formalised whenever the subject of their father arose, yet Samra's eyes were alien in that face of her sister, Rawan, who rarely forgot to doubt whether she was really her father's at all. Samra had never dared to question it, not particularly out of loyalty, but from the soul's straining for affiliation, that recklessly self-destructive desire to belong even if it were no genuine right. 'Nationalist affection' Rawan called it: the incessant curbing of those who craved guardianship of any kind; the radical stealth self-imposed by allegiance; the ultimate seduction of the simplest most culpable of lies that members of the human race are – innocently – unique.

Whether the glaring stares through the mirror were Samra's or her own, Rawan came to empathise with their lonely solitude, for not all seclusion to intimacy with one's self carries the callous sense of loneliness. However, she could not embrace the thumping thirst outside, which gouged at their grief to quench it, needing only an extra glance at her scorching eyes before she began to frantically slap herself time and again, tearing at her face, muffling her screams and relentlessly abusing herself until Zain knocked firmly on the door. 'Maluka, let's go,' he called, only for her to yell back, 'I'm coming,' whilst she soullessly pulled a small blush box from her bag and let loose a heavy pinch of white powder on the dresser table.

Fumbling with an old credit card she had found within the neglected insides of the bag, Rawan shaped the powder into a thin and impeccably neat line before pressing her nostrils to the surface of the table and violently inhaling it in one smooth swipe. Zain entered the room, just as she leaned her head back sensually, yet failed to incite the dramatic effect she was deliberately forcing. She shut her eyes and screamed silently with an agonised, contorted face. How she stretched and stiffened her arms wide on the chair in an allusion to an accursed woman being crucified was beyond him, and he could improvise no thought, save for a petty attempt to ease her distress. He paused as to what such an attempt could be, until clueless and anxious, he managed to say, 'Rawan, sorry, Luka,' he corrected himself, 'you need to leave now. We're ready, and he has just arrived.'

She turned to look at him and grinned insanely. 'There is no one in the room but me and this glorious jester here in the mirror. Let him wait for his drinks. I want to be close enough to watch him choke on them,' she announced calmly.

'Fix your face first and come out. Naktal is yours tonight, and I am here. So is Saleem. Never think that you are alone,' he assured her.

'Zain, come here.' She held her hand out for him. He drew near and squatted beside her chair.

'Don't look at me like I'm a pussy.' Rawan gazed down at him with a raised brow. 'Don't talk to me like I'm one either. Saleem tags along; he doesn't drive.' She giggled as her demeanour lightened to showcase a face whose features projected an accelerated focus, like that of someone gradually sobering from a state of deep intoxication. 'Look at me.' She raised his chin up with her fingers.

'I am.' He smiled at his friend to display his perceptiveness.

'Good,' she whispered.

Returning to the mirror after Zain left the room, Rawan dried her face and applied fresh make-up, thickening the stroke of liner, painting the lipstick with a distinct suave that was overtly sexualised and objectified, telling herself they had to be deliciously perfect, as if the whole world would taste them that night. She slid her hair over to her right shoulder, revealing a yellow eagle on her inner left blade. Zain is very fond of that tattoo, she thought as she met his eye before turning to face the dark corridor on her way to ascend Naktal's high fire-escape stairs.

***

Samra waved so her sister would spot her. Airports always bustled, but Rawan rushed with a speed no one could catch up to, running directly into a luggage-clad embrace with her sister.

'I saw this crazy movie on the plane, a Gary Oldman,' Rawan blurted.

'Oooh, Gary Oldman!'

'Yeah, it was weird though. Excessively paranoid I would say.'

'What's it called?' Samra pushed her sister's cart towards the car park.

'Tinker, Tailor something, something…'

'Why was it weird?' Samra asked. Rawan explained that she 'found the plot based loosely on stressing the issue of "trust" as well as the performance being "too staged".'

'But that's acting, right?'

'No, acting should be natural and real, as in life.'

'Hmm.' As she drove, Samra grew less attentive to Rawan's eager, albeit extremist, answers, which she adopted when critiquing almost anything. She blasted Black Theama's *Bahar* on the radio once they were inside the car, as a welcome back gesture to Rawan.

'Mama is very excited. She has taken over the entire thing!' Samra told her sister.

'How does Saleem feel about that?' Rawan asked, while Samra, perplexed and unable to link her sister's question to her own comment, merely replied that 'he was happy' then moved on to the weather.

'It's too bad you left in January. You missed the spring.'

'What are you talking about?' Rawan said. 'I hate spring!'

'Yeah, your hay fever but.—'

'No, not just the hay fever. The sandstorms. It's like the desert is throwing up all over Cairo.'

Samra did not respond, sensing that her younger sister was attempting to take on some sort of role, inconsistent with reality, and, instead, opted for a less animated drive home from her personal side. It had always plucked a nerve with Samra whenever she came across such behaviour, as if it were oddly appealing for people who had travelled to act like the experience qualified them to be strangers to their own land. Through her emphasised criticism, Rawan acted like she had left for many years when she had been away for less than one. Tunis isn't even that far away, Samra thought to herself. Surely the climate there is similar.

'How can you people drive here?' Rawan cried out, astounded at the lack of order accompanied by frequent violations she witnessed on the roads as they drove through the bustling city.

'You used to drive here too,' thought her sister.

***

Rawan stole a glance at her sister through the window before stepping inside. Samra was heavily bruised and bloodied, and a network of tubes intertwined with her body, binding her to an unfortunate fate. Yet her features remained recognisable. They themselves, in all their delicacy, were pitiless. Rawan's eyes, dark and deadened, scoured the room to land on the bed. She saw Saleem wretchedly huddled up in a corner, buried in a hospital throw. His closed eyes were pits of despair. Rawan doubted whether he was in fact asleep at all. She sat on the edge of the bed, peering across to the monitor that paced her sister's heart.

Lines.

Fuller, more well-rounded shapes that defined and danced in tune to her richer life come undone to pathetic lines. Samra's and Rawan's entire childhoods, their innocent bickering and ridiculous giggles over scraped knees, bruised palms and shared secrets; the ring Saleem had slid up her finger before she was conscious enough to weep with the joy of fulfilled anticipation; his immense love for her; the wedding dress that had watched her attack from the back seat of the car, now hanging in her cupboard like a silent witness; the sparkle in her mother's eyes, which Samra would never see again; and her insatiable dreams and longing for life and beauty had all degraded and transcribed to shallow, senseless lines.

Samra sensed the heat of Rawan's despairing body and, ever so timidly, opened her eyes. Her gaze landed on her sister's own stare. They saw each other but said nothing. Samra searched her sister's face – pleading for help, begging to be saved. Rawan, tormented by her ineptness to do anything but watch inevitability take its course, felt her chest heave. She could not stop it. For the first time in her short life, Rawan possessed no control.

Silently, Samra asked to be held. Far from longing for Saleem's arms to envelop her and his fingers to caress her hair in the sun, but, much in angst, she yearned for her sister's embrace. The one that told Samra of lost youth and of one's natural and inevitable inclination to mutual disappointments, of a clandestine language they spoke in silence. And rushing to comply, Rawan leaned over her, gently sliding one arm under her sister's back while the other supported her feeble neck, eventually managing to pull her up to her own chest. Rawan awaited a gasp, a twinge of pain. Nothing.

Sometimes in intimacy, we do not crave eye contact. It is too overwhelming, maybe too exposing. Sometimes we do not wish to be kissed, fondled; we do not even desire to speak. Sometimes, what we need most of all is to hold and be held. To revel in the restless drumming, which, in turn, speaks without fear. To hold is the greatest moment of self-actualisation, the most human act of achievement. And to be reciprocated? All that which can be spoken on this earth would fail to substitute those mutual beating of two souls who communicate their love in the smallest and most private space in existence. In an embrace.

One vibrating line, hurriedly plummeted to a horizontal assurance, although Samra's heart seemed to be beating restlessly. So restless. As if its halt would cause the Nile itself to dry up. Rawan shut her eyes, held Samra tighter, and screamed in silent despair a wave of helpless tears. No one would know how much time passed, and Saleem did not awaken. The incongruous ferocity of her fatigued heart compelled Rawan's as it broke. She fought the scene streaming within her aching skull of their childhood fights, how the only way to tear them apart from their violent grips – projected with young nails pierced into tender skin – was their mother chasing them both menacingly around the house. She would curse them amidst ingenuine threats, and for as brief as it would last, the fear of a common outcome would unify them, oblivious to their differences. As Samra's breath came to its last pause, for in Rawan's mind she had been feeling it against her neck still, Rawan laid her back on her pillow.

Hurriedly shifting her body towards Saleem, still perched awkwardly on the edge of the bed, Rawan's hands were clammy and printed on the sheets while her breathing grew heavier and intensely loud in a sort of sob unfamiliar to her. It disturbed him, and he began to fidget and arouse. Her eyes searched the room frantically, landing repeatedly on Samra's gaze, Saleem, Samra's right hand, Saleem again, the door. She was hunting anxiously for something, an answer to a question, one she clearly couldn't articulate, her eyes resorting only to appear paralysed beyond their sockets yet vividly murderous. The face of her heart contorted itself in alternation from shock, to pain, to fury and frustration, and back again in a triple loop until Saleem's eyelids lifted and he caught her gaze. And she paused in her sphere of emotions and looked at him. And for all the vocalisations of pain from loss that one could muster, he gasped in – as though in cardiac arrest – all the cruelty in the room's air and held it. They did not move, forced to listen to the heart monitor, and to the sound of all that Samra once was, departing from their lives and their mundane realm.

He would not collect her body following the coroner's examination, never offering the reason because he never really offered explanations. So reluctantly, Rawan went unaccompanied and rather irritated because her mother had refused to subject her daughter to more humiliation, protesting that she should 'just be left in peace.' Her other daughter disapproved, as it was crucial that they do everything in their power to identify and sentence the rapists.

There were four of them, as the forensic examination report had stated. They had brutalised Samra, attacking every inch of her before expelling their wretched bodily fluids inside her life-and-death-giving womanliness. They had mutilated her dreams long before she shared her last breaths with Rawan, leaving her to contemplate her losses on the hot Egyptian sand, where the sun baked their defiling remnants inside her. Samra willed herself to death at the recognition, in the care of stunned doctors, bewildered at the abhorrence yet non-fatality of her injuries. But they knew nothing of Samra. She could not live contaminated, could not have survived the sun's glare upon her after what they had done.

Cross-stitched far past the right to be washed as the sacred Islamic ritual of preparing the dead for burial dictated, Samra was patted with a sponge dipped in musk and saffron-tinted warm water then wrapped lazily like an anchovy ill-prepared. And Saleem was late to the funeral. He missed the procession and arrived as her body descended below the mourners' feet. Standing a fair distance behind them, he inattentively left his hand to be shaken with rushed and mostly insincere condolences as they passed him while exiting the burial plot. He thought of how they would all return to their homes, eat, sleep, go to work and make love to each other and life as they knew it would remain unperturbed. In forty days, they would return, cry, wail even, only to once more go about their existence as do the cattle at a slaughterhouse, mindlessly watching their fellow livestock's heads falling from their bodies and patiently waiting their turn. Maybe even chewing *berseem* as they cue.

He asked himself if he could do the same: brazenly live. To continue would be hypocrisy on his part after all the judgments he had imposed on all those people. But to die? Even to live so apathetically that it would be like dying would, too, be unrealistic. He pondered those clashing thoughts for a while, as his hand was repeatedly shaken and his cheeks kissed, one light, dishonest peck on the left, another on the right, amidst occasional earnest hugs from a few. All who remained now diverted their attention to his distraught 'would-have-been' mother-in-law, who had dropped herself to the ground beside the tomb's entrance and, shaking her frail arms to the heavens, yelled, 'You are an unjust god! I will never pray to you! I will never pray to you! You are a monster, not a god! You thief! You murderer! You tyrant!' She continued to lament amidst bystanders' pitying comments, such as 'The woman has lost her mind. Poor thing.' Others countered with 'No matter how can she utter such blasphemy?!' Saleem, as a strange pilgrim seeking death, stood alone.

The thing most discerning when solitude is concerned is hardly the independence of one's self, but rather one's competence to endure one's individuality when there is no one present to critique or applaud.

From the elevated ground he stood upon, Saleem noticed a black shape crouched far across from where he stood and a slim hand extending from one of its sides, gripping the soft, wet sand above Samra's tomb. His body shifted.

Rawan was not crying. It was peculiar. She was sitting at a fair distance from him, but he could hear her breathe as he dragged his feet to approach her. She was panting, as if on a sprint. He approached her dishevelled body, perhaps craving proximity with the one other person he knew was genuinely grieving, maybe even – he dared think – more than he was.

She was not beautiful. Not in the direct, overt sense. She was not striking, and could hardly be referred to by a stranger as sensual. She lacked the symmetry and delicateness of features commonly considered attractive. But she had the most intense eyes; they could seep their haunting coolness, their languid evil into people and drown them. You only had to possess the patience and intrigue to see that she was absolutely mesmerising. Rawan's beauty could only be recognised and appreciated by someone who wished to own the prohibited, who desired to hold water within his palms yet keep them dry, someone who craved delay.

Her hands ground the sand harder, rasping it between her fingertips until they bled. He sat beside her and the call to prayer rebounded in the dark that encompassed them together with the dead.

'*Hay 'ala al-falah! Hay 'ala al-falah!*' What was that? And in God's name, how could they do that? Was Saleem being asked to drive to the cargo village at Cairo Airport, to sit in his office signing papers or sweep the site checking shipments? Must Rawan change the return date of her flight back to Tunis and leave the next day? What was he expecting when asking them to *hay 'ala al-falah*? If God understood and would grant them a grace period to heal, then why were they hearing it, pounding in their ears like a nagging question from someone who knew the answer? '*La elah ella Allah...*'

The cockroaches emerged from their homes to serenade the dead and their new member, Samra, whose freshly watered cactuses adorned her resting ground.

They would not have been able to see each other's faces even if they had looked at one another, yet their breathing was the same, like a rhythmic warp of the aftermath to a nuclear explosion. The bright white cloud that implodes and engulfs a city in darkness, producing generation after generation of beings who may wish to believe themselves human, yet unavoidably lack humanity within and without. Rawan felt the tension of hushed air cut through her until it ripped her lips apart: 'The lawyer says we will wait until he schedules a hearing date.'

'I didn't ask.'

'I called him when we were still at the hospital … I called him.'

'It doesn't matter.'

'He—'

'How can you talk about this? How?'

She stared at him in the darkness so intently that the white in her eyes shone against the faintest light of his. 'Don't you dare sit there and talk to me like you didn't sleep last night, wake up, put those clothes and those shoes on, get in your car, drive and come here! How dare you?'

He was perplexed. And to her own knowledge, she was breaking him with every word.

She continued, 'He says we have to wait till they identify and bring in the other two.'

Saleem remained silent.

'Say something,' she said in a somewhat gentler tone of empathy.

Was his attitude a considerable betrayal of Samra? He asked himself whether or not her sister's efforts would amount to anything but more loss, more pain, more of how he felt at present.

'I don't trust that Amgad guy,' he finally said.

She paused. 'Who?'

'Amgad Acir, the detective.'

She paused again, gathering the name he was mentioning, playing with its letters in split sets to even the outcome – AM-

GA-DA-CI ... R ... like an indecipherable scribble, a symbol, lay the 'R' on its back and draw a line through the middle ... R.

She uttered in response, 'You don't trust the police.'

'Do you?' He smirked, as if ridiculing her inability to sense the irony in her statement.

She thought about his question. Needless to say, it was expected nature of her being to produce adequate answers, but, at that moment, she repressed the impulse to offer a satisfactory response and moved to her own self-reflection.

'I don't trust them,' she finally mustered.

Evening Comes

A mgad considered snapping the office boy's head off his pathetic body. He shook as he screamed into the boy's face, spraying him with poisoned spit. 'Why is Samra Yaqub's case not on my desk? I asked for that file to be on my desk before I arrived! Get out of my sight, you rotten piece of filth, and don't show me your face without that file!' The boy ran out of the office terrified. 'Son of a bitch!' Amgad cursed under his breath.

He drowned his coffee down, then checked his watch. The girl was brutally raped, he thought to himself. *Four thugs. We found two.* He scribbled words and lines and arrows, underlining some phrases, circling others, as he recited the details to himself, trying to make sense of them. *The other two escaped ... Girl died from intense cervical damage and uterine bleeding ... Ambulance didn't get there in time to minimise damage ... As a result, complications arose ... Announced dead around midday, 5th of October.*

A knock on the door interrupted him. Timidly but hurriedly, the boy paced across the office and placed a file before Amgad. 'Here you go, *basha*.'

'Knock on my door when it's 2:30 sharp. I have an important errand.'

'Yes, *basha*.' The boy scurried out of the room.

Amgad flipped through the file in his hands. He selected certain pages, separated them from the rest and placed them side by side across his desk. Singling out select photos too, he would frequently scratch his beard or shrivel his forehead in concentration. Here and there, he placed post-it-notes on the papers and photos, then scribbled words on them. He continued for hours, scouring the file, smoking repeatedly until it seemed he was finally momentarily satisfied, then picked up his mobile and commenced to capture pictures of the organised chaos on his desk. Finally, he stripped the yellow notes off and stuffed them in a plastic bag by the dust-bin beneath his desk.

Amgad rewarded himself for his hard work with a coffee break until his office phone rang. He sighed, before raising the headset to his ear. 'Yes, send him in,' he prompted.

A large, somewhat ageing man of a distinct portly build entered the office, and Amgad rose to shake his hand.

'How are you today, *basha*?' Ahmad, the lawyer, inquired.

Amgad already felt he could envision his own neurons clicking and transmitting a nebula of data, and the presence of the lawyer entering his office was the adequate increment.

'All is well, thank you. How can I help?'

'*Basha*, I've been trying to reach the lawyer of the arrested suspects, to discuss persuading them to provide information on the other two.'

Although the case was clearly vivid in his mind from endless hours spent reading dozens of reports, Amgad pretended not to know the lawyer or what he was discussing. 'I'm sorry, what case are you representing?' he asked.

'*Basha*, I am Mr. Yehia Yaqub's lawyer: Mr. Ahmad!'

'Mr. Who?'

'Yehia Yaqub, the deceased Samra Yaqub's brother, who was—'

'Ah, yes … hmm, and why are you here again?'

Ahmad regarded the detective for a moment, clearly confused. 'Well, I need access to the two detained suspects so that I can—'

'I'm afraid that will be difficult,' Amgad said.

'Yes, I know. That is why I request to meet with their lawyer … to—'

'Lawyer?' Amgad sneered. 'Mr. Ahmad, they are thugs! The defence is unwillingly obliged to handle them. This is a common case; too common now. As a lawyer yourself, I'd assume you are aware of this. It is impossible to reach the remaining suspects. I mean, the ones we found we were only able to do so because they were lagging a few miles away from the scene of the crime. Now it's up to the general prosecutor to determine their sentence.' He spoke in a monotonous unaffectedness, yet sensing the crude insensitivity in his voice, he added, 'But I'm sure nothing would compensate your client's loss.'

Ahmad was dumbfounded. The detective did not appear to be considering the matter seriously, regardless of the few staged compassionate words with which he had ended his speech. 'Amgad *basha*, I am a lawyer, and I have the right to—'

'Mr. Ahmad,' Amgad interrupted once more in mounting impatience. 'Most, if not all, rape cases have no witnesses except, in this girl's unfortunate case, the culprits themselves – in the plural sense. We were only able to arrest these men on the basis of them being in proximity to the victim directly after her attack. However, it is highly unlikely they will be convicted. If I were you, I wouldn't concern myself too much with the other two because the ones we have, those suspects, well, they'll be released before you finish your Tuesday morning coffee. Now, I must excuse myself as I have an important appointment.' Bending down to pick the plastic bag off the floor, he shoved it awkwardly in his trouser pocket then proceeded to the door whilst continuing to address the lawyer. 'But let's reschedule this delightful, yet unfortunately compromised, meeting and we can discuss matters further.'

'I had no idea that violent and criminal thugs were so indispensable to the police,' Ahmad declared furiously.

'Excuse me?' Amgad retorted.

'You seem to be more occupied with preventing me from doing my job than with doing yours.'

'You ought to be very careful with filtering what exits your mouth, Mr. Ahmad. You are, after all, in a detective's office. I could arrest you this very minute.'

'I am a criminal lawyer, *basha*. I have been threatened countless times before, and it has never hindered me from my work.'

Amgad kept his hand on the doorknob and spoke his

final words before exiting his office: 'If you regarded that as a threat, then you are clearly a very inexperienced lawyer who I presume has only been handling petty cases. Tuesday morning coffee, Mr. Ahmad.'

***

'Why are you here? You hated it here. Why in heaven's name would you choose to remain, considering the circumstances above all else?' Zain swept his left thumb across the rolling paper and smoothed down some unruly hash into a straight line. He peeped at Rawan over his glasses, waiting for her answer.

'I must do this, with or without your help.'

'This isn't about my help.'

'It's about my sister, so I cannot make sense of your attempts to distance me from here.'

'No it's not about Samra. It's about you. Are we really doing this? Because I can't talk to you like this anymore. I like to think you are many things, Rawan, but you're not an idiot.' He stood then proceeded to stroll to and fro before her, his hands moving in performance of his explanation. 'This is too elaborate and intricate and screwed up for me to believe that it's not about you.'

'Zain, that man must pay. He must be punished for what he did.'

'And you think you won't be? After you go along with your plan, you think everyone will let you out clean, if you kill a detective? Or would you opt out at the last minute and have Saleem do it? Why do you want to get rid of Amgad, Rawan?'

The light of the lanterns seemed to flicker against their escalating debate.

'Are you joking? Are you seriously trying to convince me that you see no clue how this corrupt piece of garbage is the reason those men walked free? The scum practically sabotaged the entire case!'

'There was no case, Rawan. The judge decided, not Amgad. It was a judge's verdict to acquit them.'

'And what is this rubbish regarding Saleem? The man has wept more than I have, for God's sake.' Rawan eyed Zain silently with an obliging impatience for his response. 'Zain, I just need the place for one month. Thirty days. That's all I'm asking. You've instigated fights for me. You've lent me more money than I can remember, most of which I don't recall having paid back. Do this for me, and it will be as if we are travelling together and seeing more of the world, you and I. Please, I just need this. You still remember; I know you do. You still remember—'

'All the escape plans we never saw through? Yeah ... I remember. Come here.' He held her close to his chest and heaved. 'Rawan. I'm such an ass with you. I never do you any good.'

She looked up at him. 'What are you saying?'

'I mean ... yes ... how we met, but—'

'So I score off you ... so what? Oh, come on! You love me! Stop being soppy; it's not you. Are you high? You're high, right?' She giggled, then sprang into an uncontrollable fit of laughter.

'Yeah,' Zain snickered. 'Yeah, I'm high as hell!' He laid his neck back and rested his back with her torso, still holding her against the elevated side of his ribs, across the end of the office sofa.

It was an absorbing room. It held nothing within that could resemble that of an office save for its 'declared' purpose. Like Rawan, Zain loved Andalusian furniture; he decorated the walls of the room where he spent his evenings with Arabesque-style wooden creations. The intricate carvings and jointed pieces lent the room a sense of history and authenticity that surpassed the charm of the entire city. He had bought the lamps from a grim alley in Al Azhar one damp October night and then, realising they were worth more than he had paid for them, returned to purchase another item from the *dokan* owner, and reimburse him. Indeed, day after day, month after month, his business flourished, convincing him that the lamps were his lucky charm. Their seller was just as responsible for such luck and held in high stature within the eyes of a fellow man who had scrupled himself from a similar alley to his current disposition, and Zain, overwhelmed with intense schedules, could not leave El Gouna until a year had passed. He returned to that *dokan* on a more humid October night than the year before, and as he approached the door, he heard a girl cursing from within: 'Your display is pitiful! It was bound to snag against someone sometime and fall!'

'You had it in your hands … you were asking for the price. You dropped it, woman!'

'Woman!'

'What? You're not a woman?! Sorry, princess, madame,

whatever. You have to pay for it. It's only a hundred pounds, you cheap—'

Zain could hear a faint yet audible pandemonium of bells and rustling from within.

'Oh! "Only a hundred pounds" – oh, that's ok then. Because I'm dressed well and look well-off so a hundred pounds must be pennies to me, right? You're a poor old man in a *dokan*, so I should pine "poor thing" then trip over myself and pull out those pennies, or else I'm a cheap woman? You bastard!'

The man lunged at her, aiming to slap his hand across her flushed cheeks, just as she pulled a gun from her pocket and pointed it at his stunned face. Zain ran into the store, between them and yelled at her to put the gun down.

She paused and glared at him, her arms stretched out, fixated in their pose, taken aback by his confident rebuke of her as opposed to timidly approaching more slowly to the woman who had a gun. He stared at her, as if she were a self-contained fire.

'Here.' Zain pushed a two-hundred-pound note into the man's hand just as he was about to say something, grabbed the woman's arm and pulled her out of the store.

She struggled to free her arm from his grip, protesting indignantly, but he held her until they had exited the alley. When they were near his car and she was moments from screaming he released her arm.

'How old are you?' he asked, scrutinising her appearance with the perplexed countenance a man could only give when in the presence of a woman who was both hostile and relatively young.

'What?'

'How old are you? It's two in the morning. How do you have a gun?' He blasted questions at her like a child who had just discovered he could talk. 'You look affluent. What could a well-off girl like you possibly be doing here at this time with a gun?'

She sized him up, running her eyes from the pavement he stood on to his hairline. 'That is the most sexist thing I've ever heard anyone say to me.'

'What?' Zain could not believe his ears. He gazed at her with a heat in his eyes so intense it burned him. This woman intrigued his hairs on end.

'I said—'

'I heard you,' he said. 'Did you just socially critique my question? I mean, did you just "ideologically" analyse what I said?'

'You commented on the fact that I was a woman out at two in the morning in Al Azhar.'

'You're not a woman. You look shy of twenty.'

'Just as offensive! I'm nineteen.'

There was an obscure murk floating too close to his introduction. Had he prevented her from a mistake? No. For as relatively brief as she had existed, life, meaning those who had almost destroyed her after degrading her from all she knew of herself worthy of keeping, had bid their abusive farewells in a manner which dictated a simple truth: coincidence is a lie.

'Who sent you?' She raised a single brow at him under the conspicuous light hanging theatrically obtrusive above their heads like a dramatic crown.

He smiled at her, his face shaking slightly in confusion. 'What?'

'You heard me,' she said. 'Who sent you? I know the answer already. I'm just enjoying your poorly controlled body language at the moment.'

With his own years , which at that moment seemed to almost cripple his back with their burden, his own simple truth dawned upon him, and his eyes dared not to blink at the sincerity of his ardent belief that she, like the rest of her kind, was the most unassailable, breakable thing in existence and that the harder she was, the less pliable, less volatile she could be. Damage to such a creature was irrevocable – breaking a woman, a sin.

So, as Lucifer himself only could, Zain spoke the words that would harm the least: 'I don't think you are aware of what you were about to do to that man in there, and, consequently, to yourself – let alone this air of conspiracy you are feigning, not because what you claim is absurd, but because of that pale emptiness in your eyes, assuring me that you know; you know very well there is no one who cares about you enough to send a soul after you.'

Rawan seethed silently, her body frigid with the indignation of a child tolerating punishment. The sentiments within her grew ever so placidly that, by the time realisation dawned upon her, their source had budded a fondness for himself within her too, and for no reason – save for the abject Stockholm syndrome taking effect – at that very moment, he seemed to her almost fatherly. She liked that. She liked him.

'What's your name, woman of nineteen?'

She repeatedly breathed her name a couple of times, imagining its sound if he were to say it. 'Rawan,' she replied.

Zain watched a galloping wild horse, vehement yet graceful, glide within his mind's eye across the office. He passed the joint to Rawan as they relaxed on the sofa, her bare feet stretched on the coffee table before them. 'I like the way your face looks in this light,' she told him.

'I know … I like your tattoo.'

'I know.'

Zain, put Omar Khairat's 'A Place in the Heart' on. He left her side and walked across the room to the iPhone dock, scrolling to find the track she had requested.

'When are you planning to install the aerial ropes?' she inquired casually.

Zain, still bent over his desk, considered her from over his glasses. 'Tomorrow morning. I've booked the men. I expect them by nine.' He continued to look at her. She was so beautiful, he thought, and so lost. So poetically lost.

She returned his searching gaze. 'So why have you been trying to talk me out of it, if you're so on board, you've already booked them? I mean, I did nag, but—'

'Because I only attempt to plead with those who do not falter in their decision.'

'A pointless and useless thing to attempt, right?'

'Yes, that's why I do it.' Zain walked back to her. He knelt at her feet, pulled one of her legs off the coffee table and hugged her knee with both arms. 'You can practise tomorrow,' he said.

She began to roll him another joint, grappling for what she needed from the table. 'I don't think I need to. It doesn't have to look professional. There are no references to compare me to. It must only seem erotic, exciting, eye grabbing. That's all I need for him to see me.'

'Who could not see you, Rawan? *Habebti*, you're an earthquake!'

'We feel earthquakes, Zain. I don't need him to feel. I need him to see. I must be a firework on a dark, starless night.'

'Fireworks burn out and disappear.'

'Exactly.'

'Are you sick of the music replaying?'

'No.'

'How are you going to do it? In the end, I mean.'

'With the gun.'

'That's ironic!' Zain scoffed.

'How so?'

She was so adrift in her scheme, she was practically drowning herself in it. 'You cannot erase the past, Rawan. Hell, we can't even decorate it. It is what it was. All you would achieve is a menacing, endless loop of recreating it. The desire to undo the past excites and thrills. Like that "firework" business of yours. But following the great explosion, the epitome of a seemed actualisation, you gradually dim out from self-immolation. What's left of you shall eventually become colourless, and you will lose your burning quality before you ever touch the ground … that's if you actually land. Spectators down below leave after their final gasp. And you will become nothing. You, Rawan. Imagine! Nothing!'

She eyed him absentmindedly, staring beyond his skull. 'You're not scaring me. If that's what you intend.'

'I don't intend to do anything. Leave, Rawan. Just go back. No, not back. Wrong word.' He thought for a second. 'I mean away, go away. Don't keep looking behind you. You've stumbled enough. Stop pulling at the remnants of your past and flinging them on the path ahead of you. You're so young for God's sake! You're so gloriously young.'

She put the joint butt between his lips and held his face in her hands. 'Zain, make sure those ropes are secured as tightly as possible. I've gotten slightly weather-beaten over the years.' She giggle in obsessed determination, smiling as if to shake and ground him at once so that he may eternally vibrate in the unyielding sphere of her emotions and disappear with the magnitude of a genesis bang.

Hiding Behind Trees

S aleem rubbed the ring between his thumb and forefinger. He lay in the tub, soaking in water that carried traces of his people's laundry sweat, cooking residues and urine. He could no longer wear it, having lost so much weight. Layla Chamamian's melodic voice flushed through the walls and flew in under the bathroom door, as his ageing brow fixated in its recent default of a concentrated frown.

He examined the ring. Engraved across the interior of its curvature was 19-03-2013. She loved the Nile. He had been away for two months at work in Dubai and was to miss her twenty-fourth birthday celebrations, yet when the phone rang at his early regular hour, she began to expect her fantasy's approach.

She imagined one of her friends would arrive at her home to be sure she wore a more socially promoted attire – connotative of femininity – than jeans and a top, to direct her, behind the wheel, to a remote area on the corniche and motion her to park. A few hours shy of dusk, the sky would be a clear coral as it nestled the hesitantly sinking sun amidst a few wisps of clouds. When she steps out of the car and walks along the waterside, the breaking lines of light would caress her hair, handing her golden strands to the breeze so it too could fondle them. Her friend would grab her arm and guide her to a ramp that led to a half-dozen floating yachts. They would board a noticeably neat one, and it would launch as her friends kiss her and shower her with perfumed birthday wishes. Following dinner, the same friend who had accompanied her earlier, or another, would suggest they approach one of the crew men to request dance music, and she would talk to the man in charge, then abandon Samra.

Her imagination ruled that she should turn at that moment to see where her friend had gone, and there he would be standing, with all the gentle innocence of a boy in love. His eyes would gleam at her, and, as she runs to hug the man who would have abandoned all his obligations to celebrate the day she came into the world, he would fall to his knees like in her favourite movies and look up at her as if she were a goddess on her pedestal, watching him from above as her face turns, dazzling, hoisted amongst the stars like an apparition. He would speak grandly of his utter devotion to her: 'I want to look in the mirror each morning to find you sleeping peacefully next to me. I want you to laugh into my chest and ignite my heart with your breath each night. I want to carry each of our newborn children and whisper the *adhan* in their ears as I look at you. I want to love you each day like it's my last on this Earth. And what I want most of all is for the sound with which you utter that you love me and your bright encompassable eyes as you say it, to be my last memories before I die.' And then he would ask her to be his wife, and she would weep with joy and the world would be splendid.

There was one simple problem with Samra's vision: It was not Saleem.

Being a rebel of a man, he would not have it as so; he would not propose when she anticipated him to. He couldn't. He could only be the man beyond what she expected. But Samra was a romantic puddle of dreams.

So she waited.

Waited to hear a feigned indifference in his voice over the phone.

Waited for him to show up 'unexpected' at her birthday. Waited for the music to numb and the lights to dim to find herself staring at him from across the yacht in a suit, holding flowers and kneeling. She told her friends countless times, so their unbridled tongues would betray her secret to him. But he knew, without a single secret escaping. Because he knew her.

Yet, he did not comply with her wishes. And so she waited many more months, a year, two years, three, a hundred … Who really knows for how long she must have waited? And he willed it as such so that she would lose hope, so he would know what it is she sought more: to be with him, or to experience the resolution of the story.

At least that is what he told himself. But that was not why he let her wait, because although he did not realise it, he was waiting, too. Waiting for her to abandon hope, yet choosing to remain nonetheless, so that he would be assured that no matter what life hurled upon them afterwards, she would never leave him. Because unfortunately, Saleem needed more to feel the reassurance of her unfailing love for him than to be the man who assured her of his.

So when the time came, he disregarded her dramatic and overworked fantasy, believing that a man may gratify his woman in all matters except with his proposal, for it must be an indication of who he is.

It was their yearly camping trip in the desert with the same group of friends they had always accompanied, and after the first bonfire, she agreed to stay up with him, for he had requested so, knowing the exhaustion of the day's amusement would have her fall asleep in no time.

And now *he* waited.

Waited for her breath to deepen, her lips to soften, her body to sink, heavy and limp in his arms. And because he knew her, he did not need to ask; he slid the band gently around her fingertip and just past her knuckle where it would rest so that when she awoke at the brink of dawn, and felt an odd squeeze on her finger, she would feel nothing but astounded. How simple it was, how deeply she felt for him. How devoid of distractive nonsense he had made it. He had said it all silently: 'I want to watch our last sunrise together, with you, my wife, in my arms.'

The water in the tub around him grew colder, and he had promised they would leave the world together. In retrospect, the audacity of his marriage proposal was overwhelmingly sickening. Where was it now, his crowning of her finger? In a box somewhere in her room perhaps, buried under a white satin dress and tulle, both her room and the sun and the desert oblivious to the loss of their owner.

Samra's playlist continued to drown him. How long would

it take for the soak to decompose his body, he wondered? Must he submerge his head at some point so as not to interrupt the process?

His phone buzzed for the fifth time. Rawan, again.

'Yes, I'm here. Sorry … I was taking a shower.' His throat croaked like the churning insides of an abandoned car.

'Ok. So, I've just met with Zain. All is set. I want to see you before though.'

'Yeah, I was going to call you for the same reason. I don't plan on being patient, Rawan. I'm going to see his filthy blood on the floor soon. I know I will. I am going to get that corrupt son of a bitch so soon—'

'Just meet me tonight in Zamalek, ok? We'll talk.' She hung up. Samra was also accustomed to ending her calls without a formal farewell. It had always annoyed him, but now, more and more, he found it endearing. Anything Rawan did or said that was once shared by her sister brought him peace, if that were genuinely possible.

He left the house earlier than they had agreed upon and sat in his car.

The door man ran to him as fast as his feeble legs permitted and rested his wrists on the adjacent window. 'Saleem *bey*, you've forgotten to give me the electricity money. The man came early yesterday with the bills.'

'Yes, excuse me. One second.' Saleem fumbled with his wallet.

'He was going to cut it off, *bey*, but I stopped him! I said, listen here! Saleem *basha* will pay tomorrow, so just come back tomorrow!'

Saleem handed him the money. 'Yes, here you go *'Am* Galal, thank you. And these are for you,' he added, crumbling a fifty-pound note into the *bawab's* hand.

'God bless you Saleem *bey*. Keep it. *Wallahi!* I told him not to cut it and left. Don't you worry; I'll give this to him the next time he comes. God give you patience, *bey*. God give you patience and strength. *Insha Allah* God will substitute you with the lady of ladies … with a princess!'

Saleem's right leg gave an involuntary twitch as he slammed his foot on the accelerator and careened down the street. He fumed, barely avoiding clashes with Cairo's vehicles and pedestrians headed for their Thursday evening rendezvous.

Despite his early arrival, she was there, motioning to him across the street from Diwan Bookstore. He signalled, confirming that she had been spotted and crossed over to hug her. His younger 'sister', the girl who smelled and talked and carried herself as the love of his life once had. The unruly hair that would tangle in defiant knots if he absentmindedly stroked it, the ruffian grimace she made when a passerby violated her with his tongue, even the hay fever-induced sniffle that twisted her nose, later adopted by Samra out of visual habit, an unconscious desire to conform; they were so alike that it both broke and poorly patched his heart in an endless loop. Rawan held him tight for as long as a public heterosexual embrace was permitted in the streets of Cairo. He finally released himself from her grasp.

'Take a walk with me,' she announced, and they moved past the security man eyeing them from his post on the sidewalk.

'How long do you assume you'll need before you can be alone with him?'

'A couple of weeks, I believe,' she said. 'It depends how frequently he goes there. Zain says he's pretty frequent.'

'A couple of weeks, Rawan?' Saleem felt he envisioned a heaving hourglass prance before him, pounding against the road at its feet. 'No, I need sooner!'

'Hey, listen, it's not a project! It will take as long as it needs to. You're impatient, and that's not going to be helpful by any means.' Her intonation of the last three words implied more than a simple intolerance but a reprimand of sorts.

'There are going to be a lot of girls there. Whores, every single one of them. The longer it takes you, the more we risk him losing interest. This Zain, are you sure he's a friend? You need to be safe there. This is just acting. You can't be subjected to any harm. So I think I need to meet him first. I'll know his true intentions to help us once I do.'

'Zain?' She laughed drily. 'I've known Zain for over five years. He's the only man who's had my back in this country.'

'You told me before never to trust, Rawan, remember?'

With what sound implication had he preferred at that given moment to subdue her inability to avoid inconsistency, by reminding her of words she had spoken during their first meeting? Rawan did not trust, because what differentiates docile beings from wild ones is the docile's ability to trust. A wild horse cannot calmly parade through a bustling crowd, nor can a feral pigeon stay still in one's hand long enough to carry a message. And Saleem knew this much about her.

So why did she trust Zain?

'This isn't about trust, Saleem. You do your part, I'll do mine, and we'll both get what we want. Hey, look at me.' She stopped walking and stared at him intently like he was a single lamp in a dark alley. 'I'm not going to play a belly dancer, Saleem. I am going to be … those people are going to see me like I am a dare to their wildest fantasy. And I will make them feel like when they leave that place, they leave the world. I will allow them to see and touch, to experience an illusion, and they will revel in it like nothing they have ever chased before.'

Saleem watched her verbally animated thrill at the prospect of their plan. The means through which she expressed the significance of her role stunned him, yet he was confused as to what he felt. Was he enticed, or threatened? Rawan represented for him the duality of being – at its best and most convoluted state – and whenever they were together, he would become more and more aware of the opposing parallels within him, the paradox of his own self.

She continued to convey her vision: 'As for Amgad, well, he will be drugged … the single man fortunate enough to have the illusion chase him. I will mark him and aim at the mark, and he will grab my hand and plunge that arrow right through his heart; and, should I falter, he will push towards me and end himself.' Her deameanour relaxed so vividly, even her blinking eyelids fluttered gently like a butterfly's pondering wings of fancy, which incongruous to the content of her words agitated Saleem slightly, and he felt a sudden yet fleeting dread and loneliness.

They were quiet until Rawan finished her elaborate depiction: 'You've read "Season of Migration to the North". Well, I'm Mustafa Saeed.'

***

Amgad studied the grey hairs in his beard in the mirror; there were mounds of them that seemed to have appeared overnight. He showered then drove to his barber. The skinny rod of a man greeted him with his regular salute and arched his back forward a couple of inches to shake his hand.

'Come in, *basha*. Right here, yes.' He led him to the chair and ran in for a fresh towel. 'The *basha's* machine, son. And his coffee!' He motioned to an underage assistant at the back of the shop.

'Quickly, Mohammed. I need to be at a meeting,' Amgad ordered in his bored and mandatory tone.

'Oh, *basha!* You exhaust yourself. Look at the weather outside – it's splendid. Why don't you spend the morning on the beach?'

Amgad took a few sips of his coffee, then, as the barber was about to smother his cheeks with lather, replied, 'Mohammed, you want me to stroll on the beach and arrest your peddler friends who charge the foreigners a hundred pounds for *freska*?'

Mohammed laughed as loud and amused as Amgad's rank allowed. '*Basha*, they're poor fellows. Let them earn their bread. We all have mouths to feed.'

'No one is too poor for bread, Mohammed. Not around here, anyway.'

'Yes, *basha*,' Mohammed obeyed. 'Please … this way.' He led Amgad to the right corner of the shop to wash his hair.

'Tell me, Mohammed,' Amgad said over the sound of the water, 'does Zain pass by much?'

'Zain?'

'No fishermen friends, Mohammed?'

'Oh! Yes, *basha*, Zain, yes. Not much. He came for his hair about a week ago, but I hadn't seen him for months before then. All is well, *basha*?'

'Anything new with his business?'

'May *Allah* pardon us, *basha*! I have no ears to listen to prostitution talk.'

Amgad exploded in thundering laughter. Mohammed timidly joined him out of respect.

'Prostitution? Mohammed, you are something!'

Mohammed wiped Amgad's chair by the mirrors.

'Just a trim.'

'Yes, *basha*.'

Amgad's hair flew from under the barber's hands down to the floor, like a crew of suicidal men plunging off of Kasr el Nile Bridge into the water below. Once finished, Amgad was feathered and brushed from excess hair, then he pulled his wallet from the pocket just under his gun. Handling a fifty-pound note, he smiled to himself, reopened his wallet and pulled an extra two-hundred-pound note.

'What's this, *basha*? Do you need change?' Mohammed asked in surprise.

'Here.' He pushed the note into Mohammed's hand. 'Take your wife to a cabaret and have a drink. Prostitution might get you serviced when you return home. Sometimes when a woman sees what she lacks, she's more motivated to please her man.'

Amgad turned his back, exited the shop briskly then jumped into his car and laughed with intense amusement, as looking in his rear-view mirror, he saw the reflection of his barber outside the shop, with a high salute to his head and a bulge in the front of his trousers.

He drove parallel to the sea, the waves seemingly struggling to spray the side of his face as he flew by. It itched him where his beard had been, yet he paid the stinging discomfort no regard; the damning soreness of an irritable face was of no concern to men. If anything, it practically solidified the patriarchy; the provocation of their faces placed them in the rank of species that self-inflicted their daily annoyance to feel presentable. Those who did not shave ranged from religious zealots to lazy sloths.

Yet few men to none understood the pleasure of keeping it to tickle a woman's skin. Even fewer women appreciated the excitation of a man's beard and moustache during a kiss, or their brush against her neck while making love. As a woman had once told Amgad, no one kissed or cared for making love in Egypt.

Amgad recalled her commenting on a Rushdi Abaza and Shadia scene in a classic Egyptian film, how she saw the violent, grinding manner of the kiss as an awkward, passionless act from a man gratified with the non-gratification of his woman, or at least the forceful overpowering of her. Countless women, in love with Rushdi Abaza, charmed with his on-screen sexuality; generations of women coded to believe this was love, that force meant passion.

No one kissed in Egypt. No man who considered himself a genuine product of Egyptian society knew what it meant to press his lips against a woman's, then separate them with his tongue. No man knew that to slide passionately from one lip to the other meant that he held the freshness of the sea at the edge of his mouth. Amgad would barge his tongue between her teeth and push it as far inside her mouth as it could go, because his pleasure derived from penetrating her, roughly.

The women knew not the feeling of their men's tongues caressing the curvatures of their own, stroking the very cells of their palate. The women knew not the idea that a woman's body with all its entrances was not to be penetrated, but to be slipped into.

You must approach the entrance with care, tiptoe in awe and converse with it. You must tease her, entice her to grant you the permit to enter; and, once she does, you must never forget to drop your ego at the door before treading within. The expression is to 'fall in love', not shove in love. And no one made love in Egypt.

To make love to a woman is to be your most vulnerable self. The only strength you may possess is the realisation of all it is you have to lose as you step inside, knowing you shall not leave as the same man who entered. The power lies in willingly risking all, hoping she allows you to carry the scent of her skin as you exit. Who would not care to receive such a shrouded gift?

But no man has ever made love to a woman in Egypt.

He had tried to – once upon a time, beyond his own conceivable fears, he had chosen to trust, and deceiving his own senses, he entered a woman. This woman, however, did not release the scent of her skin nor return his own to him. She engulfed him completely, and the more he entered her, the more she stripped away until one day he awoke to find nothing of whom he could barely remember as Amgad. It is impossibly cruel how those who are wronged must go on living at least long enough to pay it forward with unkindness.

Amgad continued to scratch his face as he tore along the ocean's edge. He slowed down at a right turn before approaching an expansive yet scattered array of docks at the far end of the street. Everything was sickeningly quiet. Amgad raised an eyebrow, his gaze searching. Even rodents weren't traceable.

A loud bang resounded somewhere inside a slate-black building featuring an awkwardly handwritten (albeit large) sign: 'Naktal workshop'.

Amgad circled the workplace and came upon a tall, broad-shouldered man standing outside the back entrance. He was directing five men transporting boxes and heaving steel cases, loading the contents of several trucks and carrying them to the boats docked. Amgad parked and approached the man who stood with his back to the detective. Amgad stopped. Zain's ears prickled at the halt to the sound of the detective's approaching feet and froze for a split moment before casually turning around to greet him.

'You are so loyal, *basha*. You never give up on your perfume.'

Amgad laughed, the same dry laugh he had given his barber. 'Congratulations, Zain. Has business picked up so well that you're running morning shows now too?'

'May God hear from you! No, I'm just developing the place. New equipment for the girls.'

'New girls, you mean.' Amgad grinned daringly.

'That too.' Zain turned to stroll by the docks, and Amgad followed. 'Would you like a private tour, *basha*?' Zain prompted.

'That would be a good start, yes.'

Zain signalled to two of his workers to prepare an unoccupied and dainty fishing motor-boat, and, followed by Amgad, climbed in.

The detective studied the beach as the boat took off, taunted slightly by the roar of the engine, which seemed not only to drown the voices of the sea, but to also obliterate his sense of time to a formidable extent. For sure enough, they were approaching their destination briskly.

Little wind disturbed the surface of the sea, clawing gently at the sides of a looming building, and 'Naktal' stood surrounded by docks with the air of a grand mountain that perhaps continued further below into the sea bed than one's eye or the world's light could reach. Amgad gawked silently at Naktal's monumental size from his humble angle, feeling the strain of his pitiful eyes collaborating to encompass the building fully in one glance, and the struggle of his lungs to meet such fulfilment in the scope of one breath, before both his eyes and his chest surrendered and he dropped his gaze to a glare, studying Zain who had already disembarked from the motor-boat and was beckoning him to follow further.

Naktal seemed larger from within than an outsider would expect, although the walls were extremely dark. There were no windows, and so one would assume it would feel like being inside a cave; yet the experience was not so. The space shared the ocean's scent, though there were no signs of natural ventilation, and while it seemed enveloped upon itself, the sheer vastness caused the sensation of standing somewhere on a cliff that was drowned in constant darkness. And since that very moment, Amgad would think of Zain as a 'bat', although Zain himself would have preferred to be labelled an 'owl'.

The colossal building was internally a large semi-circle, although its exterior looked more rectangular and defined. At the far centre of the hall, a stage was prompted reasonably high so that clients' heads would be levelled with the dancers' stilettos. Along the edge of the stage were high chairs and a blindingly bright bar table, while further behind, tables and chairs were neatly scattered to accommodate the more cowardly souls, those who felt that as seated spectators, they were less involved, less guilty of crossing permitted boundaries of sexual experimentation.

Amgad's eyes followed the men, who, like Solomon's ants, assembling his throne upside down from the depth and dark innards of Naktal's roof, had risen to the top floor of the building and were affixing what seemed to him like iron bars of various shapes to the grand ceiling that loomed above him.

He frowned, clueless of what exactly could be considered 'business development' by cramming the ceiling with bars and hooks. Zain eyed him, apparently amused by his convoluted expressions.

'In four days, *basha*, I invite you to a vision … something new … which I believe will flip this town on its head.'

Amgad peered directly into Zain's eyes. 'And what would that be, exactly? You found a woman with three tits?'

Zain's chuckle roared across the hall. 'I found one who can fly!'

'Just make sure she doesn't break her neck, Zain.'

'Actually I'm more concerned about my clients breaking theirs.'

'Well, you've intrigued me,' Amgad replied in his usual assumed boredom. 'As always, be careful, Zain. You are a man who has a knack for throwing away your people for your own dreams. Hopefully you won't wake up anytime soon, wondering whether it was all worth it.'

Zain lit a cigarette and blew the smoke in Amgad's face. 'Don't ever hint at that topic with me again. You have no comprehension of what you are talking about.'

Coughing slightly, Amgad waved both the smoke and his bubbling irritation with his hand. 'Fair enough. I have another word of caution for you, Zain, since we're here on a friendly basis: do not surprise me. People who attempt to are more than often gravely disappointed. It is my understanding that you are a smart and pragmatic man. Stay so, and do not veer.'

'You must have much work to get back to. Good day, *basha*. I shall be expecting you soon.' He shook Amgad's hand and turned his back, continuing to comment on the handymen's work.

Amgad put on his sunglasses and led himself out the back door, before indicating to the boat man his need to return to shore. For some reason, Amgad found himself scanning the water around him for fish or even tiny air bubbles, any semblance of aquatic life or any life for that matter other than the wind forcefully breaking the water's surface, as Naktal continued to shrink in perspective until the sun drowned it. The motor fought noisily against the breaking water, which paid back its complaints in salty spits across his face.

When he could finally see his car, he fidgeted with the keys in his pocket impatiently until the engine clapped to a stop and the men on shore grabbed the rope that had been flung over his head, tying it securely to dock. He rode his car, circled the workshop again, then drove back down the narrow street,

Arriving at the station an hour later, he honked promptly at the security guard, who anxiously jumped off his seat in the shade and let the gate bar loose from its clasp to the ground. Amgad swerved into the parking quarter and left the car under the canopy at the far right. He walked up the stairs to the station amidst salutes and greetings choked with reverence and assumed inferiority, then sped to his office.

Cases and files waiting passively to be reviewed sat in piles on his desk. As the office boy raced past him to open the air conditioner, Amgad passed him a dirty look that signalled for coffee and a gesticulating swipe in the air with two fingers to shut the door.

So We May Be Lost

Rawan watched her sweat drip below her on the wooden floorboards, yet she kept a determined grip on the hoop. Hanging upside down, her loose hair brushed the sweat on the floor delicately as she forced her two legs wide open above her head. She panted heavily, remembering to point her toes, to relax her muscles that ached tremendously in forced recollection of their former abilities.

Rawan had religiously taken on pole fitness during college yet gradually lost interest later on. She brought her legs together and curled them over the inside of the hoop, then hoisted her torso up until she could sit within the circle. Her breathing heaved her chest out and in violently as two quarrelling lovers torn between separation and union.

Her mother walked into the room. Rawan swerved round from her height and looked at her as she stared back from behind her burdened eyelids. A woman, made a mother by a man, bereaved of her eldest daughter by other men, stood before Rawan with the perplexity of a victim of time's crimes against her wasted youth and sense of worth.

'What are you doing?'

'I'm exercising,' she replied in a chilled manner.

'Exercising?'

'Yes. What is it?'

'Where were you last night? I didn't hear you come in.'

'With Saleem. We went out for coffee.'

'You left in the morning and returned so late I was fast asleep!'

'So?'

Her mother had been standing by the door; she stepped further into the room and approached her, craning her neck up to look at her daughter.

'Come down from there,' she said.

'I'm not done just yet. Did you need anything?'

'Rawan, I'm tired. Please come down.'

'If I come down, you won't be tired?' she retorted.

'Listen, I'm not in the mood for your philosophising right now. I can't talk like this.'

'There's nothing to talk about.'

She did not interrupt eye contact with her mother, who stayed fixated on Rawan with such frustration, she almost cried. Her daughter remained unperturbed.

'I'm moving out of the house in a couple of days,' Rawan said.

'Now you look here!' Her mother launched at her with a rebuking finger. 'If you think I'm going to allow you to—'

'I'm not asking for your approval; I'm informing you of what I'll do.'

'Do you have any feelings whatsoever?' Her mother broke up emotionally.

Rawan, refraining from responding to her mother's ill-advised rhetorical question, jumped to the ground. The floor creaked, suffering beneath her composed rage. She bent low to search under her bed, but stretching her right arm into the darkness and sweeping right and left, found nothing but dust.

'What are you looking for?' her mother said calmly.

'There … was … a suitcase … here.' Rawan panted, pushing her chest to the floor so she could see, squinting at the dark. She glimpsed it, far towards the edge of the bed. She dragged the suitcase to the middle of the room, unzipped it and began to empty winter clothes onto the bed. Her mother shifted her body in order to secure the cupboard door from her daughter's determination.

'So, I've lost my children? The only thing I've lived for? You're condemning me … just like that?'

'I'm sorry you feel that way, but I have a life to live. No parent, nobody owns that.'

'You think I'm going to let you act as you please? Do you even realise what talk would circulate about you? The kind of things people would say?'

Rawan's tone increased in depth and volume. 'Do you even remember Samra? "What would *people* say?" Where were people? Where are these people you're so concerned about? Where is your husband?' She laughed, perhaps with more cruelty than she intended. 'Even *he* is not here!'

'Are you judging me because he left, Rawan?' her mother replied, greatly pained.

'No, I'm answering you, Mama. I'm talking to you, but all you've ever had ears and voice for was to judge me. I'm not like you, and I'm sorry for that.' She paused, considering the truth in her spontaneity. 'No – you know what? I'm not even sorry! You've always reminded me that I'm different; I always assured you that I was, always confirmed that I knew. And I can't talk with you. I haven't been able to for years. I don't even think you care. But here's the thing: it doesn't matter to me anymore, because I will not lie to myself, and I really don't give a crap about pleasing anyone, even you!'

What her mother said next not only infuriated Rawan beyond the benefit of discussion, but also made certain that she had paid no regard to all she had just said: 'Did you do something wrong, Rawan?' Her mother was almost motionless, cold, stiff, nothing in her even twitched save for her quivering eyes that darted deep in their insane shuddering glare. 'Is that it, Ms. Open-Minded Dancer? Are you running off with some man?' The last word she spoke was no more than a dreadful whisper.

Rawan's entire body fumed, her thoughts barely able to articulate themselves within her long enough before she spat them out: 'Oh, my God! I am so sick and done with this pathetic, revolting culture! Everything is a vagina.' Her mother stiffened at her daughter's uncouth brandishing of the word, yet Rawan was undeterred. 'Everything is a God damn stiff key and a hole! You stress on them both so much, they're the only things that move anyone around here! Your husband ran after his, and now I'm running to hide what you think I've done with mine. If I was getting married and moving to the other side of the globe, you wouldn't talk shit, because my vagina would be acting accordingly. Do you even remember what your first words were when we got the ambulance call for Samra?'

'Don't you dare drag your poor sister into this! Leave her alone!'

It was Rawan's turn to act like her mother had not even spoken. 'You said, "*Ya Rab*, her wedding is in a few days! Why *ya Rab*, why?!" You care about people? How are you people able to live like this? Don't worry, Mama. You haven't lost all your children just yet; go live with Yehia in New York. At least he doesn't have a pussy for you to lose sleep over.' She smirked sourly to herself as her brother crossed her mind. 'Move away from the cupboard, please. I need to pack my things.'

Although uninterested in inducing sympathy, her mother wept. She held herself well – she was dignified, even, perhaps weeping from God's wrath rather than from Rawan's. Tears rolled down her defiant face, and her eyes seemed to be swimming in blood, yet her daughter's resolution did not falter. Unperturbed, Rawan carried select garments from amongst her drawers and dropped them into the suitcase.

'You're right,' her mother finally said. 'I should go to your brother. He is young. He probably needs me more.'

'That's the best for everyone, Mama. I will book the ticket for you whenever you are ready.' Rawan paused her packing, and with her back to her mother, continued, 'You didn't even ask me where I'm going.'

'It doesn't really matter, does it?'

'It should. I really think it ought to matter … to someone.'

**

The flat was unbearably humid. Vapour seemed to elevate from the floors. Sunlight enveloped the exteriors of the tall building that loomed over the street. Had it not been for the scarcity of immediately available and secluded residences in the city, Rawan would not have stepped foot through its doors. Saleem, however, did not seem to mind its stifling nature. He cared not for luxuries that would forsake purpose; function-wise, the place was indeed fitting. A house in Hurghada would be close enough to El Gouna without threatening their discretion, not to negate the dull and hushed demeanour of the neighbourhood; they would both be able to slip in and out daily, alone or together, unnoticed. Right from the entrance was a narrow hall leading to the kitchen, bathroom and bedroom, while the section to the left was entirely appropriate for casual, miscellaneous purposes. The entire wall to the left was composed of glass, ceiling to floor, and a wall made a grand window. Saleem asked the owner to install thicker curtains along the glass wall 'to tame the heat.'

Rawan appreciated the rustic lighting, although it was nothing fancy, caused mainly as a consequence of the building's age, which also led to a perpetual series of power cuts as the block was serviced by untended and neglected stations. Saleem's favourite feature there, however, was a significantly large log-fuelled fireplace, at the far left of the living room.

It was the most intriguing thing he had ever seen, for he could not understand why it was there, serving no purpose whatsoever; there was no exit through which smoke could leave the building and so, it could not be used. Having asked curiously on the story behind it being there, the owner had replied with a shrug of possessing neither idea nor interest, before continuing to laud the kitchen's unique tiling.

Young children portray overwhelming curiosity towards kitchens, those unfathomed spaces in the house in which they find themselves constantly supervised when entering. They are enthralled by all the possible dangers waiting to be discovered, challenged and overcome. At the first opportunity, a solo child will cross the threshold of a kitchen's doors and head to the most intriguing prohibition of all: the stove. The dare is common, known, feared by all, except the child; they light one of its rings then proceed to sweeping the tips of their hands, rapidly passing them amidst the flames without them catching fire. Why does accomplishing this grant the child great satisfaction?

Saleem however, unsatisfied, observed the fireplace searchingly, scouring its surface and interior with his eyes until he glanced an engraving smothered in oily dirt. He rubbed it furiously, revealing: 'I HOLD WITH THOSE WHO FAVOUR FIRE.'

So the house had once been inhabited by foreigners (he found himself judging stereotypically as a man aware of his people's scarce readers), which is no surprise for most cities on Egypt's Red Sea coastline. Saleem was never an enthusiast of foreign languages or poetry, yet he instantaneously grew very fond of what he read on that useless fireplace, mounted near where his head would rest when he lay to sleep each night on the room's couch.

'You said you will be living alone here, Mr. Saleem,' the portly landlady stated, apparently satisfied with how extensively she had advertised the many qualities of her flat, before proceeding to discuss the details of her new tenant. 'So you're not married,' she went on, glancing to his left hand. 'No, no ring. Because I thought you were married and was going to tell you how safe this building is if your children played out front.'

'I will need to head to the bank tomorrow to withdraw your money,' Saleem broke off, heeding no attention to her ranting. 'Let's meet here then, same time as now, preferably.'

'You will sign a contract for one year? Because I'm sure you will need it at least for a year if you are being repositioned in your job. Is it a promotion?'

'I'm not sure exactly how long my work at the airport will require me to stay,' he interjected, starting to lose his patience. 'I think it's best if we declare it for six months, and once I am given a clear idea of the duration, I will need to be here, I shall contact you, either to confirm the six-month rental period or to sign a new contract for one year.'

She did not appreciate the monotone with which he spoke, which is very off-putting for Egyptians to experience. They do not support concise answers to questions nor fervour-less talk. All must be light and scattered ubiquitously, keeping neither substance nor intention, before disappearing into thin air, as promises. Everything must be loaded with colour. Stories are enjoyed when mostly adjusted with enticing detail and accessories. There is no desire of communication lacking the weight of pretences and the lightness of insincerity.

In Upper Egypt, for example, they hire a 'face-palmer' at funerals to woe, scream and slap her face continuously in staged agony, thus arousing those paying their condolences to express their grief with gusto! One who is alien to this when witnessing such a spectacle sees grand and unified exultations of pity and despair. Yet one must enter the women's quarters to know of amused laughter and random gossip, hushed conversations on whom is pregnant, or comments on a woman's make-up at her own mother-in-law's funeral.

The men's service is worse. A parade of political criticism attempting to answer why the country is still in turmoil floats over complimentary roars to the wisest president on the planet slammed against voiced reprimands of his drinking habits. They howl over how far the US dollar's exchange has risen – because all Egyptian men are investors or entrepreneurs – all this in the foreground of an afflicted recitation of *Surat al-Fajr*.

In this country, one must remember some crucial codes of conduct: your intentions are best buried under mounds of loud feigning, yet when you speak of others, be sure to stereotype them into polarities, never forgetting that scandals are only so by their volume – atrocious is only atrocious when loud.

Needless to say, Saleem's promptness was unsatisfactory yet sufficient. He thanked the landlady for her time and left. Rawan would be bringing her luggage the next day, and he was to be sure her room was ready and all rent procedures were out of the way before her arrival.

He drove from Hurghada to El Gouna, towards the inner city, his bowels squirming themselves together from the absence of something to churn as he planned to introduce himself to Zain, this mysterious sultan of a man who was to help them beyond all risk. It was the inadvertent whim of his wearisome mind that caused him to consider his near-obsession with this Zain. Why was he so preoccupied with the man? Was it the severity of their need for him that unhinged Saleem when he frequently entered his thoughts, or the masculine protection with which he sought to blanket Rawan?

It is inconsolably amusing how a woman can survive for years, overcoming the daily impediments that block her path, managing to strategise her movements in such a country to protect herself from the perils of her own body, often carefully, seldom ignorantly, formulating decisions to struggle her way through the world, yet once a man is allowed into her intimate sphere, she is degraded in his perception to nothing short of a fragile, half-witted doll in dire need of his guarding grace and power, his heroic countenance and boundless logic, rescuing her from her obsolete mind. 'Nakhwa', the masculine patronising sense, as Rawan would describe it, was the monopoly of the East, the mark of the 'authentic' man, the most genuine official brand of his manhood. And Saleem's *nakhwa* would be spared no test with each day to come.

Parking outside 'Hydra', he opened his wallet to check its contents, unmindful of what he may find there. Three hundred pounds and some change. *Ful* sandwiches were a wiser option at the time, considering how much would be paid the very following day on rent and insurance. Saleem remembered he also needed to shop for groceries.

Pulling at the gears to exit the parking beside the restaurant, Saleem saw a police car parked a few metres away. The man who had his back against the car's left door gesticulated violently to the air as he held a phone to his head.

Saleem felt his head close to rupture; in the air's pleasant breeze, his skull felt icy and blank. He merely stared at the man, transfixed and, somehow, lonely, for the few eternal seconds he spent peering at Amgad's face. And in that endless moment, he was convinced they were the last two men on Earth. His chest constricted his heart from pounding and where moments of waiting dwelled, Saleem found himself reciting calls of pardoning requests to God, warding Satan away from his fuming heart.

Amgad ended his call, passed a glance towards the heat darting from Saleem's dark irises, then turned away, strolling to enter the restaurant.

At the onset of their strategising, Saleem had negated Rawan's idea, refuting its plausible execution since Amgad would identify either or both of them through the case documents. Rawan, having previously fled the country out of trepidation of its calamities amongst other factors, knew this well. By sheer coincidence, Ahmad the lawyer had advised that Samra's case be filed through Yehia's name, on the basis that a male plaintiff of a rape case would hold stronger in court. Amgad himself, who had spent long days stretched into endless nights as a young officer in a Nasr City precinct, bored and rended with the countless accounts of the women who filed in before him to retell the gruesome narratives of their husbands' abuse, would not have denied the male leverage in such cases.

Rawan's name had not been mentioned once in a single document, nor had she attended any trials. Ahmad, as the family's lawyer, was able to use Yehia as his legal representative in coordination with his sister and Yehia himself.

She and Saleem were precariously untold to Amgad.

Coincidentally, beneficial as it may have been, Rawan had not used her brother's name solely for cautionary purposes, and although it was a decision proved to have been favourable to their interests, her motivation was entirely of no relation to those grounds.

Yehia had never been forced to tolerate their hardships. As the youngest sibling – and only male – their mother had repeatedly shielded him from acknowledging their daily concerns, obsessively refusing to allow him the slightest assumption of responsibility. Both sisters had arguably fought against this not out of a rightful sense of injustice, yet more from concern for their brother's true interests.

Why do these women, the likes of which bored Amgad

for years on end, complain of their husbands when they are raising future ones so poorly? They moan of their men's passivity then nudge their daughters to clean their brothers' plates; they weep when their partners are unfaithful yet strip their sons of moral soundness. For if those sons fall in love, their jealously possessive mothers make sure they understand well and clear how women were made to be pleasured from and used, not to be felt.

Rawan had felt it was time Yehia put his entitled organ to the benefit of others for once in his pampered life.

She and Saleem knew Amgad had no idea who they were, which, in ironic injustice, meant that Saleem's droning looks at the detective were as satiating to Saleem as repeatedly banging his own skull against a brick wall.

Ridding Our Nights of Moon

Rawan had not painted in years. She laid her canvases face to face on top of one another, then slid a twine beneath the pile, wrapping it round and round to assure they would not separate.

Her artwork was the vessel of her time on Earth; she bled her own paint, tinting it variously, according to how much or how little she favoured the world. Its places and people, she held between her fingers and pressed against the canvases, violently or gently.

Which are more honest, more real in a painting: the lines, or the coloured strokes?

None.

It is the border, the outskirts of all the manifestation and mess, the edge of all tumult, which is where truth lies.

'I paint because I must,' she would say. 'Because I am stranded with no edge, I am safe only when I pour my existence between those borders and collect them there.'

Hence, her fascination with tattoos came as no surprise. 'Imagine it, Zain! You are the edge – holding your life's truths wherever you may go.'

'Why an eagle though?' he prodded her.

'You are so unpatriotic,' she teased. 'They should arrest you.'

'They tried! But your man here can negotiate with *Azra'il* the terms of his own death if need be.'

Zain had no cultural objections to the ink on her body; he was merely communicating the possibility of her regretting a particular motif and not being able to rectify her skin afterwards.

'That's grand, especially coming from you, my "Mr. No Regrets",' Rawan said, altering her tone to imitate her exaggerated perception of the haughty one he adopted whenever he felt inclined to parent her. 'Regret is the greatest sin our kind has ever committed. You know all those idiots who drink and sleep around then tell you, "We know it's wrong, and we pray to have the strength to stop?" Well, they're the most insanely screwed up. If you make a mistake you like, then continue to make it, perhaps even with the acknowledgment that you never plan on stopping. At least have the sense to admit that you don't really consider it erroneous at all. If you're going to go all self-righteous and pull out the I-know-it's-*haram* card, at least respect the god you claim to be experiencing guilt before. Creating a sinner is one thing; a sinner who also happens to exercise self-retardation is too much for any god to handle!'

Zain palmed his face to hide an overtly stretched grin. 'Is it still sore?' he questioned, elevating the very tips of his fingers close to her slightly swollen neck.

'No, I didn't even feel the needles.' He continued to peer at her neck. In a bizarre manifestation of daydreaming, he felt she looked fresh; oddly enough, the sheer red inflammation surrounding the bird's wings and stretched beak seemed to radiate purity in a way no woman isolated in the folds of a monastery ever could. It was the tangent between her newly pierced skin and the fact that those cuts did not bleed. Holding his fingertips steady, with the greatest proximity he could muster without touching her, the heat that emanated from her live canvas flooded his palms like the smoldering breath of a woman whom his lips had ventured to approach ever so intimately yet forbade themselves from touching hers.

***

It was incessant.

Climbing those stairs was endless and irreversible. She could have walked away in trepidation and taken heed of the foreboding that failed to call her. Rawan ascended higher and higher, swerved the bends and continued as fate would have it, until she found nothing more to mount, no further elevation to reach, approaching nowhere but to fall.

It was an infinite labyrinth of separating walls between her and the light. They chipped together like an incomplete puzzle, and glaring beams had exhausted themselves, striving to reach her eyes, always blocked, furiously in vain.

She prodded the air, avoiding the walls, advancing further within. Plato would have painlessly guided her, yet she would have refused his assistance.

The light approached. As a shying lover, it played before

her, urging her closer to it, oblivious that she was the temptress of Lucifer. In all her dangerous innocence, she lured the light itself until it fell to her feet. She stepped on it, more, closer, ever so assured.

Never had light flooded so, with such unconditional obedience to one's will; it was her slave in the night, and she, the vengeful goddess in all her splendid rage, knew how unfaltering her slave would be. Ariel did not serve Caliban so well, so willingly, with such harmony.

The music halted.

Zain's booming voice came as the truth would enter fantasy, subtle and violently surreal: 'Friends, family, dear guests, the sun is for those who require it to see, to feel warmth, to tell time. They know they must rise with it; they surrender to their dreams only when it temporarily leaves them. Tonight, I tell you of a man whose dreams kept his nights restless and his darkness welcoming. And by befriending them, he stands before you now to show you why we were created to defy, why you come here every night, why your dreams haunt you throughout your day and leave once you enter my doors. Because I have created something even greater than the sun. Your sight comes to life through the stage I stand upon. My wine gives you warmth, and instead of watching the minutes and hours of your lives trickle away as the sun bleeds itself below your feet, you come here to live! So as of tonight, life shall seep into your breaths never to exit.'

He swept the entirety of the hall once more with his eyes, then spoke for the last time. 'I thank you.'

Zain was a cliff against the ocean; their applause lapped at him from every spit of air in his circumference where he stood solid and grand. Amgad followed Zain's eyes from across the room, waiting. He did not think to look at the roof over where Zain stood, yet Saleem saw nothing besides it. He was tracking Rawan, awaiting her movement so he could safely look where Amgad sat.

At once, they were thrust into darkness. Complete and utter nothingness encompassed their abruptly hushed voices and did not last long enough before impatience was brewed amongst their restless souls.

She had already hoisted herself over the bars at the edge of the canopy's narrow ledge. Freeing two aerial-silk ropes from their knot, she wrapped both strands of thick fabric around her lower waist, alternating right to left and reversing again. After a few rounds, she swung one strand around each of her upper thighs a couple of times.

Drum beats resounded.

She pushed herself off the ledge as a swimmer commencing a backstroke into the water and watched it distancing. More drums accompanied the first. They grew lighter, patting playfully as the tender feet of a woman teasing her chasing lover to bed.

Rawan beckoned the light upon her, and it complied.

A swarm of gasps hit her bare back, which was all they could see of her. She flushed silently, heat escaping her face and heart until the latter grew icier.

In alliance with the light, the aerial ropes extended in

length, lowering her down until she was no more than a metre above centre stage.

The air was worse than still; it refused to stir, as if its movement would distract Rawan and cast her deliberation away. With her back still the only visible angle to the audience, she pointed her toes sharply forward, her elongated legs tightly stretched. The music pounced louder and more wildly.

Slowly, she opened her legs wide amidst the coloured beams breaking through her chest and splitting the crowds', exiting their backs as bright as they had entered their torsos. When her legs were completely apart from one another, forming a perfect straight line, the music stopped.

Saleem fancied he could hear her breathing sharp and light, his back firmly erect on a bar seat to the far left of the stage. He managed to faintly alternate his guarding looks from her and to Amgad, landing occasionally on random spots in the room's objects or faces.

Amgad, too, was contemplating Rawan. He stared at her bare skin, far away from his clear view, in neither awe nor indifference. Neither curiosity nor familiarity moved his irises within their shells.

And as she suddenly dropped her back in rushed abruptness so that she was facing him upside down, beats and strings reverberated around him, louder than his heart, stronger than their applause had been for Zain.

And he breathed in her scent. Tangy and moistly sweet.

He savoured it like he was tasting her from across the room, filling his dullness with the placating flavour of a woman hanging head down, her hair teasingly out of the floor's reach, her lips high above her eyes, conversing with him.

Rawan pushed her thighs back at each other and clamped hard on the ropes as she smiled, her eyes more mischievous in their rotated form. She sank her right palm into a pocket sewed somewhere along the inner lining of her costume and pulled her hand out again. Blowing the contents towards the crowd, they yelled wildly as a thin ray of sunshine blasted from the tip of her breath and danced around them high in the air.

Rawan urged her body weight to her left, and the ropes tugged heavily yet dared not defy her. She began to swing to the far left of the stage until it passed from beneath her.

The crowd, torn between screams of exultation and attentive silence, seemed to stutter in demeanour, their faces imitating the madness of the music they were submerged within.

Raising her back slightly and lowering her legs, she bent one knee higher than the other and stretched her right arm above her shoulder.

Rawan was sweeping above the crowd in a wide circular field, aiming for one table in particular. As she flew above their seats, some of them hurriedly stood up, reaching as high as their ligaments allowed, to touch her. Some barely scratched through her flouncing hair, while others made it to feel her resting palm. Others clawed at her legs violently.

Yet none could have her, because she sensed neither their

grabs nor their intentions. She sped along to the vibrating rhythm, luring him further until she approached his table. Amgad had not left his seat; he had one hand rubbing the back of his shirt collar, the other gripping the pack of Marlboro Red cigarettes before him.

Rawan flipped her body forward and landed feet first, inches away from his fingers. She stood upright; he had to bend his neck far back to see her face, yet his eyes did not aim there first.

He considered her small feet for moments; they looked constrained in 12-inch heels, her toes slightly bruised. Ascending his surveying glare, he saw she was sprayed with a copper-ish opulence entailing his hands would stain if he touched her. Her seamless black dress clenched at her stomach and went no further than a curtain of frills covering her buttocks. With his head bowed backward, the bearing of her protruding breasts pleased him to look at. He liked that they were trapped and constricted, fighting to escape her clothes from her slightest breaths.

Her collarbone extended higher up her chest, marking where her shoulder blades were, rooting her neck further up as he hurried through them, to her lips, slightly open in a reference to her other lips, the safer ones, where she had no teeth to threaten him, where her only bites would come from the scorching heat stinging his throbbing manhood.

It was ludicrous to think Rawan safe, even with herself. She regarded him intently until he was about to peer into her eyes, then split her thighs and dropped herself to sit on the very edge of the table, between his arms, her legs wrapped around the back of his chair. He held her lower waist firmly with both arms, his palms rubbing where her body touched the table. She did not flinch from their closeness yet ignored a frosty twinge where his fingers lingered. Succeeding to steady her breathing, she lowered her face to his, like a tree collapsing against a steady wall. He thought she wished to kiss him and moved his left hand up her spine, finally clenching the back of her neck. Rawan felt him against her tattoo and almost panted. When their lips had barely touched, she swept hers to his ears and whispered, 'Have a drink with me before you leave tonight,' before climbing her rope to stand and swing away from his reach.

She sped above another sea of raised hands and landed back at the centre of the stage. Immediately over twenty dancers joined her, moving smoothly in correlation to her bends and twirls.

They were undistinguishable from one another: the same height, the fair tone of skin, the same curvature of breasts. Their waists began and ended at equivalent levels, the lines of their toned thighs one. Even their smiles to the crowd were identical. It was as if Zain had sculpted and painted them with the hands of a robot, computerised to produce immaculately homogenous women, and Rawan their distinctive centrepiece.

The dancers intertwined, chasing the choreography across the stage amidst roars, gasps, applause and sexual musings. Those at the tables ordered round after round of drinks and overpriced finger-food. The women hand-fed their men endlessly, feigning an ignorance of their bulging trousers, convincing themselves that their men's drools were from thirst and hunger of the stomach and that their hearts raced solely from the music.

And Zain, who stood from where Rawan had first leapt, drank the taste of his kingdom on the sea, inspecting all, rebuffing many, concerned with none.

He saw Saleem sip through his liquor absentmindedly, looking fairly unfamiliar and peculiar to his environment, though not entirely suspicious, for a place such as Naktal attracted distinct newcomers daily. Zain nudged his neck slightly to the left to view Amgad, who sat smiling to himself in great agitation. He appeared as a man who stood between disappointment and content, his contorting mouth unable to figure out which of the two sensations to follow.

From the corner of his eye, Saleem could barely consume Rawan as she shifted with graceful violence across the stage. The sound of her feet alone was distinctly audible to him above the rest. A rhythm to which his heart alone could place sense upon before imitation, as the accordance from toes to heels to hips harmonically played a master replica at her sister. And neither depriving his sight from reaching her nor condemning it wide to recognise that she was Rawan, affected his torture in the slightest way. Through her blurred intoxicated filter, she was Samra, so proximal to his reach yet utterly absent.

Zain returned his gaze to Rawan, whose aptness suggested she had forever danced with the women with whom she flowed and vibrated beneath Zain's looming presence. Satisfied with the overview, he turned his back to the vibrancy in all its hues and roars, disappearing into the darkness of his maze. He skipped down a range of stairs, past a short corridor that lead to his locked office. He gave the key an upper jolt, making a note to himself – for what was at least the fifth time – to oil the keyhole. Shutting the door behind him, he sped to the sink at the far right of the room and splashed his face with cold water repeatedly. He ran a finger across his left cheek then placed it to the tip of his tongue to taste. It wasn't salty; his face was clean.

Zain left his face to air dry. He moved to his desk drawer and pulled out some rolling paper and a small plastic container, opening it gently before dipping the head of a paper clip inside and quickly pulling it out. Zain allowed the red paste to drip from the paper clip onto his tobacco heap then rubbed them together.

He smoked while circling the room purposelessly, casually parting a gap in the curtains and peering at the new faces dispersed amongst his nightly crowd. Inhaling from his joint smoke, he saw a man stagger slightly from his table, heading for the stage. He seemed to be in his mid-to-late thirties, but his clothing and hairstyle carried the air of someone who refused to age beyond his hipster teenage years. Zain blew once more from his joint before laying it down in the ashtray, and aimed for the door.

When he had reached the bar steps, the man stumbled slightly to the edge of the stage and began fishing in his pocket. Before he could spray the arena of dancers with money, Zain caught him in a firm shoulder grip and talked him down, off-stage.

The man nodded with straying eyes until Zain led him back to his chair.

'Ahmad, where is Ali?' Zain asked one of the waiters.

'He's with Madame Zahra.'

'Ok.' Zain gave one stern pat on Ahmad's back and routed himself amongst the many tables then motioned to Ali, whose back was bent forward in patience, smiling politely to a woman who sat beside him.

'Yes, Mr. Zain!' Ali looked at the woman, pardoning her for having to break their conversation and jolted briefly to where Zain stood.

'Ali, you need to make sure no one approaches the stage steps except the dancers and me. You tell clients if they want to leave tips, they leave them with their cheques'

'Yes, sir, sure!'

'This is not a brothel, Ali. We're not in Mohammed Ali Street here; I won't have money thrown at them like it's a tent in a *mouled*. Is that clear?'

'Certainly, Mr. Zain.'

'Zain, you are exceedingly short-tempered.' Zahra spoke to him from her seat. 'I had thought a flourishing business would have settled your edge greatly. Was I mistaken?'

She was an elegant woman, poised and proper in her appearance. Her face was not heavily painted – and where the generous years had marked her forehead and the sides of her eyes and cherry mouth, the grace with which she smiled seemed only more beautiful because of them.

In a poorly humorous attempt, Zain bent forward, his large belly bulging from all angles possible, as she held out her left palm, placing it in his, pecking his cheek.

'It's been a long time, Zahra,' he smiled calmly.

'Why don't you ask then if it's, as you say, a long time? Come, sit down.' Zahra beckoned him closer as he approached the chair opposite her. 'But I'm more gracious than you. You wandered into my thoughts, and I said I'll go see Zain; but, frankly, I have witnessed more enticing sights tonight.'

'It pleases me that you are enjoying the show, Zahra, dear friend.'

'So who is she?'

Zain laughed endearingly. 'That's all you liked, huh?!'

'*Habibi*, are you mocking me? He who raised knows more than he who bought. Naktal has always been a destination for those who seek to be pampered by dancers, and perhaps even receive more if they are lucky and correct in their approach. But this … this girl, what I've just witnessed tonight was – I don't wish to sound dramatic – intriguing, to say the least.'

'Why?' he prompted, curious to hear an articulated reason from a woman of women, perhaps to feel assured of Rawan's plan, perhaps to pride himself in having agreed to help.

Or, perhaps just so he could hear Zahra talk.

'Why? She is young – I'm almost certain she is your youngest. But she flew across the room with such familiarity, like nothing held her from falling but the light that toys with our sight in the dark you care for so well.'

'Yes, she is remarkably talented. Her physical agility is excell—'

'And there is something in her eyes,' Zahra interrupted, staring at her drink as though waiting for something to float to its surface. 'I don't know what, not a feeling; someone – there is another person in her eyes.' She looked at Zain, seeming to expect an answer to an unposed question, yet he evaded her remark and looked at his wristwatch instead.

'Zahra, you treasure hunter! You see the beauty bolstered behind the uncanny, and it draws you in. But do not run ahead of yourself; wait until you have seen her a couple of times before you deem her a gem.'

'You see? Language, words, not a thousand years unused could rust or diminish them. You just used the vocabulary of your old way to describe her. Words are like antiques, Zain, more valuable the longer they remain unspoken. And I know how proficient you once were with them, how skilled you are at recognising what is priceless, so I am confident the brief speech you launched tonight with such fervour was nothing if not assured. Needless to say, you will be seeing much more of me as of now.' Zahra twisted her neck to her left and glanced at Rawan who was flushed and smiling, her body absorbing the night's ambience, seconds before the music rose to a rapid climax then halted.

'It delights me!' Zain yelled to Zahra over the flare of applause and cat-call whistles, as he stood up to join the standing ovations. He excused himself from her table and walked to the back of the hall, heading for the dancers' dressing room. He held the door open for the train of women who had exited the stage and were running to enter past him.

'Thank you, lovelies! Let's not extend our break for too long tonight; it's very packed out there.'

'Zuzu, you're a freak! We haven't even stepped back, man,' one of the dancers breathlessly told him from across the room.

'Zuzu has no brains for you tonight, Karma, but since you're the *"revolutionary"* one, if anyone is late to follow me, it will be on your head.'

'What? Why is it my problem if they're late?'

'I don't hear anyone arguing but you. A quarter of an hour, girls.' His eyes swept the room searchingly for Rawan, finding her at the far back fiddling with feathery props. 'Malak, my office,' he ordered before shutting the door behind him.

One of the dancers was speaking audibly to Karma so that Rawan would hear. 'That lucky bitch. It's her first night, and she doesn't even have to go back out with us! I bet you she'll be in his office till the morning!'

'I swear on my honour if there's a bitch here, it's you,' Karma spat back. 'When has Zain asked any of us to spend a night with him? Did he ever touch you?'

'Who are you calling bitch, you ugly whore!' The woman made to grab Karma's face and tear at it, right before Rawan, who had witnessed the scene from the onset, slammed a shuddering slap across the woman's cheek and pulled her down to the ground from her hair.

They all stood back, including Karma, while the dancer lay pinned to the ground moaning faintly under shots of blood spouting from her injured nose and ripped lips.

'She asked you a question, whore!' Rawan blasted at the bloodied face she towered above.

'What?' the dancer pined in confusion and pain.

'She asked you a question: did he ever touch you? Huh! Did he?

'No, no,' she winced.

Karma stretched her arm daringly and touched Rawan's shoulder, silently asking for her to stop. Rawan slowly untangled the hair wrapped in her hand, lifted her weight off the mangled woman beneath her and stood up.

'The next time I hear your voice, I'll have Zain shoot you in your filthy mouth. That's the first thing I'll discuss with him in his office now.'

She Washes Her Hair

R awan dragged the chair to Amgad's right, and with a bottle of whiskey choked by the neck, she sat down, eyeing his glaring pupils in the dim light. He did not possess the likeness of a predator – in fact, if anything, the limitations of his ageing body were splashed across his hair, etched across his skin, signed in his weary feet.

Indeed, Amgad's eyes were inarguably diabolic and threatening, yet the frequency with which he dared through them had deemed their intimidation harmless by those who did not fear his 'official' authority. People like Rawan.

An undesired stillness numbed them in their shared silence as each awaited the other to initiate with spoken language or shifting bodies. Rawan kept her lashes wide open, urging him to surrender all resolve; the curiosity as to what he would say if he were to begin gnawed at the tufts of her mind and, not too soon, he submitted to her defiance.

'Why are you here?' Amgad finally pronounced.

A smile she had harmed her soul practising crawled on her face and propped itself before his. 'To dance for you,' Rawan declared.

He frowned at the animosity of her smile and the simplicity

of her answer. 'Well, uh …' Amgad smiled wide to himself. 'What do I call you again?'

'Malak.'

'Mmm, Malak, suits you … Well, Malak, it wouldn't be a first.'

'What?'

'It wouldn't be the first time a woman dances for me, although never so willingly.'

'I am glad my eagerness shows. Those without passion have lives wasted upon them.'

Amgad seemed agitated. He reached for the liquor and poured himself a glass, ignoring hers. 'You see, why do you do that?' Drinking a little, he squeezed his eyes from bitterness and continued. 'Why do people say random, grand shit like that? All of a sudden, everyone's so deep. Look at you. You're a dancer, aren't you? Yet here you are talking like you're a goddamn elitist commenting on life and other crap. "Those without passion have lives wasted upon them." Everyone in the country is an intellectual now; everyone has something to say about anything.'

'Don't you? I mean …' She poured herself a glass of whiskey and hit it against his. 'You just put yourself up there and decided someone like me can't say anything meaningful, so what's so special about you? What do you do?'

Amgad smiled again, extending his right arm and yelling, 'Amgad Acir, head detective at El Gouna local precinct.'

She snickered mockingly. 'I didn't even know there was a precinct in El Gouna till just now! A policeman! I'm guessing you didn't perform so well at school. Son of a big shot perhaps. It doesn't matter whether either factor or both led you to your position today. Here's the thing.' She moved closer to him. 'I imagine your days are spent cooped up in an office somewhere, on slow days of course; when busy, you may find yourself driving miles round and round the city.'

'No, you're confusing the years. That was a long time ago when privileged, middle-class women who had nothing better to do than nag their husbands all day for more of this or more of that, to the point of losing those men their tempers, came dawdling to me to complain after their useless friends had choked feminist rubbish down their throats.'

She continued as if he had not interrupted her, 'Then you come here. You're here, in a club, sitting with a dancer, talking with her about why she shouldn't be talking, and I'm thinking, I'm thinking, what makes you think you guys can run this country?'

He chuckled cynically at her words. 'You know something, Malak? There was an occasional highlight to listening to those imbecile women droning for hours on end. Sometimes, every once in a while, one of them would drag a witness with her. I'm still ridiculously curious as to why it was always a daughter, never a boy. You see, sons have a natural allegiance, a subconscious empathy with their kind I guess. You talk more than your own good would allow it, and what I'm thinking is, those lips can be put to much better use.' He eyed his wristwatch for a moment. 'But it is too late for me to coach you on such uses tonight.' He waved his hand expressively to insinuate a condescending impatience.

'Tell me, *basha*, what arouses a man more: what a woman is capable of doing with her body, or what he aims to do to it?'

'What do you mean?' he asked, perplexed between the arousing connotations in her words and the odd nature of the question posed.

'There is such violence in your talk. You believe your remark was sexy, clever even, yet there is an undeniable trace of hate lingering somewhere there.'

'What remark? I really should go,' he told her whilst his body spoke otherwise. Amgad remained comfortable, almost reclined upon his seat, gulping sips of his drink while feigning interest in her conversation.

Rawan, resolved to patience and austere persistence, continued to clarify the point she was making with the utmost air of indifference a suffering, half-naked, gradually intoxicated woman could muster: 'I'm asking why you would rather have me kiss you, amongst other things, than speak my mind about … well … you!'

'And do you know me to speak about me, Malak?'

'I know your claimed profession entitles you to one thing, which is to do your job. You hardly seem to be here for that purpose. You are also unfit to strut around deciding what should be said by whom and when. Yet, that is solely what you have been occupied with for the entire evening.'

'And does your job entitle or, should I say, equip you to understand mine?'

She snorted an accusing smirk at him, professing the audacity she deemed in what he had posed. '*Basha*, whores and the police are not exactly incongruous in this country, wouldn't you say?'

'Are you are a whore ... Malak?' Amgad retorted with an intensely condemning glare at her devilish painted face.

'I am enough of a woman to not require "coaching" on the uses of my own body, so considering your offer to instruct me is unattractive on my part, in that sense I am far from it. Yet I am also sitting here, with you, and I am smart enough to know why you are here – in that sense, I am very much one.'

'It seems you and I have a choice then.'

'Very much so.'

'Why?'

'Why what?'

'Why this then? Why work here? Why Zain. That is his name, yes?'

'Because he is interesting. The answer to that is obvious. And, if I'm not mistaken, I'm not the one paying him to obliterate all memory of my senseless day.'

'Well,' Amgad said after finishing his last spit of liquor and shook the glass before her as he spoke, 'this is exceptionally good stuff to be enjoyed free of charge. In that respect, you certainly are a lucky girl.'

'Not all currency is money, *basha*.' She smiled.

'Indeed, indeed. And what do you pay him with, Malak?'

'For a man who claims to be the judge of others, you are commonly assumptive. Zain does not seek to share his bed with those who work for him.'

'What? Even with someone as dazzling as yourself? I'd say he's gay.'

'He is a man who has surpassed the limiting cravings of his own body, a brilliantly self-nourished soul I would say.'

Amgad lurched back in pained laughter as he choked on his own bile rising from the depth of his stomach. 'Apparently, I know more of Zain than you, sweet thing, or you wouldn't speak so grandly of his soul.'

'I understand,' she mused. 'It is egotistically difficult for people here to understand and admire difference. For a man of law and order, such as yourself, even more so; you can only tolerate herds, you the sheep-men at the frontline. You've been glaring at me for an hour now because I, a woman, dare to argue and converse with you. You deem my mouth as any other hole in my body, to be opened for your pleasure only.'

'This equality nonsense is centuries worn out, Malak. I would assume you bright enough to not dip so frequently into it.'

'You are just less bright than you claim; this is not about gender. Take what I say and stretch it over the broader context; cultures like this one were built on the principle of subordinates. You entered your profession for the sole interest in power. You strive to maintain what you call order through sustaining the need to suppress and rule others: you dehumanise them, manipulating and contorting realities to fit your convenience. Your utopia is a world where you utilise all – you, the consumerists – for no charge.'

'I am hardly impressed. Where did you read that?'

'It wasn't my intention to impress you.'

'Right. You simply chose to strip and hang yourself off the ceiling of this place and land on my table for leisure.'

'No, *that* was to impress you, amongst everyone else here tonight; this, here, well ... how would I call this? An ugly lap dance to your ego, a cursing middle finger to this country and its forces.'

Amgad stood up, not out of anger or resentment to her words, but more of a lack of sympathy to the crudeness of her despair. 'Someday, perhaps sooner than it may seem, you will understand who your real enemy is. Until then, learn to go past the childhood innocence of recognising the culprit from his gun. There are monsters that carry roses and demons as charmingly guiltless as yourself.'

'Spectacularly insightful, *basha.*

'Goodnight, Malak.'

Amgad bent low to kiss the side of her temple, breathing her hair in before stepping away. She choked on the last trickles in her glass, coughing heavily, even more so as she suffered to prevent it while, Saleem eyed her expectantly from the far end of the hall like a gift-less child under a looming Christmas tree.

***

Rawan fled to her room minutes before Saleem slammed the flat door behind him. They had left Naktal without one another, but in coordination, they had embarked on separate boats and she had driven herself home, while he followed in a cab at the early onset of dawn. She rummaged through her drawers, clutching at a towel as she grabbed for one of her knickers. He walked through the room where she had left the door open.

'What did you talk about?' He panted from the heave of stairs he had just run up.

She fumed as the drawer, old and unruly, refused to slide shut.

'Rawan!'

'I need to wash myself,' she blurted.

'Ok, what did he tell you?'

'Extremely hot … I'm going to die in this house.' She shoved past him and dropped her clothes and towel on the closed toilet seat, managing to throw her shoes off backwards while bending low to plug the shower drain. Rawan loosely opened the cold tap and felt the water run blissfully on her clammy hand. It was so soothing, she did not wait to undress before pushing her head where her hand had been, feeling the water run across her scalp-like soil, which had been cracked and etched apart by severe drought.

Saleem toddled back to his spot by the fireplace, and, while fumbling with some rolling paper, he heard moving outside again. He ran back down the hall.

Still dressed, her hair mangled and dripping down her face smudged with wet make-up, Rawan held some pencils in one hand and Canson sheets in the other as she exited her room.

'You're going to shower, with those?'

Once again, he received no answer. Why should he expect

one from the onset? Were it not for her silence, he would have granted her mind the space to breathe, yet it remained puzzling to her how much Saleem needed to be directly informed of one's thoughts to respond with a certain limit of understanding. He was not an insensitive man; on the contrary, he spoke much of his fears with those he considered safe, a rare trait to be found in men. Yet he was someone who required – no, chased – guidance and clearly stated matters. It was not a lack of experience that led him to this necessity, but more an urgency of safety; he would rather be 'told' than risk a rarely mistaken assumption.

And she knew this of him; she knew him so well. It was not out of cruelty that she refused to ease his insecurities, yet, more so, her utter sense of loneliness was what pushed her to share with him her profound sense of loss. He saw the stream of light from within the bathroom narrowly tighten as she finally clicked the door lock into the wall.

Rawan undressed then climbed into the tub, bringing her pencils and paper to join her as she scrolled for Souad Massi to play off the phone. Her skin did not once shudder against the cold water, while the tip of a pencil she pushed against the paper chipped off moments later. Absentmindedly, she grabbed another one from the pile on her dress splayed across the floor and continued. She had loved working under the rain in Tunis' Avenue Habib Bourguiba, where, when most people escaped to sheltered outskirts or remained indoors, Rawan would cross her legs beneath the flowing heavens and pour her soul within the edges of a pile of sheets that gradually weakened in her arms. They couldn't be sold in their tattered condition and she would not have forsaken them for purchase, yet it was the lack of purpose that she liked so much, just as Saleem increasingly cherished his fireplace. It is not what we humans can do with beauty that determines it as such; beauty, like art, is not dependent on the purpose we bestow upon it. It is self-reliant, possessing its own all-encompassing soul; we are neither its sovereigns nor its patrons. We are merely put on earth to experience it, temporarily; and when we leave, it shall remain.

Rawan etched the charcoal tirelessly against the blunt whiteness of the paper, laying each one on the surface of the water. They floated like lotus before her then descended to the bottom. Some covered the others, which had preceded them. Some bent over themselves and clung to her legs, refusing to abandon their creator. How does the ultimate creator exist, she wondered, observing a particular sketch that had wrapped itself around her thigh? How did God create all, without inspiration? How can you incite that which does not yet exist?

Souad had stopped singing, and Saleem's praying voice crept from under the bathroom door. Rawan heard him like the faint mumble of life, as the dead must hear the living, oblivious of the definitive meaning of solitude, speeding past their graves in their cars. And she wept, like a mute woman who caged her curdling tears within her chest, her insides burning at the few that managed to escape her throat. She wept as though weeping would be her most loyal companion in life, as the hungry in a famine knew they would never cease to consume, even if eventually there would be nothing left to devour but oneself.

Once more, the silent absence of his voice shook her to return. She tilted the lever of the shower head and watched the godless rain beat against her skin. She lay back and felt it on her face, her eyes closed, imagining she were in another place, outside, under the sky. Saleem pounded on the door.

'Rawan, are you ok?'

She heaved her weighing body from the water and closed the taps before pulling the plug to let all escape. Her sketches ran towards the drain and clogged it, but she carried them off, laying them tattered and soaked on the sink. She dressed in her sleepwear without drying herself, leaving an abandoned towel where it was first placed, and opened the bathroom door.

He held her between his arms, and she stopped breathing so his scent would not enter her. When it was necessary to inhale, she pushed herself gently from his embrace.

'I need to sleep, Saleem. We shall talk when I am rested,' she whispered, avoiding his eyes.

'You have not looked at me since we came home,' he responded, wondering why her clothes clung to her, damp and dishevelled. He knew the night had been heavy and painful to withstand, yet in all sincerity, he felt a greater deal of sympathy towards himself than for Rawan.

She had been physically occupied throughout the entire evening, while he had been obliged not only to inconspicuously remain in one place, but to imitate the degenerate nature of his surrounding peers. He was forced to frequently comment on how aroused he was by the semi-nudity of the dancers, to feign excitement at their jiggling breasts, the way their hair beat against their seductive faces, the heat that shot off their skin and slapped their closest audiences below their belts, engorging them. He suffered through every smile his face compelled, every applause his hands staged and every gulp of liquor he consumed as his body ached in compliance to his heart. A man who had lost the love of his life, his dear companion to his future old age, the only mother he dreamed of for his unborn children, imposed to shield all despair behind the elaborate image of a fool who had no concerns for the next day, let alone the remainder of his life. Besides the entirety of this ill-fated imposition, Saleem was also condemned to watch the young woman he considered his own sister, whore herself to the lowest of life who had forsaken her sister's.

His heart had almost spilled from its resting place as Rawan dropped herself from the ledge, high above his reach. Every finger that had smeared its vile print on her skin as she sped above the tables ripped his dignity into shreds; with each repetition, it scarred him afresh. They were not worthy of defiling the purity of his late love's dear sister – and yet the lowest of them had touched and fondled her over and over again, while he could only smile and applaud. Then she landed on that monster's table, and Saleem, crushed and haunted, cheered as the thirsty and erect Amgad insatiably held her.

Saleem was an impatient man; rebellious and wounded, time was not something he could spare so haughtily. Rawan, however, perhaps governed by the artist within her, praised detail and meticulousness over launching a hasty, uncalculated arrow. Their alliance could only be fruitful if they both learned to stress the other's strengths and aided one another past their limitations. Yet, pain neither leaves its victim patient nor practical.

'You want me to look at you?' She retorted angrily yet persisting to avoid his eye. 'Do you have any idea how I feel?'

'We're not competing here, Rawan, or have you forgotten that?'

'I haven't forgotten anything, Saleem, but I'm tired and I must rest. You are unbelievably active after tonight, but I cannot entertain more than I have already.'

'Don't ever do that again,' he blurted at her, enraged. 'Don't talk like one of those girls. That is not who you are, and you remember that like you remember your own name.'

'It seems I am not the one confused with my name, Saleem. Stop looking at me like that, like I'm her. For your sake, not mine. I do not resemble her half as much as you are fond of believing. One trickle, one ounce of detail past the genes we share we stopped being so alike. She made different choices in life. She wanted different … things. I'm going to bed.'

And so, she slipped away from his sight with the weight of the lie, the fresh lie she had just told Saleem, dragging at her feet.

By the Canal

W hen the call for dawn's prayer broke through her window, from the farthest ends of the endless sea, the growing light peering at her through her curtains, Zahra had no choice but to nudge herself off bed and drag her feet to the bathroom sink. She performed her ablutions with care and ease. Neither rushing nor weary, the woman in her early fifties muttered with clarity the words she had been saying more than five times a day throughout her life. They were strange words, able at times to quiet her exasperated heart, at others barely making sense as she uttered them devoid of reflection. Many a time she had pondered how the same words, the same things, can continue to affect us differently, or even leave us entirely untouched, according to the weight of experiences we place upon them. That particular morning, Zahra's mind was distracted while she washed in preparation for prayer, as her heart held the most minute space for the god she was about to worship in ritual.

'My God, I ask for your forgiveness and mercy. I repent to the great *Allah* for every great sin.' She exerted some effort so as not to rush herself yet could not avoid the absentmindedness with which she moved from one holy position to the next. Her prostrations were messy; while erect, her hands swung lower than they should, and she paid no regard to the tufts of hair escaping her *izdal* in motion. God's light gradually entered the room and she reclused in bed, accompanied by her red bracelet of prayer beads, accustomed to their use after each prayer. Her late husband had bought them while they were in Medina together, and she had held onto them following his death. With his face trapped in her head, she pushed each amber red bead further from the next, rolling them over her index finger, thoughtlessly asking her creator for forgiveness from a sin she was not entirely sure she considered one.

Her husband had been of respected position in the armed forces. As the head of the national surveillance and tracking centre, he spent his mornings monitoring the skies of Egypt, every day during the war. Beloved amongst his peers, the man was entirely humble. His tales of devotion and love for his country comprised a retelling of his earlier hardships as a young soldier. 'I endured much barbarism in the desert. We used to shit in holes we had dug ourselves like dogs,' was amongst his favourite experiences to tell under the reproachful eye of his wife in the presence of family guests. Yet, as he was steadily promoted in his rank, he became more and more tight-lipped regarding his latest position. 'The borders of a country, Zahra,' he would explain to his wife only, 'are as a woman's honour. The problem with ours in particular,' he scoffed amusingly at the approaching analogy, 'is that she has kept her legs wide open for a long time. All whom have desired her have entered at their leisure, throughout her entire history. Nasser, God rest his soul, was the first man to act upon his manhood; jealous for Egypt's honour, he put a stop to it. After him, it is our job to preserve her chastity.'

He was many years her senior when he had asked her father – an esteemed judge of his time – for her hand in marriage. Still a man of relatively limited means but promising prospects in the military, her father's trust in his potential would materialise soon thereafter. He left her a widow, secured with a lavish home, some assets scattered across Cairo, their enviable estate by the Red Sea and an admirable pension. With such foundations to build upon and the unoccupied time of a barren woman, Zahra had managed over the years to expand their wealth. Rumours had circulated that he had once acquired a second wife to bear his children, and perhaps he had, yet for a while such tales remained only as such: postulated chatter amongst intrusive souls. Eventually, the tales disappeared, leaving only the legacy she had established and the occasional kind mention of her respected late husband.

'Yet, what about the remnants of all those former relationships?' she had asked him.

'What about what, my dear?'

'This country has always been referred to as a woman with a profuse history involving many foreign "occupants". What is to be done with those who came to be as a result? Years and years of genealogical "play". For who is really authentically Egyptian anymore but very few?'

He became slightly agitated whenever her political views differed from his; it was only then that he would discourage her from discussion for 'it is a topic far from the concerns of women. You should remain focused on prayer and blessing your home with God's word; there is hardly any need for you to engage in such matters,' was his ultimate response to her questionings. As a military man, having been trimmed and pruned to obey, then command, the two extremes determined that 'dialogue' would be as uncomfortable to him as it was alien. Not that Zahra genuinely concerned herself with inauspicious views on her country's heritage; perhaps she merely voiced topics such as these with the conviction that her opposing would maintain his interest in her.

She tended to attract his attention, seemingly under the impression that she was entertaining him, by countering some of his political beliefs. Perhaps like many women who suffer from insecurities with their partners, she remained constantly threatened by the possibility that he would eventually tire from the lack of futurity to their marriage and abandon her. And although her husband hardly seemed he would, it was apparent she had become obsessed with the notion of 'different' being intriguing, that if she were to represent herself in the image of a woman of critical understanding and a challenging mind, he would forever be drawn to her, curious and impressed. Yet, like most women of her society, she lacked the experience and worldliness necessary to realise that a man of her culture could only obey or command, incapable of appreciating the pleasure in conversing to convince, or of a relationship motivating both parties to advance themselves through daring competition. Across her lengthy life, she had not grasped the fact that suitors never sought a 'marriage of minds', which that English writer her husband read so often had referred to.

Yet what Zahra ached for more than ever was to converse

with someone, while she lay there staring at the door as if it would burst in her face with an absolution to her guiltlessness. The door, however, remained unperturbed, and the sun crept more and more intrusively into her room until the light eventually became irritable. She heaved herself off the bed, suffering in vain with the longing that pulsed between her thighs as the scent of Rawan's sweeping legs fixated with loyalty in her smouldering chest.

By the time Zahra woke up from her exhausted slumber, her phone had rung four times without intermission. She answered, her throbbing temple burning at her eyes as the voice of her younger sister, Aleya, buzzed through the speakers: 'Zahra, I've been ringing for half an hour. Didn't you pray *dhuhr*?'

'Of course I did. But I felt drowsy after and laid my back in bed a little. How are you?'

'*Alhamdulellah*, we thank Him for everything. I just visited Hussein – the son of a bitch who works there hadn't watered the cactus since my last visit; he's just good to come running like an ass whenever he sees me for money.'

'God rest his soul. May you live and remember.'

'Does anyone forget their own child, Zahra? God grant us patience.'

'*Ameen*. How are the children?'

'Everyone is well. They're asking when they will see their aunt. The girl is waiting for her results.' Aleya smirked bitterly. 'Like she'll find herself a job with that. No one running this country even thinks about these kids' futures. It's all talk on TV to silence us.'

'Don't despair, Aleya. *Insha Allah* she will find something reasonable. The kids just need to stop flying in the clouds with their dreams and accept what they can get.' Zahra yawned unwillingly, the phone sliding against her moist cheek.

'So when they barely want to make ends meet, they're flying in the clouds, Zahra? What can I say? How would you understand when you've lived your whole life sufficed? Our father's days are long gone.'

Zahra felt it wise and less time-consuming to follow where her sister was heading. 'Do you need money?'

'We just want to see you well and soon *insha Allah*,' continued Aleya, her voice slightly more pitched.

'I am not feeling well; I can wire the money for Salma like before.'

'What's wrong, Zahra? I must come see you if you're sick!'

'You will come from old Egypt to El Gouna, Aleya? There's absolutely no need. I will be better *insha Allah*; it's just a cold.'

'Oh, I know the cold of these months. You must eat better and rest well, Zahra – and if you need me, I will come to you immediately!' Aleya hurried her response, feigning concern as a voice far in her vicinity called. 'Try to come soon *insha Allah*, when your health is better. And God bless you for me, sister.'

'Bless you, Aleya. Give my regards to the kids and Mohammed,' Zahra said before ending the call.

She considered how repetitive people were; their lives were an endless procession of patterns in behaviours and arguments that were moth-eaten and lazy, their natural responses no more than lethargic expectancies of one déjà vu after the other. What, then, sustained their existence, if their sole purpose was to spin aimlessly in recurrence? Perhaps, she thought, her posed opposition was never intended to engross her husband; perhaps she had not acted in accordance with the women who shared that particular behaviour; perhaps her incentive stemmed from another source; and perhaps that source was that her soul was different than that of others. A spirit of no rhythm, one that could not perpetuate the monotonousness of being that most were lost without.

Of all the unfortunate souls, Rawan's was the most wretched of all, for while every woman longs to be the exception to her man, the sole person for which he would exempt all the rules he has established for himself, across disappointments and heartaches and years on this pitiful planet that eventually leave men scrupulous in love above all else. Rawan had found this in a woman.

It was not the sensuality of Rawan's body that beat against Zahra's vulva and sped, pulsating to her deepest point within, nor the agility and talent Zain had praised in her performance. Zahra's was not a sexual drive; she had never dipped a toe past the religious sentiments towards her desires, nor allowed them to become more than inert earthquakes within her body. Never had she sought a lesbian lover to release her cravings within a dark intimate crevice far concealed from the prying eyes of her damned society. And it was for that she became terrified, engulfed in panic, for what she had sensed of familiarity in Rawan's motion, her face, her eyes, had led Zahra to doubt whether her toe would remain dry until the day she would be carried to her tomb.

***

Rawan talked in her sleep, always. She did not mumble or utter separate incoherent words, but formed lucid, complete sentences. Saleem, aware of this since it was one of the many traits common between the two sisters, resisted the urge to pry by her bedroom door in insatiable curiousity, yet he could not stifle the gentle humming that crept into his ears whenever he approached the corridor to make tea.

He swallowed five mugs of tea that morning as she slept.

And she was barely alone. The desert roses gifted to her sat on the bedside to her right, their petals glinting as the daylight escaped the curtains' edge to touch them. 'Zali,' she said, 'thank you, they're beautiful.' Her mind recollected his countering response, 'Not when they're near you.' His face sat vividly behind her slumbering eyes as she recalled his while they gazed at her grateful face. He crept down beside her under the rain, attempting to cover her soaking head with his coat, but she shrugged at his gesture.

'Why do you like to sit like this?' he inquired with eyes that swept her face as it reddened in places he longed to kiss.

'Because everyone withdraws and I'm alone to think,' she replied, still taken by his gift.

'Would you like me to leave?'

'No! Thank you for this. I never really made the effort to try and get one, though I've always wanted to.'

'Nafta is not too far from here.' He spoke timidly. 'I can take you sometime.'

'What would I do there now that I have these?' Rawan's tone grew slightly strict, almost harsh.

'I would like it if you attended just one ring, Rawan. You don't have to be inside, obviously, but just come watch from the window.'

'Are we going to repeat this conversation yet once more, Zali?' Her reproach hurt him just as it had the first time he had asked. It did not upset him less every time after.

'It's beautiful, Rawan—'

'And I'm not interested, Zali,' she interrupted. 'I never have been.'

'You need to be. It's for *Allah* in the end.'

'I don't need to do it your way for Him.'

'My "way"?!' he blurted angrily. 'You have no *way* – I've never seen you pray, Rawan!'

'You don't live with me, Zali!'

'Dear God. Can we please go someplace inside?'

'No.'

'I'm not leaving, Rawan.'

'I didn't ask you to, just change the—'

'No, I'm not leaving *us*.'

She sighed at his declaration. 'Stop saying "us". Stop using that word.'

'I want to use it. I want to bring you to Nafta to meet my family. I'll even bring them to you if you agree; I want you to come see me in *dhikr*; I want everything with you because I love you.'

Rawan blankly looked at him, her vision hazed by the rain, his eyes fighting to blink less. Her sketches, once glued to the gravel, were now steadily pierced with the water thrusting the paper against the small, hard bumps of the ground.

'I love you,' he repeated affectionately. 'What are you afraid of?'

She hurriedly stood up. 'It doesn't seem like I am the fearful one, Zali. I'm certainly not the one who needs, the one who is lacking things in life.'

'No? So why did you come here? You've always said you came to settle, but that's just a ludicrous tale you tell to those who have no interest in seeing you. Leave Egypt to live in Tunis?' He smirked. 'Why? What could we possibly have here that you did not find there?'

Her eyes were darted at the centre of his, but it was as if they were not looking, nor at him nor at anywhere else, and while he trembled beneath his coat, her bare arms showed no goose-bumps against the frosty rain. Were it not for the colour of the pouring sky around them or the crystallised roses held in her hands, she would have appeared as a woman doused in her own sweat. The entirety of her demeanour made him anxious, as fear crept into his heart at her silence and collectedness. Neither impervious nor angered, she was warm. Warm and wildly tame.

'You are escaping,' he managed to indicate. 'Not something or someone; you are here simply for the running away. What I fear is that the cause has followed you here. You're looking at me, knowing it to be true.'

Rawan bent down to collect her tattered depictions off the ground.

'It has not left you. It's in everything you sketch. That's why you ruin them, try to drown them; you can't stop it nor will you allow it to endure.'

She levelled with him once more, still holding her gift. The roses had a sandy complexion that reminded her of Samra's. Every twinkle, flickering off their surface, resembled her sister's eyes at night, and she believed for a transient moment that Samra was indeed glaring back at her through the millions of blinking eyes Rawan had, clasped within her hands.

'Would you rather have me lock them up in a drawer somewhere?' she replied. 'Hang them across the walls of my home like hunted antlers? Give them to others so they crucify them in their own creative means? No. I don't ruin or drown them as you say; these roses that you stripped off the ground, are they less beautiful in my palms. Is their worth reduced? No. Yet have you uprooted them? Yes, yes you certainly have. This is why I came. I am a stranger of the very ground that begat me, so I chose to live a stranger in a land that didn't. My tale is not ludicrous or forged. I wish never to return there, yet I must. Samra's wedding has been scheduled. I am thankful for your gift, Zali.' She lifted the roses slightly higher. 'They're reminiscent of myself.'

She spoke in the most delicate manner, yet he breathed in the bitterness she did not convey. For seven months he had known her; and through each day, in all his spirituality and grace he discerned that he was not falling in love with a plain, warm woman. Not once had she been approachable. Despite how he knew nothing more than the Rawan of those seven months, he grew confident that her aura was not hers to project. Who had he fallen for? A lost, overtly philosophical woman, whose sole intention in life was to burn in the clandestine nature of her solitude, loved by a man of purpose yet one who condemned himself to wander with her displacement.

'I can survive without you, Rawan,' he said in the sincerity with which he had succeeded to maintain, regardless of her inventive responses. 'No one can claim my time with you has been enough to impair that by any means. Forgetting you will be simpler than drying my head from this rain. But I do not want to.'

The smile she gave him before walking away was an emblem of the particular grimace one renders, in the spilt second that follows stubbing one's toe against a wall. 'Next time you pray, I want you to ask your sheikh why you tie your headpieces so tight,' she remarked.

Zali, befuddled and numb, could only answer, 'If you come with me, I shall ask him for you.'

'Ask for you. I already know,' she said in her sleep. 'It's such a shame you don't.'

***

An obscene headache hauled at her eyes as she arose, as if they were teasingly digging themselves further into their crevices, struggling to make visible to her the thoughts within her skull through the most superficial understanding of sight. Her clothes clung to her skin and glued to the bed sheets below her, her hair adhered to her face, mangled and wet. She dug her nails under the pillow searching for the phone to know the time. Only three hours of sleep. Why had she stirred? Rawan's body was heavy and searing; a coffee would lessen the pain in her temple, which would perhaps then allow her body the sleep it required. But Zali would not. She opened the folder containing her photos on the phone, sliding her thumb up and down until he appeared, just as he had been visible as she slept, his arm behind her neck, his palm perched on her shoulder, looking at her as she smiled to her own finger on the shoot button.

'Why are you here!' she grouched to herself, banging a clenched hand to the side of her head. Saleem rang a spoon against his mug outside. She locked her phone and walked out the room, stumbling through the hall.

'Hey!' he greeted her. 'Tea?'

'No, I want coffee,' she mumbled.

'Just a second.'

She collapsed, comatose on his sofa, ogling the fireless fireplace.

'You didn't sleep much,' he shouted from the kitchen.

'It's very hot,' she stated.

'What?'

She would not answer until he returned with her coffee and parked himself at her feet, leaning his back against the fireplace edge farthest from where she sat.

'It's very hot,' she finally repeated.

'Mmm, sorry, I couldn't hear you from there.' He sipped some of his tea. 'Take a cold shower.'

'I will go before we leave tonight.' She eyed her mug, before tasting the heat on her tongue. From the corner of her eye, she could see him looking at her in anticipation and covert impatience. 'Tonight, we'll use the ropes again, then he'll incorporate the poles into the routines—'

'I don't care about that,' he interrupted.

'You don't care about that,' she mimicked. '"That" is how I gain Amgad's attention. You don't care.' She leered at him.

'When can you get him to come here?' Saleem replied, overlooking her smirk.

'Tonight,' she barked at him, still smiling, her face twisted and aggravated. 'I'll walk over and invite him for dinner. Come with me! Tell him you're a great cook.'

'No. We will not carry on in this manner.' He shook his head at her like an irritated dog. 'You will not take my concerns or inquiries as jests to laugh over.'

'You utter nonsense like you are oblivious of our plan. Your eagerness is endearing, Saleem, believe me; but, and I do apologise for having to kill that charming innocence of yours, eagerness only gets you past the supermarket door. It's not a currency used in purchase.'

'We are together, Rawan.'

'Well, until he's grabbing your ass in his hands, I can't really comprehend how we are.'

'Stop talking about yourself in that manner!' he said, enraged at her, yet all he managed to accomplish was to induce a demented, hysterical giggle on her part.

'Unbelievable! You men are, in truth, so reliably delusional! Is it the word "ass"?' she posed questioningly in a tiding wave of madness as he rammed his eyes shut at her firm repetition. 'Is that it? You survived a night of men drooling over me, came home and drank your tea damn well, but this, no? It's amazing how the only trustworthy trait your kind possesses is hypocrisy.'

'You're playing a role, Rawan!' he howled at her. They had both risen from their places, standing mere inches apart like rabid politicians with their noses sniffing each other's weak spots in the argument. 'You're *acting*! Your character's name is Malak. She is fictional. She doesn't *exist*! Stop talking like a whore, because if I were a pimp, I wouldn't have married your sister!'

Her palm slammed against his cheek with such ferocity, the blow knocked him to the side. A potent burning rang up her entire arm. He steadied himself once more with eyes wide at her glaring ones, their panting breaths echoing between them, calming steadily.

'Thank God you didn't.' She spoke into his stare, as his feet rooted before her. Rawan moved away, retiring and alarmed at her inability to impede such escalation and incapable of distinguishing her next step. Saleem's composure was escaping him incessantly. He grieved for how he had referred to Samra as his wife. His heart throbbed at the reflection that she never would be, his face ablaze with shame.

Rawan left the disgraced Saleem like a child who had divulged a forbidden secret, a lie ensnared between desire and reality, and she sped back to her room. The clean clothes she forced down her neck and up her legs pushed against her feverish skin, yet she paid them no notice; the urge to leave the house was overpowering and incessant. She fumbled with her shoes and fled to the door before he could stop her.

He would not.

Where did she wish to go? Rawan would not leave Amgad until she sank her nails in his chest and soiled him in his own blood. Fatigued beyond reason, she left the building and set out onto the main road, seeking further, narrower streets to wander in. Not the sea, she thought. *I don't want to stroll by the sea.*

There Came to Us a Day

The sun was at its highest, neglecting nothing and no one. It scorched what it could, baked what was possible and suffocated with caged heat what its light did not touch.

Egypt no longer has seasons, only two extreme polarities of intense, bitter cold and smoldering, sunny peaks. Where autumn and spring once existed, nothing remains but delay after delay. The waiting, Rawan's head resounded, for the coming of a soft breeze of mercy from stifling heat … how impatient one becomes of anticipation wed to hindrance, how disappointing after a drought to be flooded in frost, with nights of aching bones and days of filthy streets. How frustrating it must be for loitering trees to blossom, only to watch their flowers burn within mere days. How swift hope dies in waiting, how gloomy a waiting stained by hopelessness can be.

Rawan strode aimlessly, a stranger, from one alien street to the next, looking nowhere, seeing nothing, hearing only the sound of her breath trampled by faint car horns. She wondered what expression her face held yet did not bother to check in any object that would provide a reflection. Her head stung, and she began tracking shaded areas to drift to.

Zain should call me. You call him. No, I'll see him later

tonight. Call him. Why? Because you want to. Why do I want to? Because you want to smoke and not have to go home just yet ... What is that?

A scream rang from a distance, then another and yet another, louder and more strident each time. Rawan stopped mid-walk, petrified, seeking the source of the noise. She heard it again and frantically grappled to locate its direction, anxiously shifting her torso left and right. It was a woman shrieking. Rawan puffed the air in and out of her like a trackless train and jolted down the street. The screams grew fainter; she stopped and ran back up again to where she had been standing. Flashes of dust ensued. 'Rawan!' Samra yelled in her head. Rawan took the narrow one to her left, the shrill voice growing more vivid. *She needs help!*

A building blocked her path. The entire street was empty. She returned once more and sped through the parallel lane. *It's louder now! Yes it's louder. Oh, God.* Rawan saw the tubes that engulfed Samra, the blood that ran up one of them into her hand. Only now could she barely depict shouts accompanying the sound she was seeking, and they were not of a woman. She increased her pace, bounding hysterically from one trail to the next, Samra's wounded face before her. Pausing for seconds to assure her proximity to the noise, she ran with the conviction that if she were to help the woman, some of her sorrow would subdue, that perhaps even Saleem would be less inclined to stress her, that he would release his clutches from her own reasoning.

She was close, exceedingly close, just one exact turn. *Stop running. Stop.*

They were standing casually. A girl inclined against one of the buildings, two slightly older boys near her. One was holding his phone's screen high, facing the other two, all laughing amusedly at something they were viewing on it.

Laughter.

Rawan pulled at her hair, blinking perplexedly up to the sky as sunlight burnt from the glare in her eyes. The girl laughed yet again, the same sound Rawan had heard, and yet so dissimilar. *How could you have mistaken that for cries of help?* The voice in her head snorted at her. Pathetic delirium. She moved down the street, away from their company, and collapsed against a wall, weeping miserably, biting her lips and twisting her face in vexed confusion. She traced the outline of her sister's face in the dust at her feet with a finger, the face that had looked into hers moments ago as she swept the streets like a charging bull. She dug the eyes deeper so that they appeared to sink amidst her face, her tears forming droplets on the depiction. When it was complete, she no longer discerned whom it resembled more: Samra, herself or the soaked sketches back in her room. Her sobs were silent, speaking only in dragging breaths that swept within and without her, as her surroundings blurred and shifted away. Rawan, a recluse in her own body, squeezed it inwardly like an infant wailing from the horrors of birth, longing to return to the very womb that had expelled her.

Get a grip on yourself before he finds out. I'm tired. You're always tired. I want to sleep. There's no more sleep for you, Rawan; neither Zali nor Samra nor I will allow it. Enough ... Stop! Just will it, and I shall, you damned wretch!

A less familiar voice crept into her mind, an old woman holding her palm to read at the outskirts of the Avenue Bourguiba, finding nothing there to decipher, shifting higher to look at Rawan's face. 'I see in your eyes the fleeing of the dead in the grave. Trust is the sword of Lucifer himself, and you have placed yours in unworthy hands. Young one, leave this place before it floods you like the paper I see here at your feet.' *Leave that place, this place, to where? Where does one set forth to, when here and there are one, Rawan? Go to hell!* She slapped her face in vain. *Together, we go together.*

***

The maid indicated to Amgad to make himself comfortable. 'I'll let him know you're here, sir.'

He sat on the chair nearest to the door, examining his surroundings while reclining back. Major-General Mahmoud Fouad looked back at him from the coffee table, beaming proudly while lifting a giant trevally alongside whom Amgad suspected was his grandson. The pitiable capture gaped, wounded and horrified, its tail curled in thrashing pain of suffocation, trapped within a printed snapshot of time. Amgad struggled to stifle his own urge to smoke, while he waited impatiently for the presence of his host who would permit him.

Mahmoud skipped down the stairs with a greeting smile. 'Amgad, good to see you.' He motioned for him to return to his seat. 'How are you, detective?'

'All is well sir, *alhamdulellah*. I hope your health is superior and all is smooth at work.'

'*Alhamdulellah.*' He sat down at the edge of the sofa next to him. 'Work is work, and we are not getting younger, son.' He chuckled.

Amgad politely feigned amusement. 'No, sir … we are not.'

The maid approached to ask what they wished to drink and sped back to prepare their requests. The Major-General smiled at Amgad once more. 'Look, I've been told to look into a matter regarding the business practices of Zain Abdullah. Now, we don't want much detail regarding the sources of his funding; we're more concerned with the reputation of his business.'

Amgad hardly comprehended his good fortune, to be officially assigned to investigate the man who, until moments prior, had the leisure of providing him with tasteless conversations and reserved answers. The detective was so attentive, he practically sat in Mahmoud's mouth. 'The reputation?' Amgad queried.

'I am well aware of the nature of his business; that's not our issue here. What we want to look into is how this nature has or may negatively influence the street.'

'Voters,' Amgad stated to assert his meaning.

'Good man. Not the Red Sea of course.'

'I understand, sir.'

'Our Channel One and Two days are long gone, Amgad. You're a youthful man. You understand – my grandson, a mere child, asks me about my work, for God's sake!'

'Yes, sir.'

'We want comprehensive data on every actual and possible influence of a business of this kind in a predominantly Muslim country. Zain Abdullah doesn't own a tent in an alley in Cairo; his place is licensed, as a nighttime entertainment club of course. Thank you, Fatma.' He paused, taking his coffee from the maid. 'It's practically on an island of its own!'

'It's also significantly recent,' Amgad continued when they were alone once more.

'Yes, which is why we're not necessarily apprehensive. Simply cautious. Attentive vigilance is never a bad idea when your enemies are worming for trivial attestations to support their "holy" duties of spreading chaos.' Amgad nodded in approval. 'Investigate quietly. Give me a thumbs-up that he's keeping it hushed in the media, non-transparent or blatant, and your job is done. Amgad, I asked you to meet me here because the matter is too sensitive for the office, and we do not wish for questions to arise.'

'You wouldn't have assigned me, sir, if you doubted my discretion. Rest assured.'

Mahmoud smiled kindly to him, leaning his head closer. 'We are in my reception, Amgad, not locked in the study upstairs. My emphasis on your confidentiality has no relation whatsoever to my trust in you.'

'An honour, sir.'

There came a faint rustle from the stairwell, and the young boy Amgad had seen with the Major-General in the picture descended slowly, holding the iron rails and rubbing at his eyes.

'Grandad's beloved!' Mahmoud cooed as he held his arms wide for the boy, who paced across the grand reception and, approaching his grandfather, held his hand up to be lifted. Mahmoud hoisted him onto his lap and kissed his cheek. The boy swirled lazily to look at Amgad, who gave him an exaggerated smile. The child cupped his tender palm to his grandfather's ear and whispered, 'Who's that, Grandpa?'

'A friend, *habibi*.'

The boy discounted it as unimportant, simply muttering, 'Fatma said you can't take me swimming today.'

'Fatma said that? No, *habibi*, I can, but later. Grandpa will be busy just for a short while, and then we'll go. Are you hungry?'

The child nodded slowly.

'Ok, run to the kitchen, and make sure Fatma's preparing breakfast for you, ok?'

The boy pushed himself to the ground, but his grandfather held him again. 'Where's Grandpa's kiss?' he inquired endearingly.

The boy pecked his cheek, but his grandfather feigned disappointment.

'Stingy! Give Grandpa a harder one!'

His grandson raised his hands to his lowered head, squeezing it in his hand and planted his lips hard against his cheek. Mahmoud chuckled: 'Yes! Like that!' And the child sped away.

'God bless him for you, sir.'

'Bless you, Amgad. My daughter is travelling with my son-in-law, and they left him to me.'

'May they return safely, sir.'

'Thank you. So, when do we hear good news of you?'

Amgad paused. 'Marriage?' he exclaimed.

'Sure!'

'No, no sir,' he blurted.

'Why?' he queried, apparently touched by Amgad's tone. 'You've not met a decent girl to alter that rejection?'

'Decent girls are many, but no, I'm not considering it,' he tensely replied, hoping the topic would be discarded, yet the Major-General persisted. 'What is this I'm hearing? There is no man who doesn't yearn for the company of a woman and rearing children: the *sunnah* of life!'

'With my entire respect to the *sunnah*, sir, there are men who opt for comfort over such strains.'

'Strains? Oh, I see,' he cried out in comprehension. 'You've been burnt,' he chuckled.

Amgad laughed back politely. 'Hardly, sir. It is merely a matter of personal priorities and wants.'

'And since we're not in my study or your office, friend to friend, an old man to a much younger one, what are your priorities when it comes to women?'

Amgad was agitated and uncomfortable, for while the Major-General stressed how the place of their discussion insinuated an informal and friendly disposition, he was worldly enough to know it is never the location where a conversation is held that determines people's attitude towards it, but the parties involved in such discourse. And he was in the presence of the Major-General, the man who had used 'we' more than 'I' when providing Amgad's assignment. The same 'we' who was more concerned with the polls than the thriving of a legitimised 'sex' service provider, its representative now pressingly inquiring on the reasons for his stance against matrimony.

Seeing Amgad's silence in thought, Mahmoud thrust on. 'You've never been in love, my boy?'

He smiled at him bitterly, speaking with the repression of a man who had craved for so long an opportunity to bellow aloud another man's compromising secret. 'May I respond with a story, sir?'

'Indeed.'

'There is a man, a salesman at an antiques store in Dokki. He earns a decent pay that provides well for him and his wife, and he's fortunate and bizarre both at once because he actually takes pleasure in what he does. He revels in the dimmed light that plays off the crystal ornaments around him, spends hours intricately polishing every piece of Alpaca silverware; it seems he's happy, satisfied. You'd never understand why – being a quiet man who kept to himself – but, also, you could not discern a single hint that he was a man of grand dreams that surpassed tending to aged treasures.' Mahmoud nodded from time to time in attentiveness, as Amgad continued, 'He's married, and his wife is, as we say, an earring gifted to the earless – stunning! Breathtakingly exquisite!'

'You liked her?' the Major-General interrupted.

Amgad shook his head rapidly. 'I'm getting there, sir. His wife is pregnant with their first child. To anyone, he looks like a man blessed with limited but reasonable means of life and a beautiful partner to share that life with. Now, one day, a customer walks into the store, the slightest whiff of air you'd breathe around him wreaks of money. It's around lunchtime and the salesman's wife has just brought him his daily lunch of sandwiches to eat together – to cut it short, the customer sees her and is consumed, then and there, immediately. Without a moment's hesitation, he knows he'll be passing by that store every day on.'

'He tries to seduce her,' the Major-General uttered.

'No. He doesn't wish to; he's in love. An obscenely rich man, he doesn't want a lick to taste! He's after the entire ice cream factory. He targets the husband, chats him up, befriends him, tries to distinguish his ins and outs. Once he's judged the man for a trailblazing opportunist, he seals the deal with an offer.'

'What's his offer?' Mahmoud asked, hairs-on-end intrigued

'The shopkeeper trades, no, *sells* his pregnant wife, with his child growing inside of her, to the Christian tycoon, for a very lucrative price, through which he established a very lucrative business.'

The Major-General gaped at him. 'May I smoke, sir?' Amgad requested nonchalantly.

'Of course,' he whispered, infused in shock and overwhelming curiosity.

'And that is what I think of love and marriage; a quite profitable economy, but I am not a man of commerce.'

'But how did his wife agree to this?' asked Mahmoud with great interest. 'Did he force her, or was she willing?'

'Those, sir, are details of which I'm unaware.'

'Do you know this man?' the Major-General posed, wide-eyed with astonishment. 'Who is he?'

Amgad sucked a deep draught from his cigarette, before stating in malice and victory the words that exited his lips amidst the smoke: 'Zain Abdullah.'

That Could Not Pay Her Dowry

Rawan stepped into the dressing room and shut the door at the booming noise outside. It was less crowded than the night before as some of the dancers were already on stage, yet all the seats were engaged. She glanced down to the nearest one. The woman occupying it looked at her for a second, the memory of the past night still fresh in her mind, then graciously jumped off the seat. Rawan sat down, pulled at the coal-black wig at the edge of the mirror before her and began affixing it to her head, securing it firmly with pins, paying no attention to the woman who had risen from her place and was now chattering in a hushed voice with others at the back. A faint applause thudded far around them, and all but Rawan headed, giggling, for the door. It slammed shut behind them then exploded once more to an array of feather-splashed thighs and glittering breasts heaving up and down below flushed cheeks and noses in need of powdering. Their collective prattle was boisterous and annoyed Rawan, who puffed indignantly at the human ability to seek pleasure in the most repetitive and humiliating walks of life.

As she patted down the wig, a familiar face looked at her reflection, and Rawan smiled to signal that she could approach. Karma hoisted herself next to the mirror and said beamingly, 'Why would you wear that? Your hair's good.' Her tone was greatly indicative of her age, and she spoke without the vulgar facial movements that largely marked her profession. Rawan sensed that, besides her beauty, Karma seemed out of place there.

'Because men rarely seek "good"; they seek the unreal.'

'You're funny,' she giggled.

'Well you're the first to appreciate my dull sense of humour.'

'Why did you help me? I'm Karma by the way. You're Malak.' She said her pseudonym like she was informing her of it, which Rawan found thoroughly amusing.

'Yes,' she laughed in response. 'I wasn't helping you; I'm simply not entertained by women who put other women down so they feel self-worthy. That job is taken already.'

'You don't like men, do you?'

Rawan beckoned with her hand for Karma to bring her head close and cranked hers up dramatically as if to tell a secret, whispering, 'I don't think men themselves like men very much.'

'That's true; you should see the brawls that go on here sometimes! Nasty stuff.'

'Brawls?' Rawan stressed. The word did not conform to her initial impression of Karma. 'Where are you from?'

'Suez. Zain uses it a lot.'

'He's the one who brought you to work here, right?' Rawan

stood up and unzipped her jeans, maintaining eye contact with Karma as they talked.

'Yes! Did he tell you?'

'No, but I figured so because you're like an adorable little puppy, and Zain is, well, an angel, amongst other things,' Rawan said.

'He is. He's the one who organised everything for my stay here. I'm very grateful for all he does for me.'

'So why did that whore yesterday think she could assault you?' Rawan asked, removing her bra, as her bare breasts were revealed and pointed to Karma.

'Once we step through the doors of Naktal, we're all equal,' Karma stated. 'The waiters, or those who wipe the tables or clean the floor, Zain treats them just like you or me.'

Rawan smiled and shook her head to object, now sliding down an unruly leather bodice that obscured her face. 'Shit, I'm stuck. Come pull this down for me,' she muffled, choked by its tightness around her neck and face. Karma jumped off the table and tugged at it until she was wearing it properly, pushing each of her bosoms up to adjust them. Karma's hands felt tender and warm against her skin, and there was a kindness in them that lingered far after her touch.

'You don't agree?'

'Far from it. I simply know that Zain's fairness stretches beyond that. You cannot give a child sun and water and expect him to blossom; our differences are imputable to our growth. So what brought you here, Karma – you just fell in love with Zain and couldn't let him go?' she teased.

'I wanted to be like you,' she replied in brief earnestness.

'Excuse me?'

'I'm fascinated with body language. I think if our bodies could speak, they would tell stories forever. I've always wanted mine to speak the way yours does.' She moved closer to Rawan so that their noses almost touched, and announced in the lowest, gravest tone she could muster, 'Everybody here thinks I am an ignorant bimbo, and I let them believe it, do you know why? Because Zain believes in me. He told me to watch your every move and learn, because you're not staying here for long as I understand. He promised I would be your continuation in Naktal. I let them believe I am an idiot because I do not care for applause. The tales my body will tell should leave them speechless. There is too much talk in this world. Too many empty words spoken and gestures articulated in a million tones except the silent roar of one's body.'

Rawan smiled painfully to her eager sentiments, compelled by the heeding resonating in her mind with each word Karma spoke: Beware the silence that ruins you.

Karma stepped back, as if transformed from a possessed state. 'What will you do tonight?' she interjected.

'I'm going to let them tie me up and beat me to death.' She laughed, fastening a choker around her neck, and headed for the door, leaving doe-eyed Karma confused and smiling. That wretched smile her people in all innocence carried to their grave, because *Allah* loves most from all his worshippers those who are content.

She inhaled the alcohol their breaths emitted, signifying their numbers had increased from the night before. *Good. Let more come. Hell, are you full?* Zain's handymen were there to meet her at the same pinnacle from which she would plummet yet again. They handcuffed her wrists separately, and then she sat down, locking two more around each ankle. They were cold, relieving her, and taut, making her feel safe, as well as heavy, easing her mind. One of the men helped her up then walked away. The others had left too. She turned to look down in the dark, but only her ears could see. They showed her that she stood at the edge of a pit into which she would plunge, yet Saleem would not be willing to break her fall. Saleem's readiness. The worker who had helped her stand returned, dragging a cluster of chains in his hand. Rawan held out her arms so he could secure them on her and watched him moments later swiftly bend to her feet to affix them too.

'Done,' he said. 'Mr. Zain gave directions for you not to move so nothing becomes tangled.'

She nodded silently.

'Just stay there, it'll take us a minute. We've never used this reeling device before, so bear with us.'

'Take your time,' she whispered, looking back down the giant crater they stood by. 'They're not going anywhere.'

He left her once more, yet her solitude was immediately interposed by a loud churning nearby. Alarmed voices rose to her from below as the sound stirred more strident each second. She stood, tranquil, hearing the chains binding her begin to snake around themselves, recoiling to unwind. By the first sharp tug at her arms, Rawan had surrendered all agency from within as she rose higher than the summit itself. Even when her toes left the ground, she did not grip the chain at her palms to lessen the tension in her pained arms. The men reeled her in like a captured fish until she was hanging perfectly vertical at the midpoint. There were no drums playing, and once the men began her slow descent, a woeful cello hummed around her. She was lowered to face the audience, the chains at her feet loose, while all her weight hung at her strained arms hanging above her head. She felt the burn in her shoulders deepen yet kept a solemn face. *No smiles tonight, huh? ... Do not ignore me, Rawan! Oh, I see. Smiles for Amgad only. And Saleem? None for him? Enough!*

A small ring of light revealed only her face as the audience's thunderous applause splashed upon her while she was brought down. Her feet touched the ground, and the chains on her wrists dropped as light flooded the room. Her sight incited shrieks of horror amidst silent gasps. The only incongruence with Rawan's demeanour was that she held her head high, proud even. The fluctuation in the cello's rhythm signalled to the men high above and Rawan was yanked violently so that her feet no longer touched the ground once more. Her hair steamed beneath the wig, and blood flushed to her eyes. The chains around her ankles stretched tighter, and she was flipped in a non-voluntary summersault so that her back faced the crowd and her fingertips teased the stage floor. The melody echoed louder, whereas she dangled like a butcher's slaughtered cattle, her costume wrapped around her, waiting to be sliced apart.

Saleem bent his face low to conceal the heat in his swimming eyes; her testimonial made sense to him before any of her spectators would comprehend it – if they were to. Although they would have no reflections on it, save for their eager anticipation of what she would perform each following night, he would live with it, branded across his chest like the very analogy she embodied before him. How defenseless she looked! What in the world could differentiate us from all other beings if not for our power to control? What is it that inevitably drives us to project this influence on others, like they had done to Samra, when we are in such dire need of casting it within us, yet utterly useless in commanding ourselves?

Naturally, they were as dependable as ever to answer his ponderings before his very eyes. The chains binding Rawan's wrists tightened once more; those around her feet relaxed, and she was tossed yet again to stand facing them. Her feet, however, remained above the ground. The men above began to alternate their authority over the chains so that she marionetted across the stage as gracefully as they could manage. Her limbs obeyed their whim non-questioningly, while the restraints banged and rubbed against each other in disregard to the cello's melodious melancholy. The crowd was torn amidst laughs, cheers and whistles, yelling at how her breasts jiggled with each yank, asking when the chains at her feet would force her legs wide open, biting their tongues as they sexualised her vulnerability and eroticised her subordination.

When the grand conclusion to her performance

approached, the men prepared for her climax. They forced her to stand, her hands stretched above and her legs floating from the stage, unhurriedly pulling her arms and legs wide as she looked sternly to the crowd.

From amongst the swarm of viewers, a single voice shouted, 'Wider!' Many followed, repeating the same command, 'Wider! Wider! More!' They chanted fiercely, 'More! More! More! More!' like mad predators cheering at the kill. 'More! More! More!' the man to Saleem's left barked, nudging his shoulder to join them in their rapture. 'More! More! More! More!' he bellowed in Saleem's ears, which were pounding with the echo of the only word capable of transforming humans into less than animals, slaves, ruled over by their carnal madness, and Saleem would adhere to his fellow slaves on their pioneering ship of ruin. He took a long, pitying gaze at Rawan and roared, 'MORE!' in unison with them. They banged their fists on the tables together, chanting in a cohesive rhythm, 'MORE! MORE! MORE! MORE! MORE! MORE!' while Zain blew smoke at the window through which he watched, grinning, his chest inflated with satisfaction at what he had created.

When her Dionysian rave had been established, Rawan broke the grave look with which she had marked her face all along and catapulted the mob before her with a wide, maddened grin as her skin glistened with sweat. She leered at them, their Bacchus of the night, her lascivious smile insane and taunting, looming down at them as she drew a long breath in before howling, 'MORE! MORE! MORE,' an X-shaped woman roaring in conformity with their tempo.

Her wrist chains were released once more as her torso violently dropped so that she faced the ground, yet she continued to chant with them and they with her as her body flew above their screaming faces. Fewer hands clawed at her than before, while the others shouted their call of the night and lifted their fists off the tables to shatter their hands in applause inches from her sweeping face. She fed off their raving hunger and thirst with all her being, passing over Amgad, who roughly grabbed her hair and yanked her wig loose. She stopped her mantra and glowered at him in pain as her head ached where the pins had held the wig secure. *What is that look on his face?* His eyes held the disappointment of one who wished to possess the intangible, whereas the object of his desire fluttered away instantly and landed on the stage.

Still smiling wide, she glanced above her, then shifted a few inches to the side as a key dropped from above. She bent before her audience to free the cuffs from her feet; thinking she was bowing, they rang once more in applause. She released the restraints on her arms and stood as Zain had the night before, on his island of dreams, his wrecking ship of shameful departure and no destination. From her place, Rawan saw herself as a drug of the worst kind, that which attracts both rival and ally, intending only to toy with the minds of all who are led to believe that it is they who consume her and not vice versa.

Who do you trust, Rawan? I don't trust. Not even yourself? I know. I know you are the last person you trust. Because you won't leave me! I never will, Rawan. You know it to be true; it is the only thing you trust in. When all is lost and gone, I remain.

She blew a bitter kiss to the crowd and fled to Zain's office. He had left the door open for her and turned to roll a joint as she ran in, locking it behind her.

'That's mine, right?' she panted, looking at his hands.

'Yes,' he muttered, putting the paper on his desk and holding his empty palm out. 'Show me your arm.' He examined her wrist. 'It'll most likely bruise by the morning.'

Careless to his concern, she dropped on the sofa lazily, whispering in exhaustion, 'Can you finish rolling that?'

He turned his back to her and continued as she had asked. They heard someone approach the door and fumble with the handle, attempting to enter.

'What is that?' she asked from her seat indignantly as he walked to open, grumbling, 'Someone who has the gall to not knock and wants me to slice his neck,' he said as he turned the key. It was Saleem.

'I asked where your office was,' Saleem said, casually walking into the room.

'You asked where my office was,' Zain repeated on edge. 'Who the hell are you?'

Rawan sighed from her place. 'Zain, Zain, that's Saleem. Come.' She motioned to Saleem, patting her hand to the empty place next to her. 'Sit here.'

'I'm sorry about this morning,' he blurted in regret. 'Can we go home together? Please? I don't want you to drive.'

She looked at him, touched in sincerity, her eyes squinting to deliver the message after a tight smile of affection. 'I can take a taxi.'

'Please, can we go together?'

'We can't, Saleem, you know why.'

'Yeah, you shouldn't even be here,' Zain interrupted, making a wide circle in the air and pushing the lit joint in her hand.

'Can I have one?' asked Saleem.

'I ... guess,' Zain replied irritably, 'but you really should go back outside.'

Saleem shook his head. 'No, it's ok. The swine left,' he replied acidly.

Rawan shot off the sofa, spraying Saleem with remnants from the ashtray. 'What the—' She gaped at him.

'He left,' Saleem repeated. 'Asked for the check when you were unlocking yourself, and I came here right after he had gone.'

She turned to Zain for support, yet he remained unperturbed, dragging at the joint in his hand then passing it to Saleem.

'What's wrong?' Zain said, seeing as she was still waiting for his response.

'What's wrong?'

'Yes, what's wrong? He leaves tonight, he comes tomorrow.'

'We don't even know why he left this early! What if he doesn't come tomorrow?'

'Then he comes the next day, or the next,' he stated calmly.

She responded, agitated, 'Really? Is this funny to you?'

'Really. I'm not joking. The likes of Amgad have always been very frequent clients since I opened; although he's been extremely busy recently, he still manages to come when he can and drink his ass off. I'm telling you, he'll be here tomorrow.'

'He better!' she barked at them. *Why did he leave?*

Irritated, Rawan unlocked the door and stormed to the dressing room so Saleem and herself could return home. Perhaps retiring to bed earlier than last time would provide her with the sleep of which she was in dire need. Karma's broad smile was there to greet her; however, Rawan was not in the mood for the woman's constant chirpiness.

'Hey! Where did you go after? One of the boys left this for you,' Karma babbled, pointing to a large cactus wrapped in wicker on the long dressing table. Rawan pushed past her silently and returned into her original wear in haste.

'It's from a woman.' Karma spoke cautiously, not reproachful of Rawan's disregard.

She turned to look at her, with the slight mounting of curiosity. 'A woman? Why would a woman send me anything?' Rawan approached the obscured plant. 'They're not even flowers.'

'There's a note on the side,' chimed an excited Karma, pleased that Rawan had spoken to her once more. She grabbed at the note with the wild recklessness of youth and, piercing her palm, managed to retrieve it. She handed it to Rawan.

'Girl, are you daft?'

'Sorry,' she muttered.

'Why are you apologising to me? You're bleeding. Go wash your hand.'

'Wait! Let's see what the note says!'

Rawan raised a daring eyebrow at Karma, who timidly backed away to give her ample privacy. The little blood smearing the edge of the paper had not made it illegible. Rawan, examining it, read, 'Wild Thorn, please grace a wilting flower with your company and share a drink. More of you would be delightful.' She mocked under her breath, 'Ha! Wilting flower?' *We could use a drink. Leave me alone! Fine! You, want a drink? Yes, yes I do.* She rummaged her bag to text Saleem, told him to wait a while longer with Zain so they could still drive home together, and then headed for the grand hall.

Zahra's neck was sprained from monitoring the exit from where she knew the dancers fled following their routines.

Rawan had no clue for whom she was searching, yet assumed it was likely an old, sad, perhaps lonely woman who would refer to herself as the analogy in the note suggested. Indeed, she spotted Zahra looking her way, sitting alone on her table, looking forlorn moments before she could achieve eye contact with Rawan. They smiled at one another as Rawan walked over to where the woman sat, whereas Zahra stood up graciously to meet her.

'Malak,' Rawan said, shaking her hand.

'Rightfully so,' remarked Zahra. 'Please,' she gestured to the seat before her.

'Excuse me?'

'Your name is aptly chosen.'

'Oh, thank you.'

'What would you like to drink, Malak?' asked Zahra, pronouncing her name in a stressed sweetness.

'I have no preferences, really.'

'We'll have the same then,' she stated as she motioned for one of the waiters standing by, who ran to her.

'Two of mine please, Rami.'

'Right away, Madame Zahra.'

Rawan smiled to herself at the name and the typicality with which Zahra had attempted to mystify herself in the note, although she maintained an outward courtesy to Zahra.

'Thank you for the gift, madame.'

'It is from my garden. I uprooted it myself!' she boasted. Rawan continued to smile in feigned interest. 'Malak is your real name?'

Rawan was slightly alarmed with her question. 'Of course!'

'Do you like it?'

What is wrong with this woman? 'Why wouldn't I?'

'I know many who dislike their names, our foremost important word of self-identification completely out of our own choice. As if our creator willed it so, just to spite us from ever believing we are in control.'

'Well … ah, our drinks are here! I was just going to say how your non-piousness is right at home here,' she laughed, tapping her glass with Zahra's.

'I should be,' Zahra retorted, gulping down a considerable portion of liquor, 'religious. A woman with my history ought to be most pious; in fact, above others. But I've lived enough to acknowledge how it becomes much more complex than that over time. Piety is for temples, and, matter of fact is, we hardly live in one.'

Again, typical; the unquenchable need to justify sin by questioning the systems of belief. Why can't people just accept that their desire to sin is what makes them human?

'You're analysing what I said,' Zahra remarked.

'I'm thinking, why exterminate temples when you can peacefully walk past them?'

'That's a fair question. Because it is difficult to walk past what your culture is founded upon; it seeps into our being, against our power, leaving us either slaves or rebels.'

'I would agree if we were someplace else. But this is Egypt. You can be or do all that you please with slight caution of any influence you are fortunate enough to exercise through others.'

'You are young, dear Malak, and what you say is merely a tribute of how successful our system is. For it has led you to believe that fantasies are real, by occupying you with building them, then allowing you to indulge in what you created so you trust all the more your control and self-autonomy.'

Zahra's words made perfect sense to Rawan, not Malak. Malak, as Saleem had stressed, was different; she was 'dear young Malak', the temptress of desire, the simple-minded whore. Zahra was speaking to 'Wild Thorn', and Malak was not that.

Who are you going to be now? I don't know – she's uttering my consciousness like an open book, speaking with, not to, me; yet I should not let what I sense in this woman disturb the role I'm playing. Why not? You perturbed it without hesitation to less worthy than her. Who? Amgad.

'They say necessity is the mother of invention,' Rawan said. 'In prayer we ask. We ask because we crave an insatiable "more", and brave men are only champions when a threat is before them. I agree with you, Zahra ... I'm sorry, madame.'

Her eyes constricted lovingly to Rawan as she uttered her name, the countless nodes at the surface of her skin erect with ecstasy. 'Zahra please!' she remarked so Rawan would continue.

'Threat is the invention. Not that there are no dangers present organically, but the sheer magnitude publicised is nothing if not a contraption, enhanced, manipulated and forever perpetuated to validate the courage in force and the magnanimity in violence.'

She had stopped speaking, yet Zahra's gaze consumed her.

'May I ask,' Rawan requested, 'why you are here alone? Not that I am not pleased you offered that I keep you company!'

'I did not invite you to my table from the need to entertain my solitude.'

Rawan awaited her elaboration, engulfed with the sense that she was well acquainted with Zahra, further than the briefness of their encounter suggested.

Zahra continued in almost a whisper, 'I see in your eyes a sadness that I've known of myself, a woeful familiarity of your character as I saw it ever so briefly in your performances, and I wished to converse with you so that I may experience what others failed to witness.'

Rawan remained attentive and somehow engrossed, not only from Zahra's expressiveness, but from her voice and the physicality of her bearing, which spoke to Rawan in ways maybe only Zain did. Zahra continued, 'There was a time when I regularly visited Naktal. I would attend for a few hours, enjoy a glass or two, and leave. Then, not so long ago, I decided never to come again, till one day I felt trapped, caged in guilt and loneliness, of which the circumstances of both I had not an ounce of control upon. I returned that evening and attended your performance, and I found you … well, singular. I asked myself what it was that distinguished you from the countless girls I've known, and I realised yours was the face I saw in my own reflection, superficially dissimilar yet all too familiar to disregard as such. It is the likeness of a woman ensnared in suffering, seeking that which is lost. Tonight, I have become assured of my judgment – never before had I asked for company at Naktal, but for you I did.' She laughed to herself then held her arms out, cupping Rawan's palms in hers.

Rawan's mind seemed blank. She gawked at how wide and vacant it was. *Is this what peace feels like?*

'It is as if I am talking to a young depiction of myself without being accused of lunacy,' ended Zahra.

'More,' whispered Rawan as the music once faint around her halted completely. 'Tell me more about myself.'

'Whatever it is you have done, no matter what brought

you here, do not allow it to destroy you beyond repair.'

Rawan watched Zahra's face dissolve amidst the rain her eyes held back. 'What if it is not something I committed? What if I am not the perpetrator?'

'Then let what has passed settle in the past till it suffocates, and forget.'

Rawan's eerie laughter, at first a leer, rang across the now tranquil hall. 'Yes! That is exactly what they want: to forget! Not just forget; no, no, no, they want to falsify history, tweak what they can and distort what they would so that we forget so well, that when we relive the accounts, we're like a woman taken over and over again, delusional in thinking she's still a virgin every single time.'

'We cannot change that, Malak.' Zahra squeezed her hands desperately. 'We're not ready to.'

'No, no we're not. But there is a debt to be paid, and debts are not forgotten.' She pulled her hands gently from Zahra's grasp. 'You are mistaken, Madame Zahra. I am not your reflection. You are who I will become if I choose to let the past "settle" as you put it. You and I are greatly dissimilar.' She stood up, her eyes still on Zahra's, the kindness and loss in her silent face tugging at Rawan's own. 'Leave this place and do not return,' she told her in a calm tone that was respectful to her sympathy.

'Leave with me,' replied Zahra pleadingly from her seat.

'I cannot. Your notions on stability would not survive within my roaming body.'

Zahra looked at her in forlorn desperation. 'Then you have already invented the perils that demand so.'

COULD THE FORLORN NIGHT?

S aleem passed the joint back to Zain, who sat before him after locking the door behind Rawan. He eyed the man whom she spoke so little of and asked, 'How long have you known Rawan?'

'Years,' he stated, dragging at the roll against his lips then handing it back to Saleem. 'This is exceptional oil. I brought it back from Sinai.'

'What were you doing there, if I may ask?'

Zain nodded in permission. 'I have land there.'

'Land!'

'Yes.'

'Like a house?'

'No, just land. What's wrong, Saleem?' he chuckled.

'Rich man!' he commented, the *hashish* relaxing his tongue.

'Money doesn't do shit.' Zain prodded his temple with his index finger. 'It's this that tells you what to do with it. All those idiots working in the Gulf who come back here and pile theirs in the bank then live stingy—'

'When my parents and I lived in Kuwait, we knew Egyptians who compared yoghurt prices!'

Zain rolled his eyes in disapproval. 'I've seen worse, believe me.'

Saleem peered at the grey hairs on Zain's head, lingering, more than he would were he sober, on the etched wrinkles around the corners of his eyes and the dents on his relaxed forehead.

'How are you and Rawan friends? You're much older,' Saleem asked. Zain laughed heavily. 'Well, she needed a wiser mind in a situation, and I happened to be the genie of the lamp!'

'What was the situation?'

He opened both palms before his chest, replying, 'Ask her.'

'Just curious.'

'Yeah, she makes us all curious doesn't she?'

'I think she likes it.'

'She certainly does!' Zain chuckled to himself. 'But even with you?'

'Ha!' Saleem trajected in irony. 'Especially with me!'

'I noticed there was something going on when you walked in.'

'Things. She's just, well, tough.' He spat the word like an insult.

'It's a trauma of great impact, Saleem. My very late condolences to you are due, but it is our first encounter so—'

Saleem shrugged and waved his untimely gesture out of courtesy. 'It is not the trauma. It's like … she wants to do it alone, you know?'

'Not really. Otherwise you and I would not be having this conversation. Rawan realises her limitations quite well, which is, in fact, what makes our age difference irrelevant to our friendship. Besides her, I have met very few women who acknowledge the hindrances of their kind. The only issue is, she chooses to attribute them to society as opposed to admitting that they are wilfully so.'

'She's not mistaken though, is she? Your entire concept here is based on commodifying these women. Am I wrong?'

'Very. I don't dictate what they do! The audience and I enjoyed very much what Rawan executed tonight, and she wasn't sexually flirtatious for a moment on that stage.'

Saleem lowered his eyelids slightly to Zain, the way he did when someone was telling an explicit lie to his face. 'Violence is an aspect of sexual desire for us, Zain. You know that; it's commonly arousing ... Portrays domination.'

Zain noticed how Saleem's behaviour had changed in Rawan's absence. With her, he had seemed regretful, forlorn, tired. Now, however, his body language was ever more confident and relaxed, his responses elaborate, and Zain, confused and equally attentive to this abrupt shift, decided to test his intuition. 'They were very close I understand: Rawan and Samra.'

'Not really. At least, Rawan doesn't like to think so. She left Egypt for nearly a year, and I cannot say that I had seen much of her before then.'

'But Samra talked about her a lot with you,' Zain

continued, watching Saleem unresponsive to hearing her name repeatedly.

'Samra loved her sister, so did their mother of course. But from what I was told, Rawan never really healthily moved past their father leaving them. Sometimes she blamed her mother, sometimes him, at times even herself.'

'Why would she blame herself?'

'Because he was closer to Samra, naturally her being older and all; but Rawan, as I understand, believed if she had made an effort to attach him to her, too, regardless of her past mistake, that maybe it would have been harder for him to abandon them.'

'Yeah, that sounds like something Rawan would think. You said a "past mistake"?'

'Their father was a violent man, moody in temperament in a very odd way. To strangers, he was extremely gentile, a sophisticated intellectual, yet in his intimate circle, people knew better.'

'So what was her mistake?'

'She did something … it was more like she was dragged into something to be honest, out of sympathy with her mother,' Saleem sighed. 'His cold indifference to her in comparison to how he was with Samra was the punishment he executed till his own parting.'

'It must be difficult to lose both a father and a sibling,' Zain prodded.

Saleem smiled. 'I wouldn't know. No siblings,' he said, pointing to himself. 'I lost both parents very recently too, so

… I think losing people becomes less painful the older we get.'

Zain was shocked. 'How recent?'

Saleem looked at the ceiling, calculating. 'Almost two years ago. I proposed to Samra right after. Can we roll another?'

'Sure!' He stood and walked to his desk drawer. He strung his mind, thinking of a tactful approach to satisfy the swarm of questions flying around it then returned to his seat with a mask of pity glued to his face. 'Days before your wedding! Tsk tsk, there is no power but with *Allah*,' he said, peering at Saleem like a zoo visitor inspecting a caged animal. 'I keep forgetting where Rawan said they found her!' He whined in an act of desperate recollection that was interrupted by Saleem's voice: 'Suez Road,' he breathed. 'The far end.'

'Suez end? But that's a main road in the desert. What was she doing there?'

He never should have spoken. He ought to have left immediately, pretend to be insulted by Zain's intrusiveness or say he wished to check on Rawan, or any other form of silence in response. Yet, he spoke. Perhaps it was the *hashish*, perhaps the night's events had rendered him too exhausted for wisdom. Whatever the reasons were, he would regret it soon enough. The confirmation to all Zain's suspicion came in the form of Saleem shifting in his seat, vividly escaping his eyes and in a broken voice, uttering with a scandalous tone of falsehood, 'I … don't know.'

***

Neither of them spoke in the car, and Rawan felt she was

driving, although his hands were gripping the steering wheel, whereas how safe and heavenly the bed or sofa would be in a few minutes splashed across their minds louder than the crashing waves they had sailed through and by which they now drove.

Back home, as each of their heads rested in its place, once again dawn broke somewhere outside, far from disconcerting to them as their shut windows and closed curtains sealed the pink hues from their cave. Rawan had drowned, drained and been outdueled by her own body, but Saleem was another story. He tossed and heaved, and her face moved with him, pulling at his shut eyes, demanding acknowledgment, showing him she was there, stranded on the road, in the middle of nowhere, waiting for him.

He could not weep, as if his tears would be a recognition of his blunder. And there was no sleep for him either, for beyond guilt and despair lies a far worse monster that feeds off even the smoke above a cremation. As is often the case, our ancestral sayings are mistaken; it seems that to skin the sheep following its slaughter can still bring it harm after all.

And what use could come about now, from this madness? Why was he so reluctant to abandon their plan, if peace would not ensue? Because he secretly did not wish for it to, so that he may never forget her. Like a Heathcliff of the desert and sun, Saleem was haunted and prayed to remain so.

When Rawan finally awoke, many hours had passed, stretched to feel like a great deal more, as time is always entertained by the soul's suffering, for it is there that it lives its longest. She blissfully appreciated within herself the grand success in avoiding yet another restless slumber. Insomnia is the harshest torture, second to a sleep where the mind remains conscious. A favoured form of punishment in prisons and correction facilities, preventing a man from falling asleep is the most assured method of breaking his sanity. The human body can survive weeks and months of starvation, less if deprived of water, yet it takes only a few days to die from lack of sleep. And Saleem sensed his mind approaching impairment.

She sat herself at his feet as he lay on the sofa, rubbing them to indicate her mood had improved from the day before. He nodded and looked at her, feeling nauseated and fatigued.

'Are we sleeping in shifts or what?' She smiled inquisitively. 'Your face is crap!'

Saleem coughed slightly, his chest aching in response. 'Shifts? I didn't sleep even yesterday.'

'Why? Enjoying my snoring?' she teased.

'You don't snore,' he groaningly retorted, pulling his back up slightly to sprain his neck less while talking to her.

'I want to feed you. You like your eggs saucy like me, yes?'

'No.'

'I'll make them like that anyhow. Come on, get up.'

Saleem refused to stir. 'I'm tired,' he croaked.

'If you couldn't sleep all this time, you're not going to magically doze off now. Get up and eat something. I know you men never fall asleep hungry.'

'That's actually very true,' he said.

'There you go.' She clicked her fingers at his approval, clutched his feet once more then headed for the kitchen. She opened the fridge and then started a single eye on the cooker.

Why did she move like that, he wondered? Like a mirage of her; siblings were not nearly so similar. And yet Rawan really wasn't in many ways, for she was undeniably different as she had voiced earlier. It was more her physicality in which he saw the resemblance: the shape of her body; the tone of her skin, which glowed more as of late; the way her limbs and torso coordinated while she moved; the parts of her body that rubbed against one another when she showed compassion or anger. Yet her character and spirit were undeniably alien to what Samra's once were. She was more outspoken than her older sister, so much so that her bluntness had initially caught Saleem off guard the first few times they had met.

He had worked for their father's company for a significant while, securing shipments and sending large quantities of computer chips back and forth from China through his work. When Samra had secretly remained in contact with Yaqub, Saleem met her more than once occasionally, despite the fact that she was never really aware of her father's business. On the account of his death, he comforted her loss by being the sole trustee to the relationship she had privately guarded and he was the only person who knew of his burial place apart from her. His mind now wandered on their frequent cemetery visits, how strange he had found it at first that although she grieved her father's passing, not once had she spoken well of him.

'He was a selfish man,' she once confessed to him, 'beyond comparison. Mama, as any other normal human, has many faults, but he, like most men, saw past them only till he became someone. She was a good wife, tolerating his misfortunes under the belief when one day he would find his place in the world, he would share his successes with her. As a mother who invests her life in her child's.'

'Not all men are as ungrateful,' he had retorted.

'No. But most of those who live in deprivation, upon a sudden taste of fortune, will seek to attribute all effort solely to themselves. As if acknowledging their past would injure their present.'

He considered her words, trying to test whether the theory really applied outside the example of her father, then inquired on the reasons for her having maintained a connection with a man of which she thought so ill.

'Because the most assured way to lose yourself is to abandon your roots for any reason,' she had said.

'What if our roots forsake us?'

'Impossible. The earth does not purge itself of its seeds; it only works the other way around. I choose to never surrender my past, regardless of how agonising it may be. That's the only way I'll know for sure where it is I'm heading.'

She had this unworldly air about her as she spoke or moved or breathed. Like she was a temporary visitor who came to print her fingers on the lives of those in her presence then return to where she had first been, to a place beyond their petty concerns and obsessions. And she was mistaken,

Saleem thought. For with all her grand theories on belonging and continuation, on found and lost selves, at that moment as she spoke to him by her father's grave, she would never have guessed that she was heading into Saleem's arms and to her doom.

Rawan returned, layering bread and cheese on the coffee table. She picked up the mound of cigarette buds in their ashtray. 'That's disgusting!'

'Sorry,' he whispered back, returning from a distance.

'Why are you apologising to me?' she blurted, then stared blankly at his chest for a moment, unable to recall the source of her déjà vu.

'What's tonight's dazzling idea?' he mocked, suddenly salivating over the smell of hot bread and grabbing a loaf.

'Rain.'

'Rain,' he repeated almost inquisitively.

'I say let's drown the idiots!' She raised her palm to slap it in the air against his, yet he continued to bite at the plain loaf in his hand, unamused and increasingly hungry.

She dramatically frowned in disappointment. 'So did you and Zain chat?'

He swallowed a large chunk of bread and began to cough roughly against the friction it had caused along the tender lining of his throat. She beat his back in severity with her fist until he safely gulped it down.

'Thank you,' he heaved.

'Gluttonous!' she remarked teasingly, relaxing her palm

and rubbing his back as she sat crossing one leg under her, the other on the floor.

'This Zain, your friend, is an odd man,' he said.

'Mmm, why?'

'I don't see why you two are friends, or even how you could have met.'

She laughed slightly. 'Yeah, he says the same about you and I being friends.'

'We're friends?' Saleem mockingly asked.

'Sort of!' she rebuked. 'You should be flattered; I'm out of your league! But tell me, why do you say he's strange?'

'Well, for one, he seems greatly in denial regarding what he does; he doesn't like the label.'

'Because it's not as you think. He doesn't rent those women by the hour. They're just dancers.'

He bent his head slightly and peered at her in defiance. 'Rawan—'

'Really!' she defended, her tone somewhat finer than usual. 'I'm in the kitchen now, and I've talked to these women. They've not been asked to offer any services from the kind you imagine.'

'Do you sometimes sense him as a father to you?'

'I never needed a father to go looking for one,' she answered, calmly resolute.

'I'm sorry, Rawan,' Saleem said sympathetically. 'I just assumed that was the reason why you felt comfortable around him.'

'Don't be sorry – you and I have lost parents, and I do not doubt your heart while you thought so. To me, Zain is a man from whom I fear no judgment. Whether it is his character or his spirit, I cannot determine which, he makes me feel normal and safe at my darkest and most bizarre.'

He looked at her attentively whilst she spoke with apparent desolation. 'All who do or have claimed to love me do so conditionally; they love me, yet they criticise; they seek to change me.'

'Criticism is many times intended for the benefit of the recipient or to prevent them from self-harm,' he commented.

'Yes, yet even so, you cannot love an idea, a wish – you love the person before you as they are. Do you know why most relationships fail? It is because love becomes an initiative, not a response. I've learned that love that precedes cannot survive, because everything you see of the person after you fall in love are ideas and interpretations your love for them has dictated. Then, gradually, for time impregnates us with all that is vindictive, our vision clears, and what we start seeing does not correlate with what we once did. We suffer, strained between denial and stubbornness, and we strive in vain to maul the ones we love from their realities to our illusory versions of them because, in all honesty, their realities repulse us.'

'But we cling onto their hosts regardless?' he imputed.

'Yes. Because, deep within us, we realise the process is double-ended and that they, too, are as fond of our realities as we are of theirs. We cling out of fear, hoping against hope that they would succeed in altering us, yet rejecting it because we tried to change ourselves and failed. Now if this were to flip, if you were to know someone, in all their ugliness and fair rarity, and then fall in love with that, that is the only way it really works I guess.'

He could not remember how early he had fallen for Samra or why. It may have been her striking beauty, but no, that's not really as rare as people believe. How about that she came from a torn family? Yes, why not? Some men are attracted to women with such domestic environments, they're easier to tame and would devote all care and sense of security to their counterpart, the saviour. It may even have been how practical she was, that the suffering in her life had pulled her down to the ground; she would not build fantasies high in the clouds and drag him up there with her and away from reality.

But no, it was none of those things or others that fleetingly passed by his mind. It was simply that when they had met, he was ready to love. Oblivious to it nonetheless, Saleem's problem was that although his eager readiness had been interrupted by her death, its desire for such a state seemed to have survived her. He continued to eye Rawan, contemplating how readiness is the key that determines our actions, how neither intentions nor circumstances will them as much. Even our own death is set upon our inclination at that moment to exit the world, as riotously or as passively as we entered it. Did Samra know, deep within her, that she would die that day?

'Rawan, do you remember the doctor's disturbance at her death? he voiced to her as the walls of his mind imploded.

'Rawan!' her sister called loud and vivid within her own. 'Yes,' she answered cautiously.

Her body did not fail her, he thought, shifting on the sofa. Saleem's head throbbed achingly, looking to Rawan who, for the briefest of moments, resembled her sister's poise when he was lost or burdened. Without consideration, he bent his torso backwards, stretching his legs above the sofa arm, laying his head on her plump thighs.

What is he doing? Saleem's body is telling you it trusts. Why, why is he telling me this? Because he feels it, and he's allowed to. They can show anything they feel, Rawan, remember? She did not tense but felt cold and alert as the weight of his head grew all the more tangible in her lap. Saleem pressed his ear against her skin with shut eyes, and the sound of her thudding heart paced his to unwind. She looked at the mound of brown hair so close to her pelvis and stretched a hand out to touch it. The weight of his skull grew heavier as she stroked his hair gently, watching the curls wrap around her fingers. His scalp was clammy, but it did not bother her. She rubbed it, and he moaned faintly as his headache eased under her fingertips.

She smelled as the sea: inconsistent, a tempest of opposing scents splashing at his nostrils, ebbing and flowing, never stagnant, continually erratic. How could such a monotonous heart, he wondered, beat ever so humdrum in a woman so speckled? Woman? He had never thought of her with the inferences of such a word. Yet there she was, soft and subtle, blatant and peculiar, dictating that his pain be rubbed to ease with the very hand she had offended him with the day before; could there be a woman more comprehensive than her?

Try breathing in a less deafening tone. My chest is loud?!
Well, it was. Now you've stopped breathing altogether. Breathe.
Rawan! BREATHE! Her arms twitched, less apparently to
Saleem than to herself, yet he sensed it enough to respond.
He flipped himself around so that his stomach pressed
against the sofa and, craning his neck up to look at her face,
he smiled gently, a smile she reciprocated.

'Are we going to avenge her, Rawan?'

'Yes,' she whispered back, shaken to the past from her
enchanting present.

'Soon?' he questioningly pleaded, his face looking up
at her from her lap in childish desperation. *So what do you*
reckon? 'I don't know,' she replied pityingly, watching his
brow drop.

'There's been a twinge in my head.' He spoke after a
somewhat significant pause, his eyes bloodshot and almost
engorged. 'For a while now. Like a voice that concurs with
my thoughts only to mock them after.' He jammed his eyes
shut, his face absorbed by hers. 'And as violently determined
as I try, I cannot seem to distinguish anymore which of them
is mine.'

'They're both in your head. They're both you,' she
reassured him, continuing to stroke his hair soothingly.

'No.' He shook his head frantically, more times than
necessary. 'No. One is too cruel, the other inherently
untarnished; one speaks in malice, while the other comforts
me. And I am afraid of my own mind.'

Rawan had never before heard a man declare himself

fearful. On no occasion had she witnessed one articulate that form of weakness that separates humans from other life forms, a distinct type of fear that is more attentive to risks than the innate cautiousness of animals. *And this singular man surrenders his head in your lap for the taking.* She sensed his confusion pounding hers awake and pushed his head gently down so as to soothe him, asking, 'Why do you wish for urgency when no significant time has passed? Let both your voices answer that question for me so that I may understand the difference.'

'One hungers for closure so that I may live once more, while the other ridicules this, saying lost lives are not reimbursable. They cannot both be me.'

Oh, they certainly are. Tell him. Why speak what he already knows yet cannot accept?

The Father of Wilting Stars

Zali stepped from under the water, closing the tap firmly. He glanced at his reflection, seeing how darker his genitals were against the remainder of his body, like an obscure pattern lost amongst the lighter hues on a canvas. His single testicle hung beneath the phallus it had supported alone for years. Reaching for the towel, he looked at his phone near the sink, waiting for a name that would never show amongst the many insignificant ones that did. A name that embodied its holder in all her wild, ungraspable defiance.

Rawan had not spoken to him in months. The last he heard of her was a disturbed missed call attempt diverted to his voicemail, asking his forgiveness amidst broken tears, and then nothing. As unwanted as a bastard child, their connection had ended as unintentionally silent as it had begun. Zali desperately rang her countless times after that, contacting her through the networks that could reach her. She had not even bothered to deactivate her Facebook account or prevent him from seeing their pictures on her neglected page, as if in involuntary compliance to his most self-loathing wish, she may at least continue to haunt him until the end. The ghosts that lingered more loyal than their owner possessed no more than a few still images, fewer places, and almost every rainy sunset he would live to see.

Once, he had been so utterly consumed by longing that he packed a small bag and headed to the airport, becoming aware only at its gates that Cairo was a vast place in which to locate a particular unbridled horse. Now, he dressed himself upon the wet tiles below his feet, her frantic voice reverberating against the head he was now wrapping in preparation for prayer.

'Zali! Oh, my God!' she choked over the phone. 'I wish I'd never left. I should have stayed with you. Why didn't you prevent me, Zali? Why, when all my life has been one mandated act after another? One more stupid blunder followed by the next ... and I'm sorry.' She wept tremendously. 'I am so sorry for rebelling against the only person kind enough to have granted me that option ... Oh, God!'

He exited the bathroom amidst escaping vapour, riding cooler breezes to sweep it away and pried the medicine box open, rummaging for his heartburn dragees. A man at the prime of his youth and his own bile had already commenced to kill him from the inside out. I hope *Allah* forgives you, Rawan, he thought as his stomach contracted against the medication. He had not eaten all morning, and his insides bellowed for food to no avail. Ignoring his hunger, Zali slipped into his shoes and walked to Sheikh Wegdani's home up the very hill at whose foot his house stood. Passersby greeted the youth as he treaded soundlessly, ascending while the sun competed as it tirelessly did each evening to reach his destination before he himself would.

He clambered up the steps, knocking gently on the old man's door, who muffled from a room within the house moments before swinging it wide before him. 'Come, *habibi*.' He tugged at Zali's outstretched arm. 'You are late again, Zali,' Sheikh Wegdani reproached kindly as the young man stepped inside. The sheikh lived in a modestly beautiful home. The entrance was lined with large white cobblestones that hinged against one another in union. The house, too, was white, standing high amidst the sand and palm trees that loomed from the top of the hill over the homes below. There were no windows save for dozens of small pigeonholes horizontally lining the entire upper floor, while the ground floor resorted to large balconies for ventilation. One of Zali's favourite attributes of the house had been a large, blue, hollow dome, which stretched across the entire breadth of the roof, yet the sheikh had been ordered to demolish it for reasons undisclosed to him.

Zali walked into the home he was years long accustomed to. The scarceness of furniture and ornaments was as intentional on the part of his host as it was aesthetically pleasing to his guests. '*Allah* created the Earth round,' Sheikh Wegdani would say as commentary on his empty home, 'to prevent it from tipping over its axis when its riches are robbed and accumulated by a limited few. Which is a great shame,' he would go on, chuckling, 'for had it been flat, we would have slid and tumbled over a great deal of fair Western women!'

In the centre of the hall was a small fountain, whose flowing water balanced out the energy within the home, or so he was told. Around the edges of the walls, low sofas and grand cushions were situated in neat lines, broken only by arching entrances that led to the stairs ending at the upper floor, where the women resided during *dhikr*. Zali coughed loudly to announce he was climbing to the restricted quarters. The sheikh signalled along with him and they mounted to the rooftop. The sun had sunk moments before, its faint rays lingering across the very feet of the mountains around.

Zali shook hands with his peers in prayer whom were present as they waited for the rest to join them from across the many corners of the town and its myriad of outskirts.

Mohammad, Sheikh Wegdani's son, sat with his back to the sun, his father's old *oud* in hand, and began to instruct his peers that they were about to begin with the induction chant the sheikh had selected for that evening:

'*Allah's* peace upon the son of Mariam, Eissa, the soul of *Allah* who knows best of him. No one knows who his father is, for he is from the soul of the Constant One. Glory to He who conceived and forgot him. He does not know who his father is. He is from the soul of the One, the Constant—'

Mohammad's voice rang melodious, purifying their souls as they chanted along, like a common nostalgia of their present. When all those expected had arrived, the men stood shoulder to shoulder in a circle around Sheikh Wegdani until there were no gaps between them. The rest of the men formed a larger ring around the first one and so on until all were ready to begin.

The sky had welcomed the stars to their sight and the sheikh beckoned them to silence. 'Do not gaze above to see *Allah*,' he called from their midpoint, 'but feel his beloved essence within each of you, and his presence amongst our unison. Lock your arms together as brothers so that the devil may not enter amidst our prayer.' He hummed to himself, adjusting his tone in preparation; the neighbouring birds dared not whisper above them but soared in mute prostration. Sheikh Wegdani motioned to his immediate ring to begin: '*Allah*,' he hymned, slow and low-tuned. '*Allah … Allah … Allah.*' The circles around him joined in harmony: '*Allah .. Allah*,' they hymned, maintaining their eased pace. The sheikh entered their chant, his voice booming and flawlessly reverberating in accord with their mantra: 'Prayers and peace upon you.'

'*Allah, Allah, Allah*,' they sustained.

'Prayers and peace upon you, our master and messenger.'

Their pace increased ever so slightly, '*Allah, Allah.*'

'Muhammad, messenger of *Allah.*'

They leaned left and right accordingly, with each syllabic word they uttered, while Sheikh Wegdani conducted their rhythm and chant. From afar, their white turbans would have appeared as fallen stars from the night sky that descended below, bowing left and right to appease their creator, who perhaps looked silently upon them amongst the rest of his Earth people, impressed at the many fashions of worship man had managed to devise.

The sheikh maintained his relaxed rhythm while the men hurried in their pace, their movements just as harmonious, yet the changes from one position to the next became abrupt. They began to beat the ground gently with their feet, shaking the ceiling above the women from their drumming numbers.

'Oh, you who are the best of all people; oh, most generous of all people. Peace be upon you Muhammad, messenger of *Allah*,' sang Sheikh Wegdani. Birds soared in rings above the chandelier of moving constellations which the men resembled, yet none defecated on them. A few years ago upon their return from the holy pilgrimage in Mecca, Zali's parents had spoken of how the birds that flew above them, although vast in numbers, never desecrated the sacred site of worship there, upon which he had teasingly retorted against his parents, 'Perhaps it was because the birds soaring over our side of the world are as starved as the humans, their bowels possibly even emptier than ours!'

By the time Sheikh Wegdani rang his climatic phrase to the heavens, they were stirring so rapidly it was almost impossible for an onlooker to recognise when it was that they fleetingly returned to their starting upright positions. They vibrated like dying stars reaching their epitome of brightness before imploding. He signalled to them to halt. Immediately after, they broke their rings to kiss his hands and shake their peers'.

The sky covering them had darkened intensely as each man concealed his face behind his touching palms, wiping it while muttering '*Alhamdulellah*' under his breath, and made to exit, more than three dozen men coughing their way down the stairs within the house. 'God bless you,' the sheikh said repeatedly to each of them as they descended from the roof. 'Zali!' he called as he followed the departing crowd, 'a few words, *habibi*.'

'Yes, Sheikh,' he complied, retracting his steps and returning to where Wegdani stood, gazing at the stairway until it had been cleared and motioned for Zali to approach the single sofa at the far corner of the roof, from where the sheikh usually spoke during his sermons. 'Mohammad,' he addressed his son, who had been tending to the *oud* in his hands, 'inform your mother that a guest of mine will be joining us for supper.'

'Yes, Father.'

'There is really no need, Sheikh Wegdani. I must head home early.'

'Where is the *hajj*, Zali? He did not come with you this evening.'

'That is why I should return soon, Sheikh. My father awoke quite sick this morning.'

'May *Allah* assure his health in due time, *insha Allah*. Your mother, as I am certain, shall tend to him for the short while that you are here. Or would you deny my invitation?'

'Pardon me, Sheikh. Of course I could not.'

He smiled at Zali through his tiny eyes, dug amongst lines that embossed his aged face. Of the many curiosities that occupied his childhood, Zali had always heeded notice of how one's eyes seemed to decrease in size so significantly with old age. It is as if they know they have seen enough of the world, he thought as the sheikh rested his hand on his knee.

'*Habibi*,' the sheikh said gently, 'for months now, you have not missed a single prayer or sermon with your brothers, nor have you neglected your synchronism in *dhikr*.'

'And yet you seem concerned, Sheikh,' commented Zali in confusion.

'Because it is not you. Do not take my words heavily, Zali, or misinterpret their meaning; you are young and it is natural – or even expected of you – to show less discipline and eagerness in worship. Which has been the case till recently. I have never welcomed you a single evening without your father – *Allah* give him a speedy recovery – until today! And you have always been an ardent man to your creator in the past, *habibi*, just not to this latest extent of devotion.'

Zali appeared to be courteously silent, yet his stomach pained with a fresh release of bile that swam within him in torment, and his mind was no kinder.

Sheikh Wegdani continued, 'And I know too well that men flee to *Allah* mostly when they are in need; the more dire their suffering, the more urgently they seek endurance in his worship. What is it that burdens you so?'

'My *Allah*,' Zali said to recite the prophet's prayer in which he justified his biased love for one of his wives over the rest, 'judge me over what I possess of myself and do not hold me accountable for what I cannot control.'

The sheikh roared in relief, 'Oh, young Zali! Have you learned nothing of your name? My boy, we take nothing of this God-forsaken world with us to our graves but our names and the linen in which we are wrapped. To a "day where man flees from his brother, his mother and father, his companion and sons. " '

'It is out of my hand, Sheikh Wegdani.'

SAMAA AYMAN

'Zali, every single woman honoured in the holy Qur'an was only granted that status because of her connection to a man glorified by *Allah*. Our lady Mariam, mother of our lord Eissa, Assia and her nurturing of our lord Moussa, Khadija as the caring wife of Prophet Muhammad peace be upon him, and so on. A woman earns reverence and esteem only by aiding a man in God's path. That is the way *Allah* willed it.'

He spoke like Rawan's worst nightmare, which humoured Zali greatly. Anything that related to Rawan at this point amused and pleased him, possibly even his heartburn episodes. If the sheikh's words were correct, he thought to himself, it only meant Rawan was indeed one of these women he referred to as 'honourable' since her rejection of him and her sudden disappearance were why he was now such an oddly 'devoted' worshipper.

Sheikh Wegdani considered the youth's silence and opted to simply feed his churning stomach before they consumed Zali altogether. However, food was not the only offer on his mind for the young man. 'It seems, *habibi*, that you are resolute in your solemnity. Very well. Let us break bread together once more and praise *Allah* for his many blessings.'

'Thank you. I want it to be clear, Sheikh Wegdani, that I do not disregard all you have said, but it is, as I first told you, out of my control. Besides, wouldn't you say this change would please *Allah*?'

'Intention, Zali. Intents are the determinative of all we do and do not do. Come, *habibi*.' He led the young man down the steep stairs leading to the women's quarters, then to the ground floor. Upon taking a sharp turn on the steps, Zali fleetingly glimpsed two dainty, bare, pale white feet adorned in anklets that rang like soft bells as they vanished behind a closed curtain. How pretty they would look if they hung from Rawan's sun-kissed ankles, he thought. And their chiming as they shook only befitted a woman such as herself, one whose arrival demanded a musical announcement.

Mohammad anticipated them by the floor table near the fountain as the girl with the anklets returned, laying plates and various condiments on the large round table amidst them. She dressed and moved like a character from an orientalist depiction, too colourful, too embellished, her neck behind the opaque chiffon too ornamented, her eyes exaggeratedly lined beneath thin cloth covering her face – too stereotypically harem-like to mystify and intrigue anything but a phallus, which hungered to penetrate a festoon of brainless tinted flesh. She retreated to the kitchen within, returning frequently until their small banquet had been aptly laid before them, and the sheikh dipped his hand to indicate they could commence their supper.

'Um Mohammad has never requested from me to appoint help in our home,' he told Zali. 'She saw no need for them when *Allah* has bestowed upon us three precious girls.'

'May *Allah* bless them for your sake, sheikh.'

'*Ameen.*'

Mohammad realised his father's purpose and the jealous brother retorted. 'And I have always disagreed.'

The sheikh chuckled merrily. 'Oh, Mohammad, I worry

not about my old age when my daughters have been gifted such a protective brother.'

'Why do you differ?' Zali posed to Mohammad.

'Because daughters of noble families should not slave around their homes. When my sisters are to marry, my first condition is that their suitors provide them with a servant.'

Sheikh Wegdani looked inconspicuously to Zali, who grieved silently, realising the damnation of what he was about to do. 'How about the servant's brother?' Zali questioned Mohammad.

'What about him?'

'Why should he accept that his sister slave around a home that is not hers, as a consequence to her family's ill fortune?'

'A generous heart,' commended the sheikh on Zali's remark. 'Yet one that speaks of another world than that in which we live. This is the way *Allah* willed it.'

Zali recalled the phrase 'God the *Komi*' that Rawan had coined. 'Komi' was how Egyptians referred to the seven of diamonds; she used her expression to criticise on how, for many people, God was just a winning card from the deck, to be pulled out and brought up to justify even nonsense in a conversation. Yet, since when had Zali glorified her words above the sheikh's?

'Yes, my father is correct,' Mohammad asserted. 'Since when have we chosen what our social ranks dictated?'

'If we are as helpless as you declare, Mohammad,' Zali said, 'then God's order is irrelevant.'

'*Allah*, forgive and pardon us! Zali! A man binds or breaks his connection with the creator through one word! Regard caution, *habibi*!'

It was as futile and insincere as Rawan had always argued, yet he had never been as clear-sighted as he was that evening. The self-righteousness, the inability to entertain opposing albeit simple thought, the lack of principles that ought to be asserted regardless of particularity crowned by the mindless introduction - untactful and tasteless - that the two men on either side of him provided to the inevitable purpose about to present itself.

'Pardon me, Sheikh.' He spoke remorsefully as the sheikh patted his knee affectionately once more.

'Zali, how are you managing the *hajj's* work?' inquired Mohammad.

'*Alhamdulellah*, all is well. I think my father would agree the transition has been somewhat smooth and successful since his health mandated much rest on his part.'

'God lengthen his life,' Mohammad commented and sighed. 'It is when we sense the encroaching departure of our elders that we most seek to extend our own lineage.'

Enduring courteously, Zali asked for some water.

'Salma!' the sheikh called out to afar. 'Water for our guest, my child.'

Salma chimed as she walked over to their table with a jug and bent low to fill Zali's cup. He found her freshly applied perfume to be scandalous and irritant, yet he thanked her nevertheless. As she sped away from their company, he could hear the heat her steps emitted, the burning fumes of a bustling market. Zali, unable to endure the obvious any longer, addressed the sheikh with more earnestness than respect should allow: 'Lineage is not a possible concern of mine, Sheikh Wegdani, and you are a stranger neither to my childhood nor to my family. I trust then that you will understand; my condition has rendered me impotent. This is the way *Allah* willed it,' he stressed in conclusion.

They bowed their heads to the table, flooded with discomfiture and slight hints of rage. His rejection had greatly offended them, yet not as the extent of which the insolence of his response had been. Zali stood up to mark his parting, and they abruptly followed suit. Mohammad opened the door silently for him as Zali took one last glance at the familiar home in which he would no longer be welcomed to step foot.

As he descended the steps in Sheikh Wegdan's courtyard, he removed his turban, brooding on how Rawan and his single testicle shared a likeness; without her, a man was as active with two as he would be with one.

The Father of Scarred Songs

N aktal baked in the sun like a maiden, dressed and decorated in an open casket. The sign on its front wall loomed above the sea in all the defiant assertiveness a corpse could muster. Amgad's boat eased into the vicinity where shade and cool breezes resided, and he walked leisurely to the back door of the theatre hall. It was past afternoon and the men inside scurried around, adjusting seats and replenishing the bar from their reserves below. The detective strode to the far right, crossing over cables and fallen chairs until he reached the dark corridor where Zain's office was. No one paid him much attention as he headed for the door and knocked sternly at its placating wooden exterior.

Zain swung it wide and scanned Amgad's face intently. 'Amgad *basha!*' he smirked. 'I was just heading out. Let's go on a little fishing trip.'

'Let's not, Zain. I'd rather talk inside, seeing as I'm here for work. You can throw your bait with someone else.' He pushed the door wider and allowed himself into the office. Zain lifted an eyebrow while locking the door behind them. 'Work?' he repeated to Amgad, who was already seated on the single sofa to the left. 'Has the police force finally realised the benefits of exercise?' he mocked.

Amgad lit a cigarette and began to drag at its tip. 'You're teasing a detective on duty? I'd filter my thoughts if I were you right now.'

'And what duty do you have here, *basha*?' Zain asked, sitting before Amgad. 'Only so I may help of course!'

'I've been ordered to investigate your business.'

'Then why aren't you doing so?'

'Zain!' he warned impatiently.

'Look directly into my eyes,' Zain said in a bold daring tone, leaning his torso towards Amgad, 'and tell me why you, in clear violation of conduct to what I'm sure was a confidential assignment, are in the office of a man you were told to discreetly investigate, informing him of this.'

'What do you want, Zain?'

'I'm not in *your* territory, *basha*,' he replied indignantly.

'What do you *want*?!' he spat in desperation, keeping his voice low.

Zain leaned back in satisfaction, lighting a cigarette of his own. 'I want to license Naktal.'

'It's already licensed,' Amgad countered hurriedly and in confusion.

'As an entertainment facility.'

'Then what the hell do you want to license it as?' he snapped back.

Zain stood up and retreated further into the depths of

his office, blowing out the smoke in his lungs and regarded Amgad intently, watching his confusion dissolve into a dumbfounded grin. 'You're mad,' he whispered to Zain. 'You've lost your mind completely!'

'I can convince you.'

Amgad laughed hysterically. 'Who do you think I am, Zain?' he stated once able to compose himself once more. 'The sheikh of Al Azhar? The country's president?'

'It'll serve an exclusively foreign community, no Egyptians.'

Amgad slapped and tugged his own gaping mouth, burying both his cheeks inwards until his jaws ached, while Zain proceeded with his case. 'Think of it as liquor.'

'I cannot consider it so, because alcohol, Zain,' Amgad spat, almost spelling each individual word for him frantically, 'is religiously permitted for millions of citizens. Am I conversing with a child?'

'What about gambling halls?' Amgad bent his head between his legs and rubbed the back of his neck. 'They don't permit any Egyptians,' Zain ensued.

The detective raised his head once more. 'No.' He shook his head twice as he spoke. 'It is impossible – you know it to be so. Let's not waste more time than we already have on this lunacy. I'm not negotiating with you, Zain. I still have every scrap of evidence on the replicas you had your Al Azhar friend make. The ones you switched with the original antiques at the Cairo store. Nice lamps, by the way.' He glanced up at the office ceiling. 'Amongst your other past garbage. Having

171

highlighted the graciousness of my question, I'll repeat it for the last time, and I want a normal answer: what do you want?'

'The licence, *basha*,' Zain replied steadily.

Amgad rose from his place in a fit of hysteria. 'Why do you care anyhow? You're doing everything you want already! Your business is thriving. Why do you want it legal? You know how these things work, Zain! Look at it this way.' He laughed and stated matter-of-factly, 'You don't have to consider taxes!' Amgad's patience was far from subdued, as the purpose of his visit remained ignored by Zain in a singularly mutual silence regarding the elephant in the room.

'Sit down, *basha*, please!' Zain pulled at Amgad's arm, who returned to his seat and glared at Zain. 'I have something you want too.'

'Ha! You can choke on her,' Amgad replied confidently.

'You speak in spite of your heart,' Zain teased. 'Nonetheless, she's not whom I meant. I have something for you. You don't have to be the bad guy any longer; it can all appear as an innocent flaw in the investigation. The boy was there.'

It was Amgad's turn to lean his body closer. 'What boy?'

'The fiancé: Saleem. He was there at the scene.'

'How do you know this?' Amgad inquired, absorbed against his racing heart.

'I spoke with him. I'm telling you, he was there.'

'He confessed this?'

'No, but I'm sure.'

'WILL YOU SPIT IT OUT?! How do you know for sure?'

'I know when a man is lying, concealing a truth.'

'You're basing this on a *hunch*?'

'*Basha*, you have nothing to lose. Squeeze him till his eyes pop, and you'll know I'm right.'

'You know I can't do that.'

'Then find out the normal way. That is your job, if I'm not mistaken.'

Amgad stood up to leave.

'And don't forget my request. I still have much that can help you,' Zain reminded him at the door, walking to see him out.

'And I still have to report back on you,' Amgad leered, pointing a finger deep into Zain's chest.

***

Saleem sat himself at the bar as usual. He had left the car with Rawan and headed to Naktal in a taxi, quite earlier than her own departure. Having commenced on tactless drinking, he gulped one down after the next, his body responding to the alcohol much faster than was typical because of his lack of sleep, until his head felt like nothing more than a dense and obscenely heavy room full of angry people. His feet occasionally slipped off their stand, his eyes blurring at the indivisible yet incongruous faces of Samra and Rawan, his heart wearily dreading a secret.

He asked himself why he had sensed no awkwardness that morning towards Rawan, what the cause of his comfort and lack of concern were as he rested his head against her thighs. Yet, what genuinely consumed him more was her own lack of anxiety as he transgressed the permitted physical boundaries of intimacy between man and woman that she and himself had been raised to comply with. It was not the alcohol interfering with his sobriety that led to such pondering, for he had pressed his ears against her clothes to listen for chasing drums and rapid heart palpitations arising from her nervousness. And although he was no expert on the varied forms of music the heart plays, he had his theories, and he could swear hers was a harmony of excitement, the gentle tidings of a woman in exhilaration.

It sounds oddly different from that of fear. They say women's bodies possess a greater tolerance to pain than men's, that their brains are aware of this from the threshold. In the onset of fear, their brains realise there is the consequential risk of pain that would manifest in direct proportion to the assumed tolerance level – in other words, almost unbearable agony, they key word being 'almost'. A woman's brain, as a result, sends panic signals throughout the body to prepare it for the highest potential levels of harm that would naturally outcome from the source of fear, and her heart races.

The initial sound of a female heart in moments of pleasure is near silent. Why do most women become giddy when excited? It's their brains ordering their hearts to pump harder because excitement in its most raw state, if left without signals to ordain, soothes a woman.

Rawan walked into the dressing room, grinning in what she suspected was that feeling people always spoke of as highly regarded by God: contentment. She then placed herself in her seat. *Look at you all pious, huh!* She screened the room for Karma, who appeared nowhere in sight. In fact, the room seemed more vacant than usual. Zain opened the door and walked to her seat, standing with his arms crossed sternly.

'What's wrong?' she asked, concerned, seeing that she was somehow the source of his annoyance.

'Leave us,' he told the few dancers lurking about.

'Easy on this one, Zuzu,' one of them flirtatiously said while exiting. 'She's savage!'

Rawan jumped off her chair like a mad beast. 'YOU BITCH!' Yet Zain restrained her clawing hands and pushed the woman out of the room.

'This is how you thank me!' He glared at her. 'After everything?'

She stared at him in awe. 'She's the one who—'

'Not that!' he interrupted. 'Zahra!'

'What about Zahra?'

'The waiters heard you tell her to leave.'

'That's not … They misunderstood.'

'Well then, clarify if you may.'

'Zain, it's one customer,' she responded pleadingly after a few moments of silence.

'A very frequent one who also happens to be a dear friend. One whose importance is not for you to determine!'

'Hey! She asked to speak to me!'

'An absolutely common thing to happen here, which I

explained to you, along with everything else, before you came. Listen,' he said and sank to his knees beside her, his eyes burning into hers, 'you have no idea what I have paid for this.' He spread his arms wide out. 'And what I'm willing to do to preserve it.' His voice, a menaced whisper, elicited goose bumps the size of miniscule anthills across her forearms. 'Do not let this come between us, because I will not choose *you*.'

She raised her brow. 'Nobody ever has. Why should I expect any different from you?' she said in defiant reproach.

He wiped the tears falling down her flushed cheeks and stood up, retreating to the door. 'You've come early,' he muttered awkwardly, changing the topic of conversation before closing the door behind him.

It took her more than a while to prepare. She was somewhat unhinged following the sudden flux in her day from serenity, to slight shame, to disappointment, the occurrence of each sensation more perplexing than the other, the shift from one to the next too abrupt to absorb. *You're thinking of him. No, just this evening. You will dance differently tonight. You will stand closer to where he sits. You want to … What I want is to skim through this evening like a dull book that must be read, then go home. Rawan. Rawan! LISTEN!*

There were shouts resounding through the door, a couple of men brawling, their barks growing louder and less defined. She found it irritant yet insignificant and drew the pencil in her grip back to her eyelid, smearing a long, thin line slowly and with care. *They're crashing things now. Let them. I see these idiots every day – one silly nudge to the back of a car and next thing you know there are 'whore mothers' and pocket knives out. They're just innately violent and uncivilised like dogs sniffing under tails, no matter what they ride or how they're dressed. Yeah, well, one of those puppies is Saleem.* She heard him clearly yet distinctly far off, cursing amidst the clamour outside. She ran out of the room in her almost-bare attire, like a lioness pouncing to aid her mate.

Yet no one was attacking him. He was stumbling near the bar, intoxicated and raving in unrestrained yells that were not fully comprehendible because his tongue was unpunctual, accordingly adjusting itself with each word. The few men that stood by merely watched him, some even apparently amused by his performance. Those were the damned who would live and die an audience, the most mundane of witnesses, applauding this, cheering that, thumbs up, thumbs down, full stop.

'You low-lives! You killed her. Every single one of you!' he yelled. 'You raped her, you murdered her you, you mangled her corpse, ripped her open callously then stitched her up like she was a rooster for stuffing. You think it's just him we're after? No, no, no, no, every ass here has to pay up too!'

Zain slammed his office door and ran through the corridor, clasping his keys tight as Rawan pushed through the men standing to face Saleem, her eyes bursting from their sockets in frenzy.

'There she is! Your whore,' he shouted at them. 'Look at those eyes, one painted the other still untouched … little sister, my wife's—'

Rawan clasped his lips with one hand like she was

clutching a purse. He wept down her fingers that held his mouth shut as she pulled at his shirt with her free hand. Zain screamed to his men, 'Throw him outside! Throw him in the fucking water!'

'Zain, please!' she pleaded, still clinching his lips firmly.

'Shut up or I'll toss you out too!'

'Zain,' she pleaded, 'he'll scandalise us worse out there! Please! I'm begging you!' Saleem's weight was forcing her down exceedingly, falling more and more unresponsive to his surroundings.

Zain dreaded the threat she had suggested and considered the multitude of boats that would dock at any minute, and that inside, he would cause less harm if they managed to lock him up somewhere until the break of dawn. He pushed opposite Rawan and hauled Saleem's flaccid body on his shoulder. They dragged Saleem together to Zain's office and dropped him on the sofa, observing his eyes collapse shut with exhaustion.

She placed her palms on Zain's chest. 'Please forgive me! I will never bring him here again, I promise you,' she whispered. 'Nothing happened. I swear to you, they'll forget about it. They'll say it's the ranting of a drunkard. I'll take him home when everyone has left.'

'Oh no, no, that,' he said, pointing with repulsion at the sagging man on his sofa, 'is not going home with you!'

'Ok, ok, let's just talk about it when the night is over,' she said, patting his chest.

'Don't throw dust over it, Rawan!' he warned her.

'I won't, I swear. Just let me go so things look normal, ok?' She embraced him warmly. 'I'm sorry about Zahra,' she mumbled into his neck, feeling his tense shoulders gradually relax as he held her more taught to him.

'I didn't mean anything I said,' he said back in earnestness. 'I would burn Naktal down for this hug.'

'I wouldn't make you choose between us,' Rawan whispered soothingly.

'Yes, please don't. I'm quite fond of this place.' He laughed.

She freed herself from his arms and headed for the door. 'Just leave him there. I don't imagine he will stir.'

He nodded tiredly to her.

The nightly crowd gathered once more as she ran up the stairs to her usual brink. Not having given her wrists and ankles much thought, she realised they were a tinted brown in the dark. The black fabric hung from the highest depths of the ceiling, and she sat down to wrap herself well, awaiting the music that would cue her plunge. Rawan was glad to hear no distinct trace of disturbance amongst the chatter below concerning Saleem's episode, and she cleared her mind of everything but the act of entertaining the clowns anticipating her.

The tender longings of piano chords panged around the hall, while the crowd's silence ensued. She pushed her feet against the ledge and was immediately flooded in light. She looked at one of the men who had reeled her out the night before, and he bent low to turn a gear somewhere below his feet. The sound of flowing water surged along the music.

Rawan's hands gripped the aerial fabric tight, her left leg stretched vertically, her right leg was bent high at the knee, her neck sprained to face the ceiling above and her eyes were blissfully shut in anticipation.

It fell like God's million kisses in a drought, each drop chasing the next so competitively that her body was drenched within minutes. It flooded the stage floor then overflew at the edge, splashing those sitting at the bar who were too amused to care. There's something about a wet woman that arouses men, and it's not only the glimmer that's left on her skin. She becomes the epitome of fertility, the two causes of life on earth combined. The young Rawan, dripping as she gracefully spun in the air, was nature's best work on display. She hinged her left foot around a small section of the strands and bent her torso back so her hair brushed at the soaked stage below, twirling around herself as her audience alternated between praise and sighs.

Had Saleem composed himself earlier on, she would have felt herself in heaven as she danced under the rain pouring solely for her, yet his lack of care disposed upon the situation had ruined her will to take pleasure in the performance she had been most eager to implement, and he had singlehandedly transformed it into nothing but another work of hers, soaked in the rain. Her mind was split between a mechanical execution of movements and uncalculated rage at Saleem.

She wrapped her foot tighter with the fabric, then pulled herself as high as she could, climbing the strands like they were a pole. When she had reached the top, Rawan grabbed the fabric hanging loose beneath her and draped it around her waist, over and over, until only a short tuft was visible. Her hair stuck to her face, and she blew at it furiously, yet it would not budge. She bent slightly to one side, forcing her body to twirl around in circles until the twisted fabric stopped her movement. The strings of violins broke into the scene, slightly shunning the roaring piano as she released the grip on both hands and catapulted in a spiral to the ground. The fabric tugged at her thighs so violently, she let out an involuntary scream amidst a storm of alarmed gasps, while her head evaded being crushed to the ground by mere inches. Her nipples almost escaped their constrictions and she felt the water tickle at them, whereas her splayed arms stretched to touch the stage floor. The blood flushed to her head and she wished to remain, heedlessly fretful for her potentially injured thighs, long enough for her blood, now throbbing against her entire temple unbearably, to end it all.

Amgad crossed his arms far at the back, telling himself that she would not do so, that she would not hang from her lower body long enough to see her life trickle away amongst the rain of her own creation, assured that she merely considered it and that the thought would not prevail. It was a muted competition between expectation and will, prolonged by her tenaciousness and his vanity, and the victorious would be determined by courage, for it is never the cowardly who choose to take their own lives, but those who are brave enough to admit that their stay is no longer desired or welcomed.

The detective was not a man purposely conceited. For, indeed, Rawan hauled her torso in defeat, long minutes after her fall, to unwind the strands binding her in frustration. She jumped to the ground and stood steadily before the grand ovation, then moved aside, greeting her fellow dancers in applause as they took to the stage under their own manic tunes.

It hurt to walk in a normal fashion when all she wanted to do was stumble and be carried off to the dressing room. One of the waiters handed her a towel, and she patted herself carelessly with it, for the urge to sit down and rest her legs was overwhelming. She looked across the hall, seeking where Amgad sat.

Lead Her to Forget

H e did not leave his seat as he welcomed Rawan's approach with a smile. Amgad studied her determination to walk composed, irrespective of her probable injury, keeping his arms crossed while she dropped on the chair opposite him.

She attempted to instigate a conversation. 'What ever happened to good old *baladi* dancing, huh?!'

Amgad held an impatient look about his eyes; nonetheless, his demeanour remained stern in adherence to his silence. She sensed herself naked, due not to a sexual hint in his glances, but rather because the seriousness by which he prolonged eye contact caused her to feel transparent. It was insulting on his behalf to adopt such a bearing, whereas she was the one keen enough to incite his engagement in dialogue, and so she decided upon disdain and wit to mimic his silence. Purpose, or ego? Purpose. What does silence achieve? It is the passive form of influence by which we succeed in unhinging the other; the party that surrenders depends solely on their counterpart's ability to prolong the silence. She crossed her arms in imitation and glared at him through an effortless smile, enjoying every moment of his long silence, for her legs were gradually sensing less pain. His face eventually yielded against all severity as he grinned at her fortitude.

'I don't think you could dance oriental,' he teased, while she remained silent just to push him further, yet he would not budge more.

'My head still hurts from when you yanked my wig off.'

'Well you're lucky I haven't plucked your left eye out to rub it clean yet.'

'Excuse me?' she responded in alarm.

'Or was that done purposely?' he asked, circling a finger around his own left eye. It took her a short while to realise what he was referring to, as she remembered she had only applied her makeup to one eye before rushing to Saleem and had forgotten to return to the dressing room to continue. Rawan pulled at the napkin before her, but he grabbed her hand in objection. 'No, no, I was joking – keep it, I want to see which one I prefer.'

'I cannot sit like this.'

'Why not?'

'Because! It looks … odd. Or are you going to tell me your non-painted eye looks marvellous! So natural?!' she replied in a mocking, low-pitched tone.

'No, actually, I think the other one looks better,' he replied assuredly. 'More apt, I would say. But do not leave just yet.' She dropped the napkin. 'So, Malak, whereabouts are you from in Cairo?'

'I never mentioned I was from Cairo.'

'I assumed. El Gouna is a small town, and I've certainly not seen you around.'

'Why would I come from Cairo just to dance? That's not a rare vacancy to find there, I believe.'

'Ok!' he smirked, raising both palms open near either side of his head in theatrical defeat. 'So, what do we talk about?'

'About you, of course!'

'What about me, specifically?'

'Yourself.'

'My "self"? Ok. Well, my self comes here to unwind and enjoy the entertainment and company that women such as yourself offer. Men who come here don't generally tend to speak of themselves. Ergo, there's another example of the problem; you haven't really studied well.' She blanked at him. 'Research. Self-assurance is essential, but it isn't worth shit without research and preparation. Which, to return to myself, happens to be my whole life's work.'

What is this? You know what this is: he's cracking you down.

Staring at him lecherously, she said, 'Cairo was just too cruel for my liking.'

Amgad reciprocated her response with polite attentiveness, while offering her a cigarette. 'How so?'

She placed it in her mouth and bent her face to the lighter he held in his cupped hands, feeling his eyes burn her face more intensely than the flame.

'Most of what I know from life I learned there. And the world doesn't provide this education free of charge. Certainly not in this country.'

'And El Gouna's not of this country?'

'No. People here indulge in basics that the country in general lacks.'

'I find it a rather soulless place myself.'

'Because you belong to a distinct, very minor group of people who are privileged, irrespective of their space.'

Irritated, he replied 'You know that's not true! I breathe the same shit pollution as everyone else and drink the same water. I withstand the same heat, still have to move my ass from bed at six in the morning. I pay the same prices for my food and accommodation, and on and on and on. Everyone with half a brain can see this! Yet you perpetuate this idea like it's holy and not to be argued against.'

'It is not an idea, *basha*. It is a—'

'Explain how I am privileged as you claim; make a list for me.'

'I don't need to do that by any means, *basha*.' *How I wish to tear the throat he speaks from in such audacity!*

'That's my advantage? "*Basha*"? Malak, the whole population is one falsely attributed title after the next! Everyone is engineer this, doctor that – high school graduates for God's sake! Why should only mine be criticised?'

'BECAUSE YOURS COMES WITH A GUN!' she spat.

'You wouldn't last ONE day without it!'

'Oh, we did just fine! For eighteen, not "one".'

'You are ignorant beyond repair! You think your little fancy compounds, your bubbles of fantasy, are real? That what applied in those miniscule spheres is a depiction of the criminal flux that materialised across an entire country? Let us drop this matter before I upset you with what I have to say on guns. What you people will never comprehend is the sheer debauchery and external denigration one could practically swim in, if our esteem and dignity are not maintained by any means. This matter is closed. Now, I suggest you skip back to that stage like a good girl and do your job without condescending mine.'

The corrupt criminal speaks of dignity. How deplorable! Your leg has recovered; you can leave.

Rawan stood up and pushed the table slightly away from his chair. She opened her legs and straddled his lap like it were a saddle, their noses touching, their eyes daring one another. His hands gripped the sides of her chest and waist as they outstared one another, Amgad with his tense brows, his nostrils burning from her scent, and Rawan, one eye naked and another disguised, her abject pelvis jammed above his.

'You are ruining me,' he breathed. 'You deliberately drew your eyes so, to mock me. And staring at them like this is more brutal than anything I have ever done.'

She contorted her face to portray her loathing, aggravating him further as a skilled avenger, with just the right amount of passivity and forbearance, lures her enemy to pass his head through the rope and hang himself.

'Don't ask,' he sneered. 'I'll tell you how I sleep at night: I rub this.' He slid his hand down his stomach and rested it below his belt. 'Thinking of you, and when I'm finished, I doze off like a newborn. Now lift your self-righteous ass off me, before I take you right here.' He gripped her thigh where it hurt, arousing the pain once more, as she dug her fingernails into his hand to release herself, livid and repulsed. He held her waist tight and lifted her off his lap, thudding her on the table behind her, and stood to leave. Rawan panted in distress as she hugged herself on the table, her hands clammy, her mouth dry and her hair clinging to the back of her neck, more with sweat than water.

She sat completely motionless, if not for her heaving chest and the fury that obstructed the most boisterous sounds around her, waiting for the hall to clear. *Do you even consider sleep at this point, you half-painted, half-naked wretch? I need to take Saleem home. Saleem shall give you no peace, you can trust that if anything. Who has ever given me peace? Remember what you were thinking earlier on? You're wrapping that rope around your neck, Rawan. Do not take Saleem home. Send him back to Cairo. Do anything but that, and you'll drown yourself further into confusion.*

Rawan slid to the ground and strode to Zain's office, knocking firmly.

'He's still passed out.'

'We're leaving,' she said, walking past him and crossing over to awaken Saleem.

'Go home, Rawan.'

'Yes, we're going.'

'No, you go home, now.'

'Zain, I'm tired. We can talk about this tomorrow.'

'It never works like this! People don't help you only when

you ask them to – this is ridiculous! I'm telling you, this idiot has not been constructive to your aim whatsoever. Why are you dragging him around like a heavy chain around your foot or a giant leech?'

'Because he understands!' she yelled back. 'With all our arguments and all the things he could have helped with, yet for whatever reasons chose not to, he understands, ok? Now, help me carry him to a boat, please, and—'

'No!'

'How much money have I profited you these last few days?' she blurted.

'Oh! That's how you want to pitch this?'

'I've tried every way! Pleading friendship? No. Business talk? No. What do you want me to do? I am taking him home with me, so feel free to choose whichever method of persuasion suits you best and help me already!'

'You're going to regret your disregard to what I say very soon, Rawan, I promise you.'

She remained bent over Saleem's body, gasping at his weight. 'Come, carry him with me, Zain, and we'll talk tomorrow.'

'I think you need to talk tonight to that pussy over there and ask him what your sister was doing on Suez Road in the middle of nowhere.'

Rawan shook involuntarily. *What was Samra doing there, Rawan?* 'What do you mean?'

'Ask *him*, Rawan,' he concluded, wrapping Saleem's

arm around his shoulder and hoisting him off the sofa. He mumbled, still profusely intoxicated as Zain dragged his feet against the rugs in his office. Rawan slid through the back door behind Zain's desk to notify the boat man.

'And how do you suppose you'll take him up the stairs? Or off the boat and into the car for that matter?' he retorted indignantly.

'The air outside and the splashing water will rouse him a little, I hope.'

'You hope,' he muttered to himself as she signalled for the boat man to lend him a hand, hauling Saleem's limp body within. He pulled a pack of cigarettes from his pocket and lit one, and watching her sail off, he sighed, with the satisfaction of knowing that the next time he saw her there would be something new that he could use to bargain with Amgad.

When they reached the shore and Saleem was once again hurled clumsily into the car, she kept slapping him as she drove so he would, in turn, aid her in helping him climb the stairs. He occasionally opened his bloodshot eyes in the dark and slurred incoherent gibberish at her before collapsing once more. Rawan could not distinguish whether she was weary because of him, more stressed by him or enraged at him. Their irrevocable difference in approaching their common source of pain was overwhelmingly confusing, and she remembered Zali's words to her a while back, that it did not matter if we were loved so much as *how* we are loved. And although our sensations and experiences may be incredibly alike, our attitudes towards them remain far from being so. She questioned whether Saleem's behaviour in suffering could be tolerated at all for much longer than she already had withstood.

We were fine, just brilliant, this morning. You were; he clearly wasn't. He's the one who felt safe enough, determined enough to comfort himself with me; I did not transgress. He had not slept. You realise that is another form of non-sobriety, yet you wish to treat his behaviour that morning as distinct from his fiasco at Naktal – but, really, how are they any different? Because what happened in the morning was actual communication, whereas this lifeless drunk over here cannot converse for shit. Maybe, but that's just not why you're disappointed; you liked his closeness and fear that his conduct this evening is a sign of regret from his part. Why do you torment me so? I tell you all which you already know but do not choose to act upon. You treat me as a stranger who conspires against you, ignoring the ponderings of your own self. I must drive faster, as my legs are aching once more.

The street was dark, as dawn had not yet slit through the sky. She had slapped him more times than she could count, filling his face with red blotches to compensate for the tardy sun. She whispered persuasively, pleading that he compose himself enough to support his weight with her, and Saleem managed to, until they had ascended only one flight of stairs before he dropped at her feet. She slapped her own face in frustration, determined to keep the circumstances of their lodging unnoticeable amongst the neighbours, whom, until now, hardly sensed their presence because of the warped nature of their hours. How she managed to drag him to their floor, she had no recollection. What was certain is by that point she had an inconceivable amount of energy derivative of her rage, which she not only used to push him through the flat door, but perpetuated as she continued to tow him on her shoulder lividly through their narrow corridor until they reached the bathroom. She did not bother to turn on the light.

Rawan let him slide to the floor as he unconsciously pleased, while she removed her coat and stood before the sink, washing her face and splashing her bare arms and legs with the relief of cold water. Then she pulled the toilet seat down, bending low once more to hinge his armpits with her hands and sit him at the edge of the bathtub. She glared at his face for a couple of seconds before shoving at his chest so violently that he tumbled backwards into the tub, ripping the shower curtains as he feebly attempted to break his fall. He moaned from the pain, too real for his inebriated mind to make sense of. She undressed him in fury, tugging here and yanking there, until he was lying in the tub wearing nothing but his boxers. Rawan scrambled at the shower tap and screwed it open. The cold water shocked him awake, and he screamed in discomfort as it hit his skin and face. She sat on the covered toilet seat and glowered at him until he made eye contact with her.

'You little piece of shit!' she spat, rising from her place to pull his wet hair in a grip and slap his face furiously. 'You worthless moron!' she roared. 'Teenage girls are manlier than you! You do this to me?' She returned to where she sat, practically stabbing at his face with her eyes. 'What if he had heard you? Did you think about that, or were you too busy swallowing drinks like they were candy floss?'

His cognition was gradually clearing as he mustered to maintain focus on her bloodshot eyes, whimpering incoherent apologies at her.

'You're disgustingly pathetic – I can't believe I fought with Zain to bring you home! I should have let him throw you to rot with the garbage. Do you have the slightest idea what I will do to you if you sabotage this one more time?'

He blinked at her, voiceless, his tears indistinguishable from the showering water on his face.

She rose again to him in outrage. 'Answer me, you idiot! You do this to me?'

She sat back, reaching for the fallen curtain rail then standing once more, beating him with it while he writhed and wept.

'You useless, lost child! And there I was, thinking you were here to help me!'

Under the cold water shaking his wits to more consciousness, Saleem stopped crying. He forced what little energy he had in his building attempts to regain control into his left hand and yanked the rail from hers, then threw it at her stomach where it would fall to the ground, the metal screaming to silence against the tiled floor.

The tone of the voices in her head descended as the chaos

of random insults upon rage cleared so that she may perceive what had been piercing at her eyes all along. Saleem perched his back more upright and glared at her through the dark in daring intimidation.

She backed away timidly from the tub, gaping at him. 'Zain told me to … You're not … here to help me!' she breathed.

'What did Zain tell you?' he asked in the darkness.

She clenched her lips with her palm, then released them. 'Oh, my God, what did you do?' She panicked as her tears fell down her neck, yet he continued to stare at her threateningly. She ran past the open bathroom door into her room and frantically lifted the top right corner of her mattress, retrieving a gun from under it. Rawan yanked at the top to slide a bullet. She gripped the gun tightly and pointed it with extended arms in the tremble of her clammy hands. *Turn right and left; he may have left the bathroom. No. Yes, point it right first towards the other side of the corridor.*

Rawan fought to contain her gasps for air as she exited the room cautiously, struggling to detect signs of movement outside amidst the showers of water that beat to her left. She treaded, terrified, down the corridor to scour the living room and kitchen, yet he was not there. Her tears of horror trickled down her cheeks as she puffed at the air, slowly returning to the bathroom. She blinked her watery eyes as she approached the door and swerved rapidly, her gun in front of her chest.

Saleem had not moved.

She proceeded forward more assuredly as he looked at the gun pointed to his heart and spoke in calm resolute: 'I didn't do it. Whatever Zain told you of me, I didn't do.'

'You didn't come to the burial,' Rawan said, her tone pitching frantically. 'You refused to attend at the coroner's request. You fought me,' she said, amidst profuse weeping, 'against proceeding with the case! What did you do?!' Her voice, breaking as little as she could muster in feigned strength despite her crumbling assuredness that he was in any sense the man she thought he was, rang clear to Saleem.

'I didn't do it,' he whispered back.

'You were there that day.' She prayed he would deny, defend himself, explain, yet he peered back at her, voiceless. He didn't even shake his head in objection.

'I didn't do it,' he repeated.

'What were you doing there? What did you do?' she begged at his determined silence. 'Why were you there?'

'Please, don't,' he whimpered. 'Please.'

'You said you had no clue what she was doing there!'

'Enough,' he said, a hint louder and on the brink of his nerves.

'WHAT DID YOU DO TO HER?!'

'WE WERE GOING TO SLEEP TOGETHER!' he bellowed, shaking the water that continued to pour down on him as Rawan's arms spasmed under life's ruthless and inconsistent weight.

The Morning

'I was in El Shorouk.' Saleem sighed under the effort to be conscious and clear while he spoke. 'We had decided to meet at the house and … sleep together, before the wedding. No one was to ever find out but the two of us.' He wept. 'The house had been finished, and I was to wait for her there. It was only a few days before the wedding.' He covered his face with both palms. 'She trusted me, and I loved her! It was three days before our wedding,' he repeated. 'Three days! And I didn't want to tell, because she deserves better of the man she trusted than to divulge that and make her look as she does, now that you know.'

Rawan lowered her gun slightly yet did not loosen her grip. 'Did you—'

'No,' he pronounced clearly, dragging a long waft of wet air into his lungs. 'She called me less than an hour before the time we had agreed to meet, sounding disturbed. Said she couldn't come and that we would talk later on in the day. I understood. And my respect for her would not have altered regardless of her choice – I just wanted her to be comfortable.'

'Where you already there?' Rawan interrogated, slightly more at ease.

'Yes. I was preparing a surprise for her, the details of which concern no one but myself.' Saleem was silent for a while before he spoke again: 'I missed her so much this morning, when you sat beside me. So, so much Rawan!' He shivered under the cold water and his uncontrollable sobbing. 'And I don't want to eat, or sleep, or live, if her face and her scent are not with me for real!'

She stepped closer to the tub, her gun in one hand, dangling loose by her hip.

'I do not know why she decided to come after all,' he continued, 'or why she never called to inform me that she had changed her mind and was on her way. And what is going to kill me eventually,' he said, raising his voice, slamming his palms to his head in frustration, 'is that I am to blame, for it was all my idea from the very beginning.' Saleem lowered his eyes from hers in shame. 'If you believe me to be the culprit, then shoot me, Rawan. You will be doing me a great service, and I shall not persuade you otherwise. But, for Samra's sake, do not doubt my love for her.' He paused. 'Or for you.'

She dropped the gun in the sink and hoisted herself into the tub, crouching at his feet, pulling his knees towards her. He imitated then nudged himself closer to her. She bent her forehead to touch his and they wept, holding each other under the showers that could not cease on their own accord. For how long or briefly time passed, nothing was spoken save for the mutual breaths and beatings that rebounded from one mournful chest to the other and back. Rawan squatted between his legs, which embraced her thighs and back, and while she felt the water run to the most intimate crevices of her body, he bathed himself in the heat she emitted under the chill of the air around them, like a confused sun, lost, on an uncharted path at night.

And she kissed him.

She curved her lips to his more proficiently than the most complying fool. He did not refuse her, nor did he reciprocate, and Rawan, absent in the explosion of her own heart, wandered into his surrender as gently as the old lose their memory. The sound of her tongue against his lapped harmoniously with the water washing over them, while they tasted one another's tears and devoured them into their trembling bodies. She pressed the soles of her feet against the slippery insides of the bathtub and raised her waist higher than his, sliding her fingers under his shorts and pulling them down his legs, her wrist sensing his stiffness as she did so. She pushed him inside of her in one common gasp, continuing to kiss him passionately while dawn plunged into the house to pry on them through the minuscule window at the end of the tub. The light touched her bare back as she rode him tenderly, his hands limp on her feet in submission, while the tattoo on her back, reflecting through the window, flickered like she possessed wings.

They awoke in her bed facing each other with their heads inches apart. His insobriety had worn out completely and left a painful throbbing above his eyes, while Rawan arose, drenched in his scent. She opened her eyes only to find his ogling at her.

'What?' she asked softly.

'Are you hungry?'

She considered it for a few seconds. 'Not really, no.'

'I'm hungry.'

'Because you drank so much.' She yawned at Saleem, infecting him to follow suit.

'I'm going to make a sandwich or something.' He flung the sheets above him to stand then threw them back quickly, realising they were both undressed and that he did not want her to see him as so. Rawan watched him, absorbing his movements until she understood, then began to pull the sheet they slept on from under the edges of the mattress, rolling herself in it so that Saleem could cover himself with the one he had just flung. He coordinated with her until he was satisfied then left the bed. Once she was alone, she buried her face in the pillow and grinned with pleasure, the depth of her desire still throbbing at the sound of his voice reverberating across her mind. She wanted to run to the kitchen after him, drop the sheets to the ground, and have him take her instantaneously. She wanted to kiss him once more, to kiss him for hours, to feel his hands caressing every inch of her fervently. She closed her eyes and pictured him fondling the parts of her being that were for motherly nurture, to know she was his and he hers. She must have lain there longer than was required to prepare a sandwich, eat it, and more, because he returned to her fully dressed and satiated, carrying two mugs of coffee and a courteous smile.

'Thank you,' she said, taking hers.

'Has your mother tried to contact you?'

'No. Why?' *What an odd thing to think of now ..*

'Because … she's your mother.'

'No,' she repeated simply. 'What did you eat?'

'Egg sandwich. You don't want one?'

'No, thanks.'

From the corner of his eye, as he sat beside her on the bed, drinking his coffee, he perused her appearance. Her hair lay loosely over the curves of her shoulders and neck, and one eye appeared slightly smudged with *kohl*. Her cheeks seemed puffy and soft, while her lips, red and swollen from sleep, looked like their outline had been slightly smeared into her face, the way Samra's did when he kissed her profusely. And in all admiration of her tender beauty, Saleem could not quite grasp how young Rawan had taken his virginity while he could not claim hers. She knew he was thinking it, or at least had pondered over the fact at some point during their intimacy, and as his eyes bore into the side of her face, she gulped the remainder of her coffee quickly and excused herself to the bathroom.

She washed herself in haste and rubbed at her eyes and face, rinsing them completely from residual makeup, then wrapped herself in the towel robe hanging on the door and exited. Rawan saw he had left her bed, and she brushed her hair before the mirror against the wall, peering into her reflection like she was greeting a friendly face, which had been long absent, before splashing herself in perfume and running for his sofa. He sat on the floor by the fireplace, rubbing at the quote he had discovered as she smiled at him tenderly from the sofa at his back.

He was startled. 'Where is that smell from?'

'I found it in Samra's room.'

His brow contracted with burden.

'Is it upsetting you?' she asked anxiously.

He stood up and walked over to where she sat and joined her, laying his head on her chest. He closed his eyes and inhaled the scent mingled with the suppleness of her breasts, breathing deep, his nose as the eyes of a blind man in the light.

He whispered with muffled lips, 'I'm not the first you—'

'No,' she interrupted.

'Did you love him?'

She paused for a while.

'I don't mean to—'

Rawan interjected once more: 'He saved me once, and I thought that was love.'

'Tell me.'

Tell him about Zali. Why would I talk of Zali? I just assumed there would be more you could say about him than anything else. Zali? 'I met him in Tunis. I had acted thoughtlessly on a certain situation, and he was there at the right moment to save me from the harm I had risked inflicting upon myself. We started being in a relationship after, and one day it happened.'

'And things ended when you returned here?'

'No, I fled to here … to leave him.' *What are you doing? Why are you lying? What do you want me to do?*

'What was his name?'

'I don't want to talk about him.' *Which him? Will you stop?*

'I'm sorry,' he said regretfully, yet she shook her head and held him tighter to her chest. All of a sudden, he jerked his head away from her, his body tense with the rapidity by which the mind imposes random thoughts. 'I'm going to kill Zain!'

'You're not going to touch Zain,' she pronounced calmly. 'We've shown him enough ingratitude as is.'

'Gratitude? He made you think I murdered your sister!'

'Can we just forget that, please?'

'That man is odd from every aspect you can consider, Rawan!'

'That man and I have a history, which you do not understand; my judgment on him is the correct one, while yours is lacking.'

'I'm going to ask around about him; I'm telling you he's not trustworthy.'

'You will do no such thing. What is this?!' she questioned resentfully. 'You burden us with equal – if not higher – responsibilities and afflictions, and then deem us beneath your abilities? Everything we do is interpreted as influenced and not of our own choice, the rationale of our thoughts is never satisfactory to you, our judgment on matters always potentially impaired. Why are you so threatened, so obsessively unwilling to accept that you are just as damned and foolish as we ever could be?'

'So you agree you're foolish?' he grinned at her enthusiasm.

'Do not tease me, Saleem! I'm sick and tired of being

treated with the impression that your dangling genitals are an extra brain with a bonus licence to rights that we lack.'

'Hey! Stop using that language with me – I mean it!' he warned.

'Stop prioritising the vocabulary I use over what it is I'm saying.'

'Are we really fighting again?'

'That's your decision. I, for one, see no reason to argue if you respect me and what I say of Zain, whom I know much more than you ever could.'

'Fine, Rawan, do as you please. I was only voicing my worries for you to consider.'

I long to bite at his lips as he lies against me so. 'I'm hungry,' she blurted.

'What do you want to eat?'

'I don't want to eat,' she breathed, sliding herself further beneath him so that his pelvis pressed against hers.

He bounded off the sofa before his body would react to her advances and shot to the kitchen. 'I'm making you a sandwich,' he called as Rawan rested patiently, waiting for his body and heart to persuade their master at a more leisurely pace.

***

It was a long and droning phone call, but she succeeded in convincing Zain. He pleaded that she maintain her politeness long enough for Zahra to forgive her transgression, and Rawan promised him she would do so at all costs. Assured by Saleem that he would not step into Naktal as long as Zain wished so, she left the house and descended the stairs, heading for the garage.

It was a decent drive to Zahra's house. Zain's directions were too clear for her to follow, and so she found herself honking at her driveway before ample time had passed in preparing the last-minute apology speech entirely. A tall, slim man ran to the gate and inquired whether Madame Zahra was expecting her, after she asked that the lady be informed of 'Malak Zain's' request to see her. Rawan examined herself in the rearview mirror until the man returned to cast the gates open. She drove further, admiring the swirling lagoons that spun around the grand home before her, which stood amidst the water like a hoisted trophy. The entrance was opened before she had exited her car, and she knocked firmly then stepped inside. Zahra herself was there to greet her warmly, which chiseled somewhat at Rawan's own anxiety in further aggravation, and she beckoned her welcomingly to advance within.

'I knew immediately it was you when Ismail informed me,' she assured her.

'Thank you for agreeing to my unscheduled visit, Madame Zahra.'

They sat at the far end of the grand hall that was Zahra's reception area. Rawan complimented the oriental architecture of the interiors to her home, and the serenity the expansive windows screened of the gardens outside.

'I have come to apologise for my inappropriate conduct

earlier and my ill manners. Zain has not sent me; I am here on my own accord and wish to tell you that you remain much welcomed at Naktal whenever it pleases you to visit.'

Zahra smiled wider. 'Do you know that I picked that name for it?'

Rawan shook her head in response, satisfied that she had apparently resolved the predicament she had caused Zain.

'What will you drink first, before I tell you the story?'

'The same as you.'

'No, I am fasting today.'

'Then I am happy just talking to you.'

'You must have something!' Zahra called for the maid to request juice and sweets for her guest. 'I have been fasting every Monday and Thursday since my husband passed away.'

'*Allah* rest his soul.'

'*Ameen.*'

'So … Naktal,' Rawan reminded her.

'Ah, yes. Zain is quite a skilled calligrapher. He's done many plaques for me.' She waved her hands to the walls, indicating various quotes on hanging canvases. 'You've never seen any of his works?'

'No. I didn't know he painted.' Zain? Thought a bemused and yet slightly amused Rawan. *Zain making art?*

'Well, calligraphy is not really painting; it's a more disciplined form of art, because you must adhere to the letters that you will design and lay out in an inventive way. Anyhow, one day I asked him to do this one.' She pointed at the canvas above her head. 'An *ayah* from Surat Yusuf, my favourite in the Qur'an, and he became greatly fond of that word in particular.'

'It doesn't bother you? I mean, the purpose he used it for?'

'Well, no. Language was neither invented nor is it monopolised by God, Malak. He used a man-made invention to communicate with us through it.'

'But God created everything.'

'Yes. Nonetheless, language is more complicated than that. It is the way we choose to structure and manipulate it that makes it what it is, and that is of our own doing, not Allah's.'

Rawan nodded courteously.

'So, what did I miss of you last night?'

'I danced under the rain. We, well, Zain, installed a diversion from his main water pipe that would flow into a series of showers from the ceiling, and it rained on the stage.'

'Water … interesting. And are all these various ideas yours, or Zain's?'

'No, they're all mine.'

'What influences you to each one? What inspires you?'

'The audience.' Zahra egged her to continue by not responding. 'The first night only was when I designed the performance purely of my own inventiveness; the concept behind every show after that stems from my interpretation of the audience's experience. If they appear to seek aggression, I nurture their desire for violence. Should they crave sex, I become the goddess of fertility, and so on,' she elaborated in an explanatory tone oozing with childish eagerness.

'Do you always speak with such untroubled confidence?'

'It is more an understanding of Zain's vision; he wanted to become a creator, and he employed me for my own fire.'

'And yet you do not defy him, nor, as I see, has your fire extinguished under his rain.'

'Thankfully so, Madame Zahra. You cease to exist once smothered, wouldn't you say?'

Zahra studied her face and cheeks, noticing the change in their colour and the newly introduced brightness of her eyes. In fact, apart from her voice, Rawan was significantly altered. She held herself more comfortably, smiled more to herself than to Zahra. Even her own scent was unrecognisable. Then, as she touched her neck casually, lingering at her collarbone, breathing out a tender sigh, Zahra knew.

There is a distinct air about a woman who is sexually gratified. It is as if she is discovering womanhood for the first time. She embraces her body more deeply, almost thanking it for the pleasure it grants her. The words whispered in her ear as she makes love transcribe across her face and her features become increasingly striking, long after they have been spoken. Her senses relax, for she is no more a wild hunter, but a tamed storm. Yet, most unmistakably, it is the manner in which she breathes, guarding a secret seeping from her very pores, one far too lively to shun its announcement.

The Father of a Nostalgic Sun

A mgad looked back at himself in disdain as if his depiction in the mirror were a mocking imitation of his every movement, trapped between a frame, suspended upon the wall. He had not given Zain's ludicrous request a moment's consideration, let alone stop to imagine the general's response if he were to inform him of it. Still, he had indeed spent most of his time in bed thinking of Zain and how he was rotting long past his expiry date, his stench reeking fast and dangerously. Apart from revising the forensic report of the scene and finding any information there which he may have overlooked, it was near impossible for Amgad to prove Saleem's involvement, had there actually been any, without interrogating him. So, ultimately, Zain had been of little aid on that regard. Amgad scratched his beard before the mirror, assessing how Zain may be put to better use were he to convince him that his request was under consideration.

He dragged his stare away from the man before him to the lowest corner of the mirror, peering to the reflection of a photo on his bedside table. His father's face was too small to view clearly from where he stood, yet, as is the case with everything to which one grows familiar, the image planted in his mind from having examined it countlessly over his long years made the miniscule and distant reflection quite vivid until every detail. The old lieutenant sat on his wheelchair in formal attire, his left leg clearly absent through airy trousers, with his son perched on his right knee, both beaming eerily at Amgad through the glass between them. How can one's smile contain such irrevocable contempt, he wondered? However, if he were to pose a more sincere question to himself, it would have been more apt to ask: why do I continue to produce, collect and retain such things as photos, which across my history have caused more suffering than pleasure?

He turned to the table and, removing the t-shirt in which he had slept, gazed at the gun next to the photo. Amgad walked to his wardrobe to search for a freshly ironed shirt to wear, then looked back to his gun. He reached for his phone from under the pillow and pursued to dial.

'Zain.' He paused. 'All is well, yes. Listen, I want you alone now.'

***

Zain curved the paper in his hand around the moist tobacco, licking the tip as he watched Rawan advance through the hall from behind his curtain. She let herself in through the door he had left unlocked and beamed at him as she entered the room.

'That's for me, yes?'

'Isn't it always?' He raised his brow at her, smiling. 'What has you so amused?'

She grabbed the joint from his hand and placed it in her

mouth, while he lit it. 'I left him with a clear understanding that he wasn't to come here again until you say otherwise,' she told Zain.

'And you're all adorable right now so that Zain would say otherwise, right?' he grinned.

'Maybe.'

'Just give it a few days and we'll see. Tell me good news on Zahra.'

Rawan gave him a thumbs-up as she inhaled a drag of smoke. 'Done.'

'Good. Listen, I'm postponing the shows for a while. I want you to be, shall we say, traditional, tonight especially, and we'll take it from there.'

'Why?'

'I'm under investigation,' he explained.

Rawan coughed violently. 'Why? By whom?' she cried in alarm.

'Who do you think?'

'Why is he investigating you?'

'He's been assigned,' Zain ridiculed.

'Assigned? Why now? How do you even know this?'

'It doesn't matter. This is not worrying at the slightest. I am simply being cautionary.'

'How traditional?' she asked as they dropped on the sofa together.

'Enough to seem normal whilst maintaining the status of the place. Can you dance without turning Naktal into a low-class cabaret?'

She nodded in comprehension. 'I don't have a suit though.'

'Rawan, there are dozens in the dressing room! I'm well prepared. Anyhow, it's not what you wear that they come for now. Those idiots are so addicted, they'd stand in line to see you yawn and they'd still walk out with epiphanies.'

She giggled at his description, watching him look at her expectantly.

'Saleem wasn't there. I asked him.'

'And believed him too, apparently.'

'It's not what you ... He wasn't there and I'm sure of it.'

'She wasn't my sister, so I couldn't care less, personally.'

'Really, he—'

'Rawan,' he interrupted, 'whatever you believe is entirely up to you. Just try to assure your certitude is where it should be because I do not trust this man.'

She rolled her eyes. 'Believe me: the sentiment is mutual.'

Zain laughed drily. 'He doesn't trust *me*? That's endearing, seeing as he's been so helpful to you, much more than I have,' he mocked.

'He's important to me, Zain. Just as you are, only ... differently.'

'I don't understand. Why are you blushing?'

'I'm not!' she responded in a high pitch.

'Oh, God. You know what? I don't even think I want you to answer that.' He rose from beside her, then turned around with a tormenting gaze. 'You love complicating things for yourself, don't you? Like everything that's happened is not enough already as is!'

'Hey, what the hell?!' she said indignantly.

'Stupidity. That's what I think of this,' he muttered, looking up to the ceiling. 'Sheer recklessness.'

She stared blankly at him, her face increasingly flushed.

'I hope you haven't shared a pillow with this man just yet, Rawan.'

'Don't make me get up and punch you in the face!' she warned.

He looked at her in baffled awe. 'Is this how you respond to a man you once claimed dearer than your own father?'

'How very paternal of you to zip me up in a belly-dancing suit and applaud my flexible waist,' she stated calmly, heading for the door.

She walked to the dressing room, glancing at the hall on her way. It felt lonely knowing Saleem was not out there amongst them. Not that his presence provided her with a sense of security, but that only through his absence did she become conscious of the air of companionship that existed between them. There are those whose company reminds one of one's self, when confusion circulates with a want of tangible self-definition. And Rawan knew no more of oriental dancing than the movie scenes she had ridiculed since childhood. Zali once told her she would look 'magnificent' in such a costume, whereas she had responded by referring to him as 'a stereotypical man who lacked imagination and the originality of thought necessary to appeal to her interest.'

Karma was pulling at something clasped in another dancer's hand when Rawan walked into the room. They were tugging against one another, screeching wildly, and she could not tolerate their voices for more than a few minutes.

'Hey! Enough. Take this outside,' she shouted at them.

The dancer gripping at Karma's hand looked at Rawan and spoke defiantly: 'You still think you have the upper hand over anyone else? We heard him scold you yesterday.'

'Do you want to hear the sound your neck makes when I snap it?'

'You're a freak!' she yelled at Rawan. 'Tying and drowning yourself like a lunatic, desperate for a few claps! I feel sorry for you.'

The last sentence rang within Rawan as the dancer turned her back to walk beyond the curtains separating the dressing room and the closet further within. Rawan yanked one of the table lamps from its socket and swung it with all her might, crashing it on the woman's head, who let out a single gasp of shock and fell to the floor. Karma screamed in panic and dropped to examine the dancer's injury, her shrieks increasing as she saw her palm tainted with blood. And Rawan stared speechless at the body Karma was splayed upon – the hair moist and twisted – looking back at her like a dark face with no features. *I know: you need to sleep now.* She collapsed at Karma's feet.

In seconds, the room was packed with horrified women, while others ran across the corridor hysterically amidst the roaring music to bang on Zain's office as he swung the door wide in fury at their tantrums. They dragged him back to the dressing room, whimpering half-sentences and stuttering words amidst tears, where he walked in to find a pile of sequined lace and bare skin shaking at two bodies on the floor. Before stepping forward, Zain pulled his keychain from his pocket and locked the door firmly.

'If I hear a single peep out of anyone of you,' he boomed at them, returning the keys to his pocket, 'I swear by my honour, I will slit your throats one by one.'

They stared into his maddened eyes as their voices died down, until all they dared to project were a few barely audible sniffles and stifled coughs.

'Move,' he ordered the dancers attempting to revive Rawan, and they backed away from her limp body. He tossed her over, checking her head, and saw she was not visibly injured. Zain bent to his knees and pinched her nose tight with one hand while the other clasped her lips shut.

'You'll kill her!' Karma cried in terror, yet Zain, continuing to suffocate Rawan, glared at Karma so threateningly that she escaped his eyes and held her palm up against her neck.

'Come on!' he begged Rawan. 'COME ON!' Her body remained unresponsive, but he did not blink, peering into her face and tightening his grip. *Rawan! Breathe! RAWAN!* She twitched, spluttering against the palm that held her mouth shut, and he instantly released his grasp, grabbing her to his chest while she coughed and gasped for air. He pulled at her hair frantically in relief, hugging her harder and staring at the other woman collapsed behind her. When Rawan's panting had subdued, he carried her to a chair then returned to the dancer. He checked her pulse with his fingers. The bleeding had stopped, and he saw it was a long cut against her scalp. Zain stood up and walked to the door and unlocked it. He called outside, and a couple of minutes later, returned with a glass of juice, which he handed to Karma, beckoning her to force it past the dancer's lips. Karma's hand shook as she heaved her lifeless head up and pushed the rim of the glass against her mouth, spilling drops down her slightly moving chest.

The sound of waiting is vile yet never scarce, and torment, being the most devoted companion to those who wait, mauls at its acquaintances with every ounce of negativity and bleakness their desperate imagination can muster. All those present in the room could do nothing but watch passively as Karma spilled drop after the next, sobbing at the limp head that had been bickering with her less than half an hour earlier. And, in due time, the dancer let out a long, faint moan. Zain, who had been standing by, hauled her from under her shoulders and dragged her across the room, then supported her back with a large cushion on the floor, wedged against a wall.

'Who is responsible for this?' he stated clearly, inspecting each face before him, as the dancers stood like soft soldiers in an array of colours, rigorous curves and waves of hair.

Rawan sat completely quiet, almost huddled on the seat, her tilted back facing Zain and the others. Her mind was blank, her head sore from the fall, and she remained guiltless and non-defensively silent, almost as if the question he had raised was of no interest or connection to her, when, from the separating curtain, Karma's feeble voice came in a low, dreadful pitch as she lifted her head to respond, 'I am.'

Turning to her without the hesitation to ruminate her answer, Zain uttered determinedly, 'Get out, now, and do not show your face before mine again.'

Karma lifted herself off the floor, stumbling to carry her bag while putting her coat on, then, with her head levelled, strode shakily past the room. Before reaching the door, she swept her palm against Rawan's shoulder and smiled at her as she passed her chair. Rawan caught her eyes in the mirror and did not flinch as she watched her exit the room silently, leaving the door open behind her.

'I want you all on the stage in five minutes,' Zain said louder then walked over to Rawan and carried her off the chair, leaving the room with her arms tight around his neck. As they crossed the corridor, Amgad glanced his way from afar, and Zain, noticing his expression, shifted his body to the side so Amgad would could not glimpse Rawan in the dark.

'Take the keys from my pocket,' he said, directing her to slip them into one of his occupied hands most reachable to her so he could let them into the office. They barged through the door clumsily, and Zain settled her down on the sofa then bent his chest over hers, with her face between his hands to examine her eyes. 'Are you dizzy? Hungry?' he asked.

'Thirsty,' she muttered in all innocence. He left her side and walked to the small refrigerator at the right end of his desk, grabbing a bottle from inside. 'Zain, show me one of your canvases,' she said as he handed her the water. He strode to the window, pulling the edge of the curtain to survey the stage. 'One of my what?' he responded casually, focusing his attention on the performance and the faces of his audience.

'Why don't you just install cameras across the hall and view everything from your desk?'

'It's a different experience. You're young, so you wouldn't understand. You know when porn videos were first introduced in this country, I all but rolled on the floor from laughter that stitched at my sides. It's fascinating how your generation can still feel anything with all this crap shoved down your throats.'

'I just thought that cameras would make things easier for you.' She shrugged at him, still gulping her water slowly.

'Maybe some things are meant to be enjoyed through the effort you exert in them. That's why I admire you actually; you are more a fraudulent than a regular thief. It's easier to break into someone's house and steal their money than to cunningly persuade them to place it willingly in your hands, but there is no fun in the former method. Plus, deception is more creative; there's a story involved.'

'I'm fraudulent, Zain?' she responded resentfully.

He returned from the window to her side, snickering in amusement. 'I'm just teasing you, Rawan. How are you feeling now?'

'Better.'

'Good. Now tell me what happened.'

'Nothing!' she exclaimed. 'They were arguing, and then Karma threw something at her head I think, and she fell down.'

'Hmm.' He smiled. 'And you were so utterly touched, you fainted on the spot too.'

'Hey! She admitted it was her fault.'

'Oh, don't misinterpret my comment; as long as someone is held liable, I don't really care who is guilty and who is innocent.'

'You don't care?'

'No. We're all guilty. The only difference is who is insignificant, worthless enough to bear the accountability and who is of more importance that they may be reprieved for a while. But, in the end, we all pay, one way or another.'

His work. You wanted to see his canvases. 'Oh, show me some of your calligraphy!'

'My what?'

'Zahra has your stuff hung in her house. It's really good. I like your lines. So well-defined.'

'I don't have any here,' he muttered.

'Ok, do one for me now. Write my name?'

'Rawan, I'm tired.'

'Come on! I really liked them.'

'What else did she tell you?' he posed before elaborating his question to seem less inquisitive: 'Generally, what did you talk about?'

She stared at the wall behind his face for a short while, rummaging through her mind then declared, 'I know the story behind the name of this place.'

Zain roared in brief laughter. 'She told you that? And did you consider me obscene after such a tale?'

'At first, yes.' She giggled. 'But then I mused over it more on the way here, and, I have to say, it makes sense.'

'Yes, I thought so myself. Oh, I'll drive you home today and take a taxi back.'

'Why? I'm much better, really!'

'No, I insist, and there's no need to nag otherwise – it's done.'

'Where is your house?' she asked in surprise, as one who discovers a very regular fact all of a sudden.

'What do you mean?'

'What do you mean what do I mean? Where do you live? I just realised I've never visited your home!'

'You just realised that now?' He chuckled. 'You must have really bumped your head severely. I am a citizen of the revolving world, my dear.' He spoke dramatically, jesting at her question.

'Zain,' she breathed in amazement, 'do you live here?' And then, racing further into the past in retrospectively obvious curiosity, she blurted, 'Have you always lived here?'

'I'll leave that to your brilliant intuition. Now rest a short while. I am going to go chat with Zahra, and I'll be back by the time we are leaving. Where is your bag, Rawan?' he added casually.

'I—' She paused to remember. 'I left it in the dressing room, I think.'

'Ok, I'll bring it to you, don't worry about it.' He crossed the room and dimmed the light significantly then left. She heard him click the lock from outside.

Rawan stretched on the sofa and looked at the lamps shimmering from the ceiling, their light splashed across the walls, flickering steadily. She pulled her hair back from underneath her and dropped it over the sofa arm against her head, the dark strands swinging loosely, high above the ground.

Amgad is probably outside. I will not speak with him tonight if I remain in the office. Is that bad? It's not productive. Why do you think he comes here anyhow? For the same reasons that the rest do, I guess. Why does Zahra come then? To see her friend Zain most likely. She seems keener on seeing you, though. Everyone is; everyone wants to see the woman who shapes then responds to their whims. Perhaps I will even shoot myself on the stage for them soon. That would certainly impress me! Yes, it would, wouldn't it? What might Saleem be doing now? Rolling a joint, she thought and grinned. Thinking of me. He's not thinking of you. No he is. I know he is. It's not you he entered yesterday, you know that. He didn't enter anyone. I did that for him, and he submitted.

She sat up and rubbed her nose, peering at the desk in the scarcity of light then stood and walked over to it, sweeping her palm searchingly for the drawer knob. She opened it and fumbled around for Zain's rolling paper and oil, but only the oil was in the drawer. Her eyes scoured the desktop, landing on the bag of tobacco with the paper stuffed inside. Rawan gripped the ingredients into her hand then shut the drawer, pausing. She glanced to the bottom of the door, squinting to detect any shadow upon the floor, but saw only a solid, thin line of bright light from outside. Opening the drawer slowly, she began to empty its contents onto the desk itself. Scraps of paper and receipts filled the desk: bank statements, torn business cards and an old address book – a document hoarder's paradise. *What is it that you are searching for? Nothing. I'm just curious and bored.* Then her eyes rested upon a singular, raven black shape, almost greasy-looking in the darkness, and she pulled at it to find that it was a rolled sheet of paper pushed to the deepest edge of the drawer's interior. She loosened the cylinder from its confinement and spread it out wide on the desk.

It was a large horse caught in mid-gallop, sketched with ink, its body embossed in blocked swirls of jet black. She stepped further back to admire the intricacy of the patterns on its body and, moments later, smiled deeply as her eye made sense of the shapes spelling out her own name, penned with the sharp turns and flicks of Zain's calligraphy.

NEVER

Zain, assured by Rawan that she was indeed well, accompanied her until they reached the doorstep then hugged her tight and sped back down the stairs. She heard Saleem praying near the window, his back to her as she shut the door and shook her heels off.

'Look what I brought,' she sang in announcement, shaking a bottle of rum in the air like a trophy. He tilted his head to the side, inspecting her face with a bewildered smile, then bent low to fold the prayer mat, placing it on a side chair.

'Oh, come on … You drink!'

'And you are Satan's female version.' He laughed.

'Who is to say the devil's a male?'

'Fair point. Why are you so pale?'

'I'm pale?' she checked her face in the mirror by the door. 'Ah, no make-up.' She walked over to the kitchen, poured the rum into two glasses and carried them to his sofa with the shut bottle gripped under her armpit. She handed him a glass, which he eyed yet did not accept.

'Suit yourself,' she said, returning her extended hand, yet he yanked the glass from her as he laughed quietly.

'Yeah,' he said, frowning as it burnt at his throat. 'It's not the worst thing I've done.'

'What's the worst thing you've done?' she asked, raising the glass to her lips.

He didn't pause to think: 'Jumping on my mother's stomach till she had a miscarriage.'

Rawan choked as she swallowed. 'What the—'

'Yeah. I was very young, and the kids at school told me that my parents would get rid of me when the new baby would come – children, you know? One of them had seen a movie where the woman lost her pregnancy by beating at her stomach. So, I waited till my parents were asleep and ran into their room so innocently, claiming playful intentions, while I jumped up and down on her belly. She didn't yell at me to stop nor did my sleepy father intervene.' Saleem looked oddly calm to her as he told the horrific tale.

'Idiot!' remarked Rawan, yet deep down she felt a hint of admiration towards him. There was something peculiarly endearing about his blatant honesty and self-criticism. Something refreshing.

'How old were you?'

'I don't remember.'

'So, you smoke *hashish*, drink wine and you're a baby killer,' she stated in a staged formal manner. He snorted, standing up to roll a joint.

'Your turn.' He pointed to her from the fireplace, behind which he kept his tobacco and hashish.

She leaned her back to relax on the sofa. 'I rented a prostitute for someone.'

'You're joking!'

'No really! I went up to a prostitute, gave her money and the guy's address.'

'Why couldn't he just do that himself,' Saleem asked, returning to the sofa.

'Is that mine?'

'No. Roll your own.'

'Saleem!'

'What? I made it for me! There's plenty there, so make yourself one.'

'Fine, don't touch my rum.'

He gaped at her, amused, then handed her the joint before bending over the coffee table to prepare another. 'So, why couldn't the guy do it himself?'

'Oh, he didn't know. It was my idea. I was trying to convey a message.'

'What was the message? "You are my favourite person in the world, enjoy"?'

She lit the end of the joint. 'He just had a hard time understanding that not every woman is a whore.'

'Deep.'

'You know what? I think this country would become a significantly more pleasant place to live in if they legalised prostitution and *hashish*.'

'And theft. And murder, and—'

'I'm not joking,' she interrupted.

'You think as a child, I would say; or, at least, the naïveté of your statement shows a lack of mature and informed thought manifestations.'

'And you only say so because I included sex into the idea – you would far from see a problem in running to any store or kiosk and buying some *hashish* with your tobacco.'

'Whoever said it was more difficult to obtain than that?'

'Consider it: they'd be providing legitimate and organised means for many people to relieve their personal needs while keeping the rest of us safe.' Her closing words carried a bitter note.

'She would have still been attacked, Rawan,' he whispered breathlessly, 'and Amgad would still have manipulated the case just as much as he has in actuality, and we both would grieve no matter what the law dictated as prohibited or legal.' He consumed the last drops in his glass then refilled it, while Rawan watched his eyes fade into obscured vision, into the distance.

'My father,' Saleem continued, 'once spoke of this man who was the minister of interior affairs at some point during his life – I cannot recall the dates exactly. He told me this minister managed to clean the streets, literally, from *hashish* and more hard-core drugs. Needless to say, he was replaced within less than a year. The point I'm trying to make here is, think of lawfulness as you would of martyrdom, only to be praised and preached yet never to be genuinely sought after or self-implemented.'

'Your analogy is inaccurate. The way it usually happens is that those seeking martyrdom horrify and kill innocent people.'

'Yes, but it is not the act itself that is disdained but the belief that propels it. People are murdered every day; that is not the issue. What ruling bodies are concerned with is the threat of a principle or idea taken literally. Believe in what you will, as long as your conviction is figurative; transgress beyond that and you're a menace, because you make your belief a reality on solid ground that carries the urgency to be acknowledged and dealt with.'

Saleem noticed the glass in her hand was empty, so he held both the glass and her hand with one of his to steady it as he filled it past half its volume. She felt his cold fingers against her heat and almost shuddered at the rush that reverberated to the lowest point in her back and lingered there.

She drew in the breath so distinct in sound and length signaling one is about to speak, then hesitated, allowing it to exit her speechless mouth, and he, synced to her body with a floating mind and the gentle introduction that liquor creates shortly before sheer intoxication, deciphered the intention of her breath.

'What is it?' he encouraged.

'Do you feel sometimes that you are more pushed or dragged than advancing wilfully in life?'

'Sometimes, yes.'

'Because this is how I feel about everything.'

'Even the people you meet?'

'Why would they be an exception?'

'Since we make them so. We make choices when it comes to people – we select something someone said and adopt it. We choose whom to trust, whom to disagree with, whom to love.'

'You don't choose whom to love. That just happens.'

'Yes, it happens and then it stops happening the very moment it does, and from then on it's a choice of whether you want it to or not. Once intentions are in effect, you cannot claim that anything is beyond your own will.'

She drank slightly, watching him fill his glass a third time. Saleem was not tasteful in the manner with which he drank; he was almost sealing his glass to the brim like it were beer and gulping it down one draught after the next. They alternated between smoking and drinking, until the room fumed with clouds of a sweet scent, befuddled breaths and the haunting potency of erotic yearning. When Saleem's limbs eventually weighed down, and his eyes were less focused, his lips appeared moist and tender, so much so that Rawan felt she would tear them off his face with even the slightest grip of hers on them.

She shifted her body towards his until their noses almost touched, then spoke into the whiffs of smoke between them. 'I love you, and I want to love you.'

She held his face between her hands and thought of how one's features look very different from such proximity as he stared into her wide and receptive eyes. She bit his lower lip gently then started pulling at his shirt, his hands rising up and dropping back down as she undressed him like a puppet. Rawan leapt from the sofa to tug at his trousers, sliding all the clothing below his waist just past his knees, yet she did not undress herself. She sat upon his thighs and ripped at her underwear until it became a torn, useless piece of fabric and threw it aside, where it landed on the corner of the fireplace, clinging by mere threads. Saleem peered into her eyes without touching her as she lifted her torso higher then jammed him inside of her in an instant. She could not translate his gaze, which seemed not to be one of attraction but more that he was almost inspecting her, studying her movements and her own bodily response to them. Before she could proceed, he wrapped one arm around her back while supporting her head with the other then stood up and laid her slowly on the sofa, looking at the confused face now beneath his.

'I have been thinking of you all day, Rawan,' he whispered into her ears, 'and I want to love you too.' He undressed her amidst kisses, caressing every new section of her body that he bared until she lay below him in all the vulnerability of a woman exposed in the clear light. Saleem slid tenderly into her once more and began to move unhurriedly inside of her, kissing her lips passionately. He did not increase the pace with which he made love to her, nor did the way he timidly approached her lips each time to kiss them roughen. She could not decide which was more soothing: the lack of force in his movements or the fact that she had never felt so much of a woman in anyone's arms as she did that dawn. He was not consuming her. His touches bore not the stench that accompanies an air of authority and possession – he gave liberally to her body all that his was taking, so that their energy shot across one individual breath to the other in the cyclical motion of eternal being, and she finally understood why he had been frowningly inspecting her minutes earlier. She finally realised why this form of intimacy is related to sleep, where life as we know it returns to oblivion, and sight is restricted neither to light nor unsealed eyelids.

He did not crave her surrender, but took pleasure in her responsive caressing of his shoulders, the reciprocation her lips showed to his, the thumping heart that beat against his own as their chests pressed together. When he was about to climax, he held himself back until he sensed that she too was approaching. All from a man who was tasting a woman for the second time in his entire life, simply because he knew what it meant to have something so dear to one's self stolen away, and he would not rob Rawan of her spirit as one not half the man he was had robbed him of Samra.

Saleem carried her to bed as the sun ascended to their windows. She slid under the sheets and clung to his chest like a child, content and yearning for sleep, while he held her head beneath his chin and dozed off silently. For how alike falling asleep and shared intimacy may be, there remains one major difference between them: once deeply submerged, sleep can be an awfully lonely experience. So while the couple's heads sank into their single pillow, each mind manifested its own particular hauntings.

Samra came to him, condemning and reproachful. She was not weeping, which he considered a worse reprimand. She scolded him: 'You have not come to see me.'

'I do not want to see a dried cactus where you are invisible.'

'Not the cemetery, Saleem. Come to see me.'

'Where?'

'Come to see.'

Zali removed his turban and placed it on Rawan's head.

'You walked in the streets like that? With this on your head above jeans and a t-shirt?'

'You look funny,' he said and laughed.

'Yeah? Well this is how you look wearing it too. It's almost archaic, Zali.'

'So, I asked Sheikh Wegdani about this, and he looked at me and said I pardon thee *Allah*.'

'He doesn't even know.' Rawan giggled confidently.

'Wait, wait, and then I ask some of the other guys, and all they say is: «tradition, *habibi*, tradition»'

Rawan sniggered at the way he mimicked their voices.

'But that's not what it's about, Rawan, do you see?' he posed in a more serious tone. 'It doesn't matter what we wear or if even our leader understands why we wear it; it is the substance in the act of prayer, the supplication to God, which He receives each night, the unity through which His followers present themselves to Him.'

'I told you, Zali, I do not believe in a god who entreats his people differently. The god I pray to expects of me what he does of you. Once there are women joining you, I will be at this sheikh's door even before you leave your own home. Until then, I am very satisfied to pray in the corner of my bedroom.'

'The women perform *dhikr* too! Down in the—'

'Once they *join* you, I will come,' she repeated. 'Do me a favour, Zali, and research your religion's history. When the prophet prayed in Mecca, the women prayed along with him. They didn't pitch a tent far behind him and crawl inside to prostrate in concealment. Look at our mosques now. Back in Cairo, I would be infuriated by the massive halls wide enough for elephants to roam in for the men, while we are all crammed in an obscenely limited room on the top floors. Never mind the fact that there are elderly women who can't climb those stairs, but some would even have to go on the roof because the rooms were too small to accommodate everyone. The roof, Zali!'

'We pray on the roof.'

'You're an idiot with a turban I just stole; I will not return this, you know. But really, just forget this futile invitation and let us eat something. I'm starving.' He extended his arm to her, and she placed her hand in his as he led her further into the avenue. They crossed the street and headed towards Restaurant Le Caire, which seemed less crowded than usual as it was early afternoon. Rawan pulled him to the table far at the back so she could watch the people entering and exiting the hotel on the other side.

She found them to be most intriguing, the lodgers of Hotel Africa, and their array of demeanour peculiar amongst the typicality of faces in any regular street. She liked the way they would all turn in their tracks to examine their surroundings, as if their interest was not directed to their actual accommodation but diverted to everything exterior to it. They would either praise or complain about random happenings or aspects outside the hotel, and Rawan enjoyed their expressiveness and animated limbs as she tried to decipher from them their views on such external affairs. Zali watched her face, amused at the focus with which she delegated between herself whether or not the new tenants who had just arrived were pleased or dissatisfied with the hotel's outdoor setting.

The waiter came, and they both ordered fish *tagins*, while Rawan continued to stare at the world from behind the glass of the window beside her. She watched a small boy fling his little hand from his mother's grip and run into the hotel without pausing to look around first, wondering to herself when exactly the child would grow to imitate his parents and what causes these youngsters to eventually neglect the eagerness with which, as all the children she had witnessed, barge into the hotel without a backward glance?

'Come to see, Saleem,' Samra repeated one last time before her image shifted to become nothing more than a bloodied corpse on the African sand.

FOR NIGHT AND DAY

When Zain rang Rawan's phone, it vibrated with an irritant buzz against the bedside table while she couldn't recall having removed it from her bag at all. As she pushed her back up against the headboard to awaken fully, her eyes widening with the growing consciousness of her weak muscles, she saw that Saleem had left her side and realised he probably brought the phone near her before heading to the shower. The sound of water spraying and hitting his body travelled to her ears, and she considered joining him, yet Zain would not relent his attempts to call her. Tired and curious, she picked up the phone and yawned at him. 'Yes, Zain.'

'Sorry to wake you up; I just need your assistance with something.'

'What is it?'

'I need you and Saleem to be here much earlier than usual as I must head out for a few hours.'

'You want me to bring Saleem, you said?'

'Yes, I want you to be here in an hour at the latest.'

'Ok, but I don't really know what we'll do once we arrive.'

'You don't need to do anything. Just make sure the hall is well cleaned and the girls are ready.'

'Ok. Where are you now, Zain?'

'I'm leaving in a few minutes. That's why I need you to hurry.'

'Ok, don't worry.'

'Rawan,' he stressed, 'no craziness while I'm gone, I beg of you.'

'Enough, Zain! Just hang up so we can get dressed.'

'Ok, bye.'

She ended the call, pleased that the ban on Saleem's admittance into Naktal had been lifted so promptly, and stood up in her bedsheet, walking to the bathroom.

'Saleem,' she called from outside the door.

'What?'

'Can I come in?'

'No. I'll be done soon.'

She looked blankly at the door, slightly abashed. 'Ok, but we need to leave quickly.'

'Why?'

'Just come out.'

Rawan passed the corridor and strode to the sofa to gather their clothes from the floor but saw that Saleem had already done so. She heard him exit the bathroom and walked back. 'We must leave. Zain needs us urgently.'

'Why does he need *me*?'

'Just get dressed, Saleem! Please.'

They were out of the door almost half an hour after Rawan had ended Zain's call, and she recited to Saleem what had been requested of them. His incessant arguing as to why he should accompany her clueless, and her patient and repetitive attempts to explain that she was clueless herself but that they were obliged to help nonetheless, distracted them both from the car parked at the end of the street through which they drove. They sped past Zain, who bowed his head to conceal his face, almost crouching in the driver's seat, awaiting their departure before turning his car around, heading to their building.

***

Rawan decided, as always, to follow her own accord, and ordered the handymen present to install the poles Zain had stored away. The wind, particularly tempestuous that day, heaved the water with more strength than usual, and she could hear it slapping Naktal from all sides. Assured by Saleem that he would not drink himself to stupor, she crossed the hall to the dressing room. It was vacant, save for the cleaning lady who was playfully holding one of the costume bras to her own breast; her figure foreign to what the glaring light of the mirrors in her backdrop were accustomed to; her emphatic singing cut violently short the very second Rawan stepped in. She bowed her head in embarrassment and dropped the gold-sequined bra to the floor then proceeded to polish the mirrors silently as Rawan raised an eyebrow at her. Rawan examined the cleaning lady's face from her favourite chair, a few inches from where she stood, and she found her to possess youthful features, bordered by a veil which kept sliding down her forehead as she worked. 'How old are you?' she asked in staged nonchalance.

'Twenty-three.'

'I've never seen you here before.'

'I leave early, miss. Sometimes even before Mr. Zain wakes up.'

I knew he lived here! 'But he awoke earlier than usual today, right?'

'Yes.'

'Are you comfortable with your work here?'

'Very. Mr. Zain is an angel to me and my husband, Ali.'

'You're married?! Where are you from?'

'We're both from Suez, miss.'

Rawan searched her bag for the cigarettes and lit one, motioning for the cleaner to continue with her work. Whether it was of sheer boredom or the early wake-up call, she found herself sinking deeper into the chair until the last thing she was conscious of was the sound of the door closing and the image of the woman in her mirror with drooping eyes amidst dark sockets.

The mother followed her child into the hotel while their luggage was carried from the trunk of their car. 'Rawan,' Zali said. 'Rawan!'

'What?' she whispered distractedly.

'Food!' he announced.

She turned her gaze from the window to him with a smile

and glanced to the ceramic bowl at the table then shrieked, staggering back and knocking her head against the wall behind her.

'What?' Zali questioned, his eyebrow high in defiance while she gaped at the bowl filled to the brim with blood, hair and bones. Zali's face contorted into Zahra's as she grinned to Rawan, offering her a spoon while asking, 'Do you know what "Naktal" means? To seek measure.' She dipped the spoon into the bowl, advancing it to Rawan's lips to feed her. A cold draught of air blew against Rawan's face as she tried to move away from Zahra's extended hand.

'Shake her,' a voice rang in the restaurant.

'I'm not going to touch her – you wake the freak up.'

Rawan opened her eyes in panic to find the dancers staring alarmingly back at her, enflamed and weary in the mirror. She wiped her mouth with the back of her hand and shook her head to cease her chest's winded puffing. The dancers scurried around her getting ready, and she paid them no regard until her anxiety lessened and she noticed what they were wearing.

'No, no,' she addressed them in a drowsy manner. 'Those are for the second performance. I... Zain,' Rawan corrected, 'needs at least ten of you wearing corsets and tights. They're putting the poles up onstage.'

'He didn't tell us this,' one of the dancers argued.

'Have you seen him since you all arrived? He informed me before he left.'

'Where did he go?' another posed.

Rawan glanced to the ceiling from their nuisance. 'I'm not his wife. Just change your outfits.'

A voice mumbled from amidst them. 'You sure act like you are.'

Infuriated, Rawan stood from the chair and clenched its back with her clammy hands. 'You know, you're absolutely right,' she said calmly. 'Wear whatever the hell you like. Let Zain deal with you when he returns.' She barged past them to the curtain and disappeared behind it for a short while. When she returned to their view, there were dancers who had already begun to dress as she had indicated while the others took longer to deliberate her directions. She sat back in her chair and turned a deaf ear to their mutters and bickering as she dabbed a sponge of concealer beneath her swollen eyes.

'Those who are joining me need to leave in ten minutes,' she called to the room in its entirety once she was ready. Rawan opened the door and nearly rammed into Zain's chest. 'Hey! How did your errand go?' she asked, closing the door behind her.

'Well. Why are the poles on the stage?'

'What? Oh, my ... I completely forgot, Zain!' she exclaimed, wide-eyed. 'Are you upset? I can tell the girls to change.'

Zain's attention seemed diverted from their topic of conversation and he simply wavered her suggestion casually. 'No there's no need to. Let's just keep it less crude tonight. As much as you can.'

'I will. Just call those idiots in there to come out.' She checked the watch on his wrist. 'We're late.'

Rawan passed the dark corridor to climb the steps at the far end, leaving a distracted Zain at the dressing room's door. Once she had crossed her maze of darkness, she strode carefully to her left until she stood above the centre to the edge of the stage. The tall pole that stemmed from the ground metres below rose to level with her belly as she sat down before it, wrapping her legs and arms around it in an awkward embrace. Music broke into an instantaneous roar with no subtle introduction as the lights around her beamed on the dancers at the stage floor, who had commenced to swing around their own respective poles while the audience applauded to the music's pace. Rawan shifted her buttocks off the ledge and slid rapidly down the pole, which held no friction against the suppleness of her thigh stockings. She beamed at the crowd as soon as she landed directly at the edge of the stage, immediately moving in accordance to her rehearsed programme.

Saleem's head was bent low, focused on something in his lap that Rawan could not see, then he left his usual seat at the far left of the stage bar and made his way to the middle at Rawan's jumping heels. He smiled to the men cheering her, whilst signalling her to approach him with his index finger. Teasingly, she clasped her pole with both hands and hoisted herself slightly high off the floor then, alternating her grip, flipped herself so that her body hung upside down before him. She daringly pushed her torso forward, her hair brushing the drinks at the bar as Saleem placed what looked like a two-hundred pound note, folded in half, between his teeth and pushed his head until her red lips met his, tugging the money from his mouth. The man to his right patted his back and gripped his shoulder in admiration as he searched his pocket in an attempt to imitate Saleem, yet Rawan snubbed his advances. By the time her feet returned to the floor, Saleem was out of sight and, pulling the money from her lips to inspect them, she found a written note folded within: I'm leaving for Cairo and will be back tomorrow.

Confused and startled, she desperately scanned the hall to seek his face, yet he had already left. Rawan turned her back to the audience for a moment and stuffed the note beneath her breast. She continued to twirl around the pole non-attentively, bending her knees with the other dancers, splitting her thighs apart and flipping her hair in a robust rhythm before climbing the pole once more as high as she could, and descending again to the ground in circular motion. *What happened? Why is he going to Cairo? He's probably just bored with you. I don't understand. This is very abrupt. Only to you. Perhaps he has been planning it for a while. Perhaps he does not intend to return. I'm feeling sick.* She sensed the concerned expression on her face and forced it into a fanatical grin below an icy glare.

Every feature of the face can be manipulated except the eyes. They are too unruly, and one who masters the power to influence them is most dangerous. Samra once told her that the only people who can truly control the look in their eyes are those who are misplaced, like great actors adept in playing roles alien to themselves. Yet one who is neither nor seeking to be lost will never forcibly alter their expression. Rawan, caught between Malak and herself, steadily managed to stretch her eyes into a beaming smile to the cheering crowds at her feet.

When she and the dancers halted with the music, she exited the stage from the far right and sped through the corridor. Zain was clearly not in his office, for he had not left the door unlocked for her as usual, neither were her incessant knocks answered. Dancers sped past her towards the dressing room, in preparation for their next 'traditional' performance, whereas she treaded back to the hall, scouring the room for him. She glanced him wave to her from a far table at which he was sat with Zahra, and she approached them, making her way between the strewn tables and standing guests.

'Malak, Zain was practically boasting about you, as always.' Zahra grinned to Rawan.

Rawan occupied the seat nearest to Zain. 'Well, he should! I almost break my neck every night for him.'

'Ali!' Zain called. 'Ali! Drinks here, please. No bill.'

'Ah, you see? Omnibenevolent Zain and his great generosity!' exclaimed Rawan.

Zahra laughed to Rawan, inquiring. 'So, how is it that you know the mighty Zain?'

'Yes, that is a question I am personally deeply eager to hear an answer to.' It was Amgad. He peered down at them from where he stood by Rawan and began introducing himself to Zahra. 'Detective Amgad Acir. May I join you?' Far from awaiting approval, he pulled the seat between Zahra and Rawan then sat down.

An onlooker would have supposed them a highly odd bunch, an assortment of appearances, ages and sex. Nevertheless, the tension reverberating from one seat to the next as Amgad had joined them resembled less of a poker game and more of a naïve staring contest. Who would be the first to break the silence amongst their ring, they all wondered? It was Zahra who opted to speak first and foremost, as the old do.

'Detective, do you live in El Gouna? I have not had the pleasure of walking into you before.'

'I am originally from Cairo, madame, but my services were required here rather recently.'

'Amgad *basha* likes to think of himself as an indispensable General of the police force,' Rawan mocked, focusing her gaze upon Zahra, 'when he is merely a detective.'

'I'm sure he is a fine one,' Zahra commented in assumed civility to Amgad, yet she was still confused by his intrusion upon their conversation and assembly.

'Malak is a young, lawless rebel. Naturally, her views on my profession are harsh and her judgments haste.'

Ali returned to their table, carrying an array of drinks and placed them all in the centre to indicate each type. 'This is vodka tonic, gin, whiskey, martini and a margarita.' They chimed their thanks to Ali as each selected their pick.

'He brought five,' Zahra noted. 'Will someone be joining us?'

Zain looked at Rawan, who shook her head to him inauspiciously.

'Not to worry. Malak will probably need many more drinks before the night is over,' Amgad said snidely.

Zahra's patience began to wring against her fondness of Rawan, and she shot the detective an irritant look. 'I have not seen Malak drink herself to intoxication once, detective.'

'And I have yet to meet a woman who should, more than her. Wouldn't you agree, Zain?'

'I do not discuss politics, *basha*,' Zain said, his statement causing Amgad to roar in amusement.

'This is not politics, dear Zain. It is the gentle sex that we are discussing.'

Rawan giggled half-heartedly. 'And you, of all people, wish to discuss women? Let me tell you something, *basha*. Talking of women in the presence of two Egyptian ones is not a wise path to take. I suggest you select another topic to make your invasion of our gathering more … worthwhile, shall we say.'

'Oh! I apologise. If my attendance is unwelcome, I shall leave immediately. Zain? Is it unwelcome?'

'Not at all, *basha*! Perhaps Malak simply disliked your remark.'

'Tell me, detective,' Zahra interposed, 'are you here tonight on duty?'

Amgad grinned to Zain. 'That is yet to be determined.'

'Do not be surprised, Zahra,' Rawan, noticing the woman's confusion, intervened. 'When have any of them fully comprehended the stance of their job? It is far from unfitting that the *basha* here strut around leisurely, clueless to his true disposition. If women are to be referred to at all in this conversation, it should only be to highlight how whimsical a man in Mr. Amgad's profession is often found to be.'

'What do you think of Malak's performances, Madame Zahra?' Amgad posed, his eyes targeting Rawan's with a confidence that irritated her.

'I find them entertaining on a most conceptual level.'

'Yet, although she does not solely rely on the physicality that dancers fixate upon, and attributes an idea to each performance, still, how many of her audience would say they enjoyed anything other than the nuance of her approach?'

'Not many, I would assume.'

'Exactly. The problem is it's only a matter of time before her brain exhausts all concepts for surprise. She'll start repeating her ideas, over and over, till spectators bore and Zain eventually replaces her.'

Zain looked at him calmly, careless to argue, unlike Rawan who was once more compelled to interject:

'It is understandable why you would think this way; men of power hardly consider the reality of life that all things must end at some point or another, and so you believe everyone is equally trapped in the obsession to remain. Zain will need to replace me much earlier than you refer to, because I do not intend to remain a spectacle of Naktal long enough till the exhaustion of my own creativity.'

'It is far from an obsession, Malak,' Amgad argued. 'It is simply human nature. Survival of the fittest.'

'That's a theory construed for animals, actually.'

'Existence and survival is innate in everything, and as much as we are all equally flawed, no one can endure while they demonise themselves. It would do you well to exercise the same leniency and abundant frequency with which you absolve yourself upon others.'

'I agree,' Zahra said. 'My late husband was a loyal man to his home and a dedicated lover to his country, and while he belonged to a force of command and power, he would have gladly sacrificed his life for it.'

Rawan smiled to Zahra. *Yes, the grand estate I drove to yesterday was indeed one of patriotic love and sheer sacrifice.*

'Your husband, he was—'

'A military man,' Zahra completed for Amgad, whose hostile features smoothed into apparent affection.

'*Allah* rest his soul.'

'*Ameen.*'

'He passed away on duty?'

'No, no. Lung cancer. He was a loyal smoker. As yourself,' she added, watching Amgad light his fifth cigarette since he had joined their table.

That's most probably not all they share in common.

It is interesting how in such groups, each individual assumes a role that harmonises smoothly into the presence of the 'whole'. It happens so organically that one cannot simply specify why a particular role has been successfully adopted by its particular individual, and, once assumed, it becomes dominant over the person's entire being. The four gathered at that precise table were each consumed by their respective parts. There was the rebel, too young to have acquired a comprehensive and informed view, more bitter than constructive articulation necessitated; her adversary, impervious and unreceptive to her attempts to persuade; the peacemaker who smiles and pats everyone's back; the silent observant, master of the very ground upon which their feet rested, watching them from his proximal remoteness.

She Likes Day's Songs

The lock did not show the trouble he had anticipated as the key turned smoothly, and he clicked it open. He treaded timidly inside and shut the door behind him, the dust beneath his feet flying to escape being smothered by his shoes as he climbed the stairs to her room. Saleem pressed his palm flat against her door and sensed the wood complain of neglect under its crusty paint and lack of warmth then turned the handle and swung it open. He had been there before. Countless times in fact. Once to fix her balcony door, once when she showed him the options for her engagement dress because she liked all three and couldn't decide and once when they sneaked there to kiss while her mother was downstairs in the kitchen. The other times he could not recollect as vividly.

It was too tidy. Everything was in its proper place, almost holding an abysmal resemblance to a hospital room following the death of a patient. For how organised and neat it was, Saleem felt incapacitated with sickness. He dropped his weight from his shaken legs to sit at the edge of her bed, his stomach unsettling him greatly, his heart heavy and cold. 'Come to see me. Come to see,' she had implored him, and his mind could think of no other place to go to. He had slept with her sister twice – once of his own accord and complete wilfulness, the other without his utmost rejection. Whether Samra haunted his dreams purely as a manifestation of his guilt or through her soul's own genuine seeking, Saleem found himself staring at the dent in her pillow, which remained more faithful than its maker.

It is strange how our traces linger more devotedly than ourselves. The scents we left behind, our possessions, the thoughts we took the effort to pen down or verbally voice to someone, the motionless images we chose to preserve, the weight of our body upon the grass, our memory printed amongst those of others, branded across their minds. They are the only proof we actually existed, that we were not figments of imagination. Even our own flesh, which we waste our lives slaving to please, becomes nought but dust in the wind. Dust signifying nothing, carrying no meaning, following no purpose. And Saleem cared not to seek dust, buried in decomposing cloth below his feet.

He loved Samra. And he believed he loved Rawan too. Yet he could not bear both facts together, simultaneously burning at his conscience and mauling at his mind. He left his place and walked over to Samra's cupboard, prying it open. She wafted into his breath so much he could almost feel her fingers against his lips as they once touched between kisses. Saleem breathed in her scents deeply, so ungenerous to exhale that his head felt lighter as he almost dropped to his knees and turned to sit inside the cupboard, enveloping himself in her hanging clothes before pulling its door in so that a single vertical line of light sliced his body in half. He hinged the door against his shoes and spread his arms wide to hold her dresses and scarves and trousers, bringing them closer to his face and nose, then leaned his head back against the interior of the cupboard and stretched his arms either side of its base.

His left hand touched something hard under a pile of folded shirts. Saleem felt around until he grabbed at the object and pulled it closer to the light. It was a leather notepad, similar to the hardcover textbooks and old novels strewn across Cairo's streets. He loosened the grip of his shoes from the bottom of the door to allow more light and opened the notepad.

It was Samra's diary.

He knew it for sure, for he was looking at her favourite literary passage written in her own handwriting. Saleem read under his breath the lines she cherished from Salah Abdelsabur's 'The Tragedy of El Hallag', his eyes foggy with silent tears as the words she had chosen would inevitably speak more to him, 'a homeless celestial child who had strayed from his father', than they once signified for her. He flipped the pages, searching for nothing save for the woman he had come to find, the woman who now, supposedly, shared with her sister his heart.

She had never shown nor mentioned the diary to him, and while he was well aware of her fondness for certain literature, Samra had never spoken of her dedication to document her thoughts amongst other things. By examining the dates on the top right corners, he saw that she retreated to her diary almost every other day as his fingers traced page after page, detailing various events of the past year. He knew not whether to consider the discovery a blessing or a cruel curse, for he saw her mouth curve to enunciate the words as he read, heard her voice stress this word, pause at that, and rush through those in all her past animated spirit burnt within his memory. He came across his name many times, smiling from the midst of the cupboard as it peered back at his teary eyes from under his fingers, speaking to him what Samra had at times been too coy or too fearful to tell.

Saleem probably sat there for hours on end, reading and laughing, weeping and turning page after the next until they became empty. He stared desolately at the words unwritten, the scraps of her warm heart unpenned, the dreams foretold that would remain with her, only for her. It was deafeningly lonely. He had to flip the pages back and read again, for he had skipped the last few entries. Saleem's palm swept across the dates, pausing at September 26th: 'My baby arrives tomorrow. I have missed her like the night sky longs for the sun, no, like the sun yearns for it, so it may rest and extinguish. She is the friend I have not chosen, the face boasting my familiarity, the laughter in the dark before sleep.'

His heart warmed as he transcribed Samra's words onto the image of Rawan, which moved before him, then turned the page.

September 28th: 'I want to do it. It feels right with merely a supposition of wrongness. He is the man of my life, and if I am devoted to him half as much as my heart tells me, what is there to be concerned with? Saleem is my home amongst the wreckage and although planning such an emotional meeting seems erroneous, the intent alone is flawless and beautiful.

He is mine and I am his, irrespective of announcement, regardless of the day our bodies shall become one.'

October 3rd: 'Broken.'

The single word hanging awkwardly, abandoned in an otherwise emptiness, plucked at the corners of his mind as he hastily sought the next page. He caressed the date mournfully, her last entry in the diary: October 4th: 'Broken. Beyond disappointment or belief. Her voice wrings my veins less than the fact that I did not slam the door open and confront her. What am I to do with this wedding encroaching so dreadful now? Who is this Zali who has over a few trivial months become closer to her secrets than her own sister? This home, home! This "house" is moth-eaten and collapsing, its former inhabitants forever scarred, condemned to venture away from one another to foreign lands where they may lick their wounds with dry tongues till they become arid and itch. I have watched each of them leave, one after the other, and yet still clung to their roots till my nail-beds bled. Father, brother, sister, wasting away into their own fantasies of how their lives "ought" to be, while I tend to an aging mother who has no one but I to watch the silver invade her hair. No one but I, who will still listen to her tales which have become so torn and expended, reduced to no more than that godforsaken apology of a lover who does not cease to wrong his love.

Is it not terribly strange when they do that? When the two phrases, "I am sorry" and "I did not mean to," accompany one another from their mouths? As if one's intention has the slightest effect on the pain caused by his doing. As if I would hurt less, knowing that your aim was not to hurt me, like stabbing someone then imploring their skin not to bleed. I know not whether I should feel betrayed or sympathetic. How long has she kept this from me? Her love for the man whom I am to give myself to entirely tomorrow? Would it make a difference to know? Who is this Zali whom she rejects his love over the phone with the passionate confession of her adoration for Saleem? This is intolerable madness. I have heard my sister's muffled tears over a man she shall never claim to another I may never know.

And I can do nothing. Nothing but ask her to free an hour or so tomorrow at noon, with the excuse that there remain things to be arranged in the flat.

All I know of tomorrow is that Rawan and I must talk, alone. Even If I have to drive us to the midst of the desert, away from the world, then so be it!'

Saleem gripped the edges of the diary until the leather almost bent, tearing at his brain to remember the call he had received from Samra telling him that she would not meet him at their house. Was she already on the road by then? Was Rawan in the seat next to her? No, he thought to himself, calming the paranoid conceptions that swam behind his frown. His phone rang from the bed beyond and, clutching the diary in his moist palm, he ran to find Rawan's name on the screen.

'Hello?' she said.

'I cannot return this evening. I will be there tomorrow,' Saleem said.

'What's happening? Are you all right?'

Was he to ask her right then and there, on the phone; to confront her?

'I have to go,' he blurted, hanging up. She rang once more but he had already silenced the phone. Saleem dropped on the bed and pulled at his hair in confusion. The simplest lesson his father had taught him rang behind his ears along with suspicion and near breakdown, and he shook his legs together with intense anxiety, as it became a lesson grander by context: 'Act fast or you will find yourself immobile with self-delay and impotence. We are both violent and pacifist beings by nature, yet more prone to the latter were it not for the sense of urgency.'

He grabbed his phone and called Rawan.

'Saleem, what's wrong?' she cried in alarm.

'Send me the lawyer's number.'

'Lawyer … what?'

'The lawyer, Rawan!' he yelled. 'The lawyer you hired for Samra's case! Send his number and name now!' He ended the call abruptly before she could question him further, yet minutes later, she did indeed forward him Ahmad's number. He rang it repetitively, but his attempts were unanswered. Saleem groaned at the ceiling and muttered wordless pleas for help. He checked the time to find it was perhaps too early in the morning and stood from his place, with the diary still in his hand.

He left the room door open before bounding down the stairs and out of the house. There were more than a few taxis rushing past the street. He hailed one, which stopped a few metres past where he stood. It hastened during the route as if the driver were synced to his passenger's frantic urge then finally stopped at the main entrance to the hospital as Saleem had requested of him.

He felt the malady in his stomach heighten as he dragged his legs up the steps, clueless of his destination. Patients being pushed in wheelchairs passed him, nurses and doctors strode too hurriedly for his weary eyes to track, more patients leaned over family members as they treaded slowly in recovery, a panting woman was escorted to the delivery room, another wept hysterically as her husband argued with her mother over the ungodliness of an epidural. Lives and deaths passed by him as he recalled the single loss that had been amongst them months earlier in that very building of tears. Weeping that accompanies sheer happiness and grief, regardless of their vastly opposing nature, tastes just as saline in both.

Saleem approached the reception table and asked for the doctor who had supervised over Samra during her brief admittance at the hospital, only to be told that he was absent that day. He inquired for her patient documents and the receptionist asked to see proof of his kinship, upon which he pulled a fifty-pound note from his pocket and pressed it into her hand. She left her chair and asked him to wait a little, whereas he attempted to contact the lawyer yet again. He heard his voice in response through the headset and exhaled in relief. 'Mr. Ahmad, I apologise for hassling you. This is Saleem Salim. We were your clients for a case some months ago? Rawan and Samra Yaqub?'

'Yes, yes I recall,' he replied with sympathy. 'What can I do for you, Mr. Saleem?'

THE KING'S DEBT

'I need to meet you urgently and, of course, will reimburse you for your troubles or any nuisance this may cause to your day.'

'No need, Mr. Saleem. I am not scheduled in court this morning. Can you come to my office now?'

'I was hoping I could meet you outside. There may be errands we need to run together.'

'Where are you now?'

'I can meet you at the hospital. Do you remember where it is?'

'I remember this case very well, Mr. Saleem, and I am happy to help. I will be there as soon as I can.'

'Thank you very much, Mr. Ahmad. May *Allah* bless you.'

'And bestow His mercy upon us all, my son.'

Saleem could not sit down. He paced back and forth on the few tiles in front of the reception desk until the woman returned, shaking her head apologetically at him. 'All her papers were sent to the ministry of justice months ago. If you had told me it was a crime case, I would have explained earlier. Here.' She handed him his money back, shaking her head in refusal. 'Please,' she insisted, 'I did not help you.'

'You did what you could. It is my error,' he answered.

'Bless you,' she replied in gratitude, and Saleem walked back down the hall to wait for the lawyer outside.

He inhaled at the air like an asthma-ridden, old man, whilst he stood miserably stranded on the pavement until a car stopped near him.

'Don't park, Mr. Ahmad,' Saleem said, opening the passenger door and sitting beside the lawyer. 'We want to go to El-Sayeda, the morgue.'

'Is there any new information regarding the case?'

Saleem squeezed his eyes as they drove past the shade at the hospital entrance, plunging into the burning sunlight. He held in a draught of air then breathed, 'Samra was not raped, Mr. Ahmad.'

***

Rawan sat in the bathtub, ripping at the papers against her knees with a pencil, the surface of her skin practically pierced with goose bumps. She shivered in the cold water but would not budge from her place nor lift her hand to heat the showers that fell over her head.

I don't understand what's happening. What are you sketching there? What does he want from the lawyer? Rawan! Focus! What are you sketching? He's going to ruin everything. He thinks he's helping, but all he has done is one mistake after the next and that could jeopardise all I have toiled for! Rawan, listen to me, ignore these thoughts and tell me what that image in your lap is. And I sent him the number. Why did I do that? Because you don't listen; because you ignore me! Look: are those Zali's eyes? Yes. A very accurate depiction. Focus on that now.

Her phone rang. She drew it from on top of the closed toilet seat and answered mindlessly.

'Rawan, no poles and no aerial shows tonight, I'm reminding you,' Zain said. 'What's that sound?'

'Nothing,' she answered, closing the tap. 'Saleem is in Cairo,' she said, more to the wall before her than to him.

He was quiet for a few seconds. 'Really. Why?'

She shook her head. 'I don't know.'

'How long will he be gone?'

'I don't know,' she repeated.

The sound of his mouth chewing on something reverberated rather irritantly in her ear. 'I have to go,' she said.

'I'll see you tonight, Rawan.'

She stared at her call log, looking at Saleem's name, then held her phone above the water. She lowered it down gradually until it swung from her two fingers that were pinching it before watching it callously thud to the bottom of the tub. Zali looked back at her with condemning eyes in an otherwise featureless face.

***

'Whatever happened I have no clue, but she wasn't raped. I … I feel it.'

'Pray upon the prophet, my son,' Ahmad implored Saleem.

'Peace be upon him.'

'Why are we heading for the morgue? The report was delivered to me already, the rape indications clear and noted.'

'I am not crazy, Mr. Ahmad,' Saleem fumed.

'I did not say so, Saleem. I am merely encouraging that you seek reason.'

'Where is the report?'

'In my office. Would you like us to turn around and head there?'

'No, no. I need to speak with someone, anyone, from the morgue.'

'Anyone we speak to will not have an ounce of recollection of this case – the bodies that pass under their hands are more than the hairs on their heads!'

'Then I guess I'll have to find someone bald to speak to,' he said and jumped from the car before it had fully stopped. Ahmad ran behind him into the building and presented his ID to the officer at the entrance, who admitted them both. The stench of refrigerated corpses panged against their nostrils long before they even approached the fridges.

What must they be thinking, Saleem wondered, these frozen dead? Are they lonesome, craving contact with the grave, or seeking the company of family prayers that can cause no influence upon their deeds long done? Do their stiff bones and icy skin miss the pleasures they once exulted in, or have God's invisible men already begun to seek retribution for their unpaid debts? The lawyer's voice roused him from his distant thoughts, and he turned to find him in conversation with an employee of the morgue.

'Yes, here is the document authorising my permission to inquire on the deceased.'

The man inspected the paper handed to him and excused himself beyond the corridor. He returned after half an hour with a thin folder and opened it in his hands. 'You want to see the report only,' he said, exchanging glances with Saleem to indicate he was convinced, 'yes?'

'Correct.'

Saleem breathed down the man's neck, scanning the report, and in an incomprehensible way, hoping that his suspicions would be falsified. He read until the bottom of the page and felt a cold emptiness in the entirety of his chest.

'I would like a copy of this report, please,' the lawyer requested.

'I can't give you one. You must collect one from the prosecution office where your case is being handled.'

Ahmad tried to distract the man, seeing what Saleem was about to do. He leaned his palm on his shoulder in the brotherly fashion through which one may instigate conversation. 'But as a lawyer, I am entitled to—'

'I don't issue any documents or copies for lawyers or even to the president himself!' he pronounced dramatically.

Saleem pulled out his phone and snapped a picture from the back of the man's neck, who heard the sound of the camera click and then shut the folder quickly. Saleem grabbed at Ahmad's shoulder and ran to the main door as fast as he could. The employee shouted at them to stop, but they had already reached the front steps, as Saleem yelled at the lawyer to give him the car keys. Hearing the hassle and shouts, the soldier at the gate dropped the lunch in his mouth and darted towards the car that had already sped down the street before he could even glimpse its licence plate.

Ahmad directed Saleem across the roads to his office in Nasr City, as he watched his clammy hands grip at the wheel in shocked fury, the heat of the noon air stifling them as the car's air conditioner was faulty.

Arriving at the office, sticky and dying from thirst, Ahmad dragged Saleem past his employees and ordered the secretary against any disturbance. As soon as Saleem slammed the office door shut, Ahmad immediately crouched on his knees, inspecting the cupboard at the bottom of his library where he archived the hardcopy documents of his cases. Saleem was on his toes and absorbed in all the random, farfetched and plausible outcomes of their search that he sat himself freely at the desk as he held his phone to print the photo of the coroner's report he had stealthily procured.

'I found it,' the lawyer announced non-animatedly. His aging knees cracked as he rose from his position and placed the report on the desk near Saleem's hands, while the printer ejected a single paper. Ahmad held it to examine then lay it next to the report on the desk.

'This is the report released from the prosecution office?' Saleem asked.

'This is the one handed to me, yes.' He gripped Saleem's shoulders, who banged his forehead on the desk, digging his fingers across the back of his head, groaning in frustration.

'Saleem, listen to me: the photo you took is of less quality, and the man's fingers are covering sections,' he pointed across the paper. 'Do you see?'

Saleem spoke from his bowed head, his voice muffled against the desk. 'You saw it, and I saw it.' He raised his head to glare at the lawyer. Ahmad looked sympathetically back at his burning eyes, before Saleem continued in the tone only another defeated man would recognise. 'This report

Amgad Acir gave you, as released from the prosecution office, contains different information from that issued by the coroner, and, yet, it is the same handwriting and signature.'

'Why would the coroner draft two different reports?'

'He didn't.' Saleem shook his head wearily.

'Then how could they—'

'Tell me, Mr. Ahmad,' Saleem interrupted, his eyes pleadingly peering to the lawyer for an answer, 'why would someone forge a report to state "cause of death: cervical hemorrhage" and then manipulate the case so as to acquit the suspects of rape, for insufficient evidence?'

Ahmad maintained his supportive grip on Saleem's shoulder. 'If you take this to court, it will count for nothing. The report has probably already been destroyed by now. You know how it works here. A single matchstick is all it takes, and for someone who, for some reason, went through all this trouble to hide a truth we will never discover, setting a building's archives on fire or simply bribing an employee to act similarly are equally petty deals. It's a wonder they hadn't destroyed this already.'

Saleem staggered from the armchair behind the desk and walked towards the door, leaving the papers behind. 'There is no wonder, Mr. Ahmad. No wonder. Incompetence is our middle name,' he breathed from the door, his heart weary.

'Where are you going, my son?' the lawyer called to him desperately.

'To buy matchsticks.'

AS IT PASSES THROUGH PATHS

Rawan dropped the brush in her hand and ran to the door, her wet hair bouncing against her waist, her towel forced in an awkward knot against her right breast while she muttered, 'You have your keys, Saleem!' She had soaked for long hours until her skin wrinkled so much, her fingers were almost numb. Rawan flung the door wide with relief for his return, only to find herself looking at another face entirely.

Amgad pushed past the door and shut it casually, surveying the entrance and the living room to his left, speaking in a deep, calm voice: 'Zain told me you were alone. He was also kind enough to give me your address.'

She forced her face into a soothed smile and welcomed him, motioning to the sofa near the fireplace. 'It's a great surprise from Zain! Please, make yourself comfortable while I change into something appropriate.'

'Of course. Can I make myself a coffee whilst I wait?'

'It would be very rude of me to allow such a thing!'

He shook his head to argue. 'Not at all. I know you like my coffee. I see the kitchen is well kept. I should have no problem finding my way around. Please, take your time.' He pointedly encouraged her to leave, standing up and heading for the kitchen. Rawan walked calmly down the corridor while she heard him light the stove, then bolted into her room and locked the door. She scurried to the bed, lifted the mattress and retrieved her gun. As Rawan brought down the mattress slowly, she glimpsed something sparkle on the floor under the bed. She stooped to the floor and lay on her stomach, reaching an arm beneath the bed and sweeping the dust back and forth with her left hand until she felt a rough object. A recognisable texture, as she pulled it from its crevice to find that it was one of the desert roses, chipped off its larger body and neglected in the dark. Rawan jumped to her feet and looked confusedly to the bedside table where Zali's gift had been placed since they moved into the house, yet it was not there. Disturbed, she walked back to the door and opened it silently, the gun secure in her hand. Peering to the right, Rawan saw Amgad standing near the sofa with his back to the corridor, raising a mug to his lips with his left hand as the right hid in his pocket.

She treaded mutely, her arms extended and ready to shoot him, until she stood mere footsteps away.

Amgad's eyes widened as he sensed her and, laughing amusedly without turning to look at her, he took a further sip of coffee.

'You don't think I'll do it?' She spoke in response to his confidence.

'Oh I know you will,' he asserted.

Rawan pulled at the gun and pulled the trigger under her trembling fingers. Nothing. He spun around, applauding her enthusiastically then placed the mug on the coffee table and pulled his cigarette pack from his pocket.

'In an odd way, I'm so proud of you, Rawan.' He grinned as he lit the cigarette, now hanging off the tip of his mouth.

'Malak,' she breathed, standing rooted to the ground stiffly yet looking like a weather-beaten piece of clothing hung out to dry.

Amgad shook his head in disagreement. 'I lied when I said it suited you. It's a very poor choice, I like to think you are too smart to have selected that one in particular. Or was it Zain who picked it for you?'

But Rawan was not listening. She held the gun closer to her eyes, inspecting the malfunction. *What's wrong with it?*

'Great man, Zain,' Amgad continued. 'He did that.'

He approached her, holding his hand out for the gun. 'Here, let me show you.' Amgad took it with no force from her hands and opened the latch at the bottom. 'You see? No bullets. You had one ready to fire though. Poor man nearly shot his own thigh. So if he broke anything in there, it wasn't his fault, ok?'

Zain did this? Why? Where are you?

'I have to go. I have work in a few hours,' she said, taking the gun back in her hand and staring at the ground.

'Rawan,' he sternly responded, throwing the cigarette furiously into his mug, 'I think that's more than enough now.'

Malak, my name is Malak.

'Zain will be furious if I'm late.' She turned towards the corridor, but Amgad yanked her arm harshly.

'I have been more than patient with you!' he warned. 'This

ironic role you've assigned me … ridiculously stereotypical. The innocence of your immature defence mechanisms is off-putting to say the least.'

'Zain is my friend. I should not keep him waiting.'

'Zain is not your friend.' He spoke in a monotonous tone to state the obvious. 'Zain is a man hired to watch you, because you are an idiot who is so inventive at pushing herself in harm's way; you're practically Satan's favourite child.'

She turned her face from his, escaping his gaze.

'Rawan, look at me. Rawan, please look at me. Please!' He pulled her to his chest and dragged her down with him until they both dropped to their knees.

'Please, my love!' Amgad held her face between his palms and stared at her with imploring eyes of despair. 'I wanted to die when you left!' His eyes watered. 'I almost killed Zain when he lost track of you that day you travelled! Oh, look at me, my love, please!'

I must call Zali … and Saleem … Where is Saleem? 'It's almost dark outside,' she whispered, struggling to release herself from his clutches, but his fingers dug deeper into her skin as he embraced her in desperate severity. Rawan grappled against his shirt frantically, groaning at her weakness.

'Stop. Stop it!' he told her warningly.

'LET ME GO, YOU LUNATIC!' she screamed at him, sensing her throat slice in injury.

Amgad pushed her with such force that the gun flung from her hand, and she fell on her back. 'I am the lunatic?' He glared at her. 'Me? What can I say?' He watched her pull herself to her feet, panting. 'You are right: only a mad man would love such a deranged woman, and only an even greater fool would clean up her messes, ONE AFTER THE OTHER!'

My messes?

'Oh! I apologise. You are Malak, the exotic dancer, not Rawan, the FREAK WHO CRACKED HER SISTER'S SKULL!'

Liar. He's a liar!

Rawan looked at his face for a split second then burst out in giggles. 'That's your best attempt? That's your genius version? And did I rape her too?'

He pulled at his chin with one palm, his lips speechless and his eyes bloodshot.

'Tell me,' she said, standing defiantly. 'Really. This tale sounds interesting. I'm all ears!'

'This tale,' he repeated blankly. 'This tale … Ok,' he puffed. 'I guess it is role-shift time now; I can play doctor. Where were you when Samra was attacked?'

'Home.'

'Really?' He smiled bitterly. 'You mentioned in the interrogation that she had asked you to pick up her wedding dress from the store.'

Rawan blinked at him. 'Yes, and then I returned home.'

'How did you bring the dress home?'

'I put it in the car and drove home! What is this nonsense?'

'What car, Rawan?'

I'm late. 'I'm late.'

'What car, Rawan?' he repeated, glaring into her eyes. 'Samra had the car with her from the early morning till the ambulance came to the scene.'

Rawan shook her head, pulling at her hair as her lips trembled. 'I mean … I took a … taxi from—'

'Unless of course you picked up the dress *together* while *she* drove. She wanted to speak with you as I understand, and the rest you know just as well as I do.'

'You're a sick liar,' she mumbled wearily.

'I pity you, Rawan.'

His words slapped her stomach from the inside as the face of the dancer she had attacked in the dressing room seemed to re-utter them now. The dancer repeated the phrase over and over, her voice slowly warping into Samra's. The dressing room collapsed, and Rawan stood facing her sister, surrounded by nothing but sand and the mirage of distant buildings.

'I pity you, Rawan,' Samra said, her hair gleaming in the roaring sun that burned against Rawan's squeezed eyes. 'You should have told me. I should have known since you first felt this! What am I supposed to do now? How am I to explain to Saleem why my own sister cannot attend my wedding, that's if there will even be one?!'

'Samra, I'm telling you, you misunderstood. I would have said anything so he would leave me alone!'

'Yes, you could have said anything. Anything other than passionately confessing your love for your sister's fiancé!'

'It's not true!' Rawan yelled desperately.

'I see Tunis hasn't affected your tendency to lie much.' Samra stepped away from Rawan and the car, farther into the desert. 'I have to call Saleem,' she remembered aloud.

'Why would you call him?' Rawan panicked, yet Samra had already pulled her phone from her pocket, muttering under her breath so inaudibly that Rawan did not hear her words from where she stood. 'I need to tell him … that I can see him today.'

'Samra, stop.' Rawan walked to her.

'One second,' she replied absentmindedly as she held the phone to her ear.

'Stop! Don't tell him, please!'

Without a moment's hesitance, Rawan stooped to the ground, pulled a heavy stone and bolted towards Samra, who stood with her back to her sister. Rawan hurled the rock with all her might on Samra's head. Before she could construe why, Samra let out a choked scream and collapsed. Rawan ran to check the phone before even comprehending what she had done.

She gasped for air, watching Amgad's face. 'You told me she was raped,' she whispered through her wet lips. 'You … I didn't do it.' She wept.

'She would have had you locked up, Rawan! You called me, and I was there in minutes, but I had to wait a while after I arrived before requesting the ambulance. I had to do what needed to be done.'

'You told me—'

'Listen to me! It's DONE!'

'You did this!' She staggered, trying to keep her feeble legs firm as Amgad rushed to catch her weight before she fell. He carried her to the sofa and sat crouched on the floor at her feet.

'Rawan, I love you. I have loved no one but you, and I would have done what I did a million times if it meant saving you from yourself. What are you staring at?'

She returned her gaze from the fireplace to his eye, but he had already looked in the direction of her focus. He stood up and grabbed the torn underwear caught at the corner of the fireplace and stretched it before her face.

'What is this?' he scowled at her murderously.

She tried to leave the sofa but his hand grabbed her hair tight. 'WHAT IS THIS DOING HERE?' Amgad flung it at her face while she pierced her nails in his hand and jumped off the sofa, yet he pulled at her feet so that she fell to the ground.

'WHAT DID YOU DO, YOU WHORE?!' He slapped her over and over until her nose bled and the left corner of her lips sliced open. She grimaced at him, her eyes wide and daring.

'You come here,' she said, panting as her blood dripped to his palm, 'with all your self-righteous saintliness only to tell me that I am the devil? That I am a whore for not having kept myself exclusively your whore? You love me so much that you took me over and over then said I couldn't be your wife.' Maddened, she grinned.

He released his grasp off her face yet his body continued

to pin hers to the floor. 'I never said that! I did not betray you, all this time away from me! I never said I didn't want to marry you! I did not betray you.'

'No? To break my spirit is not betrayal? To rid me of sanity? To have me trust completely that the man taking me so avariciously had a phallus for a heart? In case it never crossed your mind, "because" is just as cruel as "never", and all you ever gave me was excuse after the next. You served me an appetiser of intrigue, followed by a starter of lack of trust. The main course was your fear; and for dessert, the sourness of your male ego. Your love, *basha*,' she mocked, 'has reduced my understanding of life to it being nothing more than constant choking with the tragedy of God giving me brief spells of air, as a tortured prisoner may eternally suffer yet never simply die.'

The twist of a door key clicked from afar before he had time to respond, and Saleem walked in, pointing a gun before his chest. Amgad jumped from his place and pulled his own to aim back at Saleem, while Rawan scampered off the floor and grabbed her own from beside Saleem's feet to point it in Amgad's direction, only to find that Saleem had his aimed at her chest.

Saleem looked at her. 'I never asked how it is you are in possession of a gun.' He shrugged. 'It just never occurred to me for some odd reason. But it looks like you're not the only one whose friends lend guns to, Rawan, although mine isn't licensed.'

'Saleem—'

'I don't know how she died, but I know you *do*.' He stared into her face accusingly.

'She doesn't remember,' Amgad spat at him to reply on her behalf. 'She's forgotten! I suggest you do the same and forget too. Forget or be forgotten. That's how the world works, right?'

Saleem turned to him. 'No, *basha*, actually it doesn't. You see, there is a debt passed on to us, only to be reimbursed with our own blood. And we have yet to satisfy it, for the debtor still stirs in her grave, buried in the dirt of this very land. A debtor that remains unsaturated, insatiable, unrepaid.'

'Put your gun down, and I will let you walk out without a scratch. How much more blood could this land need, Saleem? Isn't it enough already?'

'Apparently not. Look at us! The angel is not an angel; the devil is just as much innocent as you'd argue against … and Samra? Well, hers is the crime with no culprit, and no justice has been served.'

'The justice you seek is unsustainable. You will only continue to pile one overdue bill upon the other. This is what we understand while you still fail to even acknowledge.'

'It is not our understanding that you strive for, *basha*, but our acceptance. This entire performance has been orchestrated for one purpose only: to reach my consent. And that I shall not pay.'

'Well, I guess that's why she assigned you such an insignificant role!'

'Don't listen to him, Saleem—' Rawan exclaimed.

'Man to man, let me put it to you this way: look me in the eye and tell me Samra was ever half as interesting as Rawan. I mean, I never met her, but I can tell you assuredly that compared to her sister, she was nothing.'

'I stopped listening after "man to man".'

'Saleem! Shoot him!' she cried.

Amgad took one look at her face, glaring in awe at the callous ardency of her demand, and shot Saleem in the centre of his chest. Rawan dropped to the floor beside his lifeless body, grappling at his shoulders so his back leaned over her chest and pressed her palms over his rushing wound. Amgad examined her face then pointed his gun to the wall behind where Saleem had stood and fired another bullet. She stared to the fireplace blankly as her arms weakened, and she let the weight of his body slide to the side. Amgad crouched to his knees opposite her and said calmly, 'Go wash your hands, Rawan.'

AND TO THE MELODY SHE DREAMS

Fadya ran to her father, who elevated her effortlessly into his arms.

'Happy birthday, Dudu!' he cooed, while she wrapped her small arm around what she could reach of his neck.

'Papi, do you know what uncle Mahmoud and Yusef got me?'

'What, darling?'

'A pony like Yusef's but with a green saddle!'

'Ah! You like green,' he said dramatically, circling past the pool as he noticed his wife cross her arms over the edge. 'Fawzeya!' he called to her, and she swam closer to him. 'The general is here and you're not even dressed? Please get out of the pool now and hurry.'

Fawzeya watched him walk up the steps beyond the garden that separated their guest house from the mansion and submerged her head under the water. She closed her eyes, remembering Zain's palm on the bump in her belly that was now Fadya, and held her breath. Her daughter had none of his features, neither when she was but a newborn nor now as she stepped into her fifth year. Fawzeya thought of how trivial blood is when its influence is compared to time. For time can bring you to or drift you away from people, places, ideas and dreams, so that when enough of it has passed by, what our roots once determined become nothing more than the pigmentation of our skin or the height to which we grow.

Fadya was Kamel's daughter in every manifestation of the word: her face expressed her thoughts in imitation to his, she voiced concern and disapproval or amusement and excitement like she were a smaller and more delicate reflection of himself in the mirror. Even her nimble left thumb curled over her right, just as Kamel did, as she knelt in prayer before the cross.

Fawzeya used to pray, some years ago, until one day she decided to stop and see if God would care, but he didn't and so she never resumed. She wondered if she never rose her head from the surface of the water, whether anyone would care apart from Kamel. She doubted if Fadya would even notice.

Yusef chased behind the little girl as she ran back to where her mother had been swimming but could not see her in the brief amount of time she spent sweeping the water with her eye until her own tender spirit distracted her. She plodded on the grass near the pool and Yusef joined her, crossing his legs in imitation.

'My grandpa is going to take me fishing again tomorrow,' he boasted to impress her.

'Why can't your daddy take you?'

'He's busy,' Yusef said, clutching a pinch of grass between his fingers.

'Sometimes Papi is busy too, but I don't like fishing anyway.'

'Why?'

'Because the fish die, and then they can't swim anymore, so they can't be fish again.'

'But it's fun!' he argued.

'Watching them swim is more fun,' she explained, opening his clasped hand with her fingers and wiping it clean from the dying grass he held.

I dearly thank my family for their support, particularly my mother, Altaf Nour, without whose daily renditions of «when is this book of yours going to be done?» The King's Debt would be no more than a few dabbling notes. Many heartfelt thanks to Sherine Elbanhawy and the wonderful Rowayat family, who saw more in my words than words and ultimately welcomed me into the publishing world through my short stories and first novel. A special thank you to Yasmine Elbeih, Amr Shehata and Liz Mastrangelo for their valuable feedback and edits.

As a reader, I am deeply thankful for the sea of writers whose works and perspectives have etched little by little the fabrication of my being as a budding writer. J. B. Priestley and Dennis Lehane, thank you for your gripping and thrilling inspiration.